THE RULE OF 3

FIGHT

FOR

POW3R

ERIC WALTERS

SQUARE
FISH

Farrar Straus Giroux

New York

SQUARE
FISH

An Imprint of Macmillan
175 Fifth Avenue
New York, NY 10010
fiercereads.com

Square Fish and the Square Fish logo are trademarks of Macmillan
and are used by Farrar Straus Giroux Books for Young Readers
under license from Macmillan.

Our books may be purchased in bulk for promotional, educational, or
business use. Please contact your local bookseller or the Macmillan Corporate
and Premium Sales Department at (800) 221-7945 ext. 5442 or by
e-mail at MacmillanSpecialMarkets@macmillan.com.

Library of Congress Cataloging-in-Publication Data

Walters, Eric, 1957–
    The rule of three : fight for power / Eric Walters.
      pages cm
    Summary: "In a world gone dark, life goes on for Adam and his fortified
neighborhood—but the trade-offs made for safety and security are increasingly
wrenching and questionable"—Provided by publisher.
    ISBN 978-1-250-07358-7 (paperback)
    ISBN 978-0-374-30180-4 (ebook)
    [1. Electric power failures—Fiction.   2. Survival—Fiction.   3. Neighborhoods—
Fiction.   4. Science fiction.]   I. Title.   II. Title: Fight for power.

PZ7.W17129Rv 2015
[Fic]—dc23

                                                                    2014037070

Originally published in the United States by Farrar Straus Giroux Books
for Young Readers / First Square Fish Edition: 2016
Book designed by Andrew Arnold
Square Fish logo designed by Filomena Tuosto

10 9 8 7 6 5 4 3 2 1

AR: 13.0 / LEXILE: 730L

*To all my readers who patiently
waited for the second book!*

THE RULE OF 3

FIGHT

FOR

POWER

"Swing us back around!" Herb yelled.

I banked the ultralight to bring the wreckage back into view, and gasped. The dust and dirt rose in a column, forming a cloud that towered higher and higher into the sky. Through the haze I could make out two thick concrete pillars soaring upward but supporting nothing. The rest of the bridge was gone—collapsed and crumbled under the force of the explosives that had been wrapped and wired across the span, then detonated.

"I can't believe it's gone," I said over the intercom.

"Not gone so much as rearranged," Herb said.

I looked below. The explosion had sent the bridge to the valley floor. I could make out the hulks of shattered vehicles— the two dozen trucks that had been on the bridge only a minute before.

A couple of the trucks had caught fire and were sending out black smoke. Most were simply on their sides, smashed in pieces scattered among the rocks, some partially submerged in the river or covered by the chunks of concrete and mountains of asphalt that had come down with them.

We'd done it. We'd blown up the bridge and all the trucks that were on it and all the men who were coming to destroy us. Just seconds before, they had been racing across the bridge to kill us—my family, my friends, my neighbors—and destroy all that we had worked so hard to build. And now they were lying at the bottom of the valley, dead. And because they were dead we could live.

"Nobody could have survived that, could they?"

"Adam, I can't imagine it would have been possible to live through that," Herb said.

"How many enemies are down there? How many men did we kill?"

"An awful lot," he said.

That boggled my mind. Just three months ago, we had all been leading normal, everyday lives. And then the computer virus or whatever it was had come out of nowhere and cast us all into the darkness. We'd walled off our neighborhood, and outside those walls we'd found enemies among former friends. And now we had taken part in killing dozens, no, *hundreds*, of men. But what choice was there? They were coming to destroy our homes, take all the things we'd worked so hard to create, the things we needed to survive, and they would kill whoever stood in their way. It was us or them. So it was them, down below, lying in the wreckage.

I couldn't allow myself to feel sorry for them or regret what we'd done. I knew they wouldn't have felt sorry for us— they wouldn't have felt anything.

"Bring us down," Herb said.

"How low do you want me to get?"

"I want you to land."

"Down there?"

"I'd like to get as close to the site of the collapse as possible. Can you do that?"

"Sure, I guess so."

Running alongside the river was a small paved strip—what used to be a walking path for hikers, and cyclists, and mothers pushing babies in carriages. It wasn't wide and it hugged the curves of the river, but I'd spied one section that was straight enough and long enough to be a landing strip for my ultralight.

"I'm going to tell your mother what we're doing," Herb said. Then he spoke into the walkie-talkie. "This is Herb. Captain, can you read me?"

There was static and then my mother's voice. She was holding a position a short distance from the bridge site. "Roger, Herb."

Along with her voice were screams of joy coming through the radio: celebration. The squads gathered around my mother were cheering the deaths of those murderers who had plunged into the river. It had happened right before my eyes, I was *seeing* the results below us, but still it was hardly believable. A mixture of emotions—joy, sadness, grief, confusion—washed over me. We were going to live, we were going to survive. *Their* death meant *our* life.

"Captain, what are the plans to secure the crash site below the bridge?"

"Already working it through, Herb. I'm going to ask Brett to leave half his team at the top of the ravine to control and offer protection on the east rim and for him to lead the other half down to the site of the wreckage," my mom said, sounding like the former police chief she was.

"I'm also sending two squads, one north and one south of the collapse site, to seal it in on both sides."

"Excellent, that will give us the coverage we need to

secure the site. We're going to put down . . . if we have your permission."

"You're going to land?"

"Roger on that, Captain. With the site secured we'll be fine. That's why it will be good to have Brett's team down there with us. Why don't we send almost everybody else back to the neighborhood, just in case? No sense in winning the battle but losing the war."

My mother hesitated. "Is there another threat that you've seen from up there heading for the neighborhood?"

"Nothing."

"Okay. I'll let them stand down, go home, and spread the news. We made it."

"Affirmative."

"And, Herb? You need to take care of my son," she said.

"You've got that backward, Captain. Adam's the one taking care of me."

"Then take care of each other until I see you. I'm heading back with the reserves. I can leave Howie up here in command."

"Good idea. It should be you leading the way back and telling the people that they're safe."

"I guess it will help them trust that we know what we're doing. As if."

"You read my mind," Herb said. "It'll also help them deal with the bad news that's going to come."

"Over and out," my mother signed off.

"Bad news?" I said. I'm sure my voice had a panicked tone.

"Not today, Adam. Today is only good, but bad news will follow, sooner or later," Herb said. "And when it does they'll need to remember your mom as one of the leaders who brought them through this crisis successfully so they can trust her to lead them through the next one."

"Got it," I said. Suddenly we hit a patch of rough air and the ultralight dipped and shuddered like a roller coaster. Herb gasped and grabbed hold of the windshield frame. I smiled to myself, amused that I was probably the only one who knew that fearless Herb was afraid of flying.

"I'll put us down there," I said.

I eased off the throttle to reduce our speed and got us lined up on the path. The slower the landing speed, the shorter the distance I needed to land on. Now we were angling into the river valley, and the cliffs on both sides protected us from crosswinds. We dropped down, lower and lower. The river was off to my right, and the eastern cliff face to the left. Up ahead the cloud of dust and smoke rose peacefully into the air. I could almost taste the dust in my mouth, and the smell of the explosives and car fires and burning gasoline was already sharp.

The walking path rushed up to meet us. It was much narrower than the roads I was accustomed to using as landing strips, so I had to be more precise about placing my wheels on the asphalt. If one of them dropped off onto the softer and rougher ground beside the pavement, the whole plane could spin out or even flip over. Maybe this wasn't such a good idea, but it was too late to argue. Besides, after dodging bullets and explosives from people and a plane trying to shoot me down, I knew a strip of grass wasn't going to kill me.

I hit the right rudder to put my front wheel directly into line with the center of the path, and pulled slightly back on the stick to soften our descent. I eased off the throttle even more, slowing us down but still listening for the sound of the engine, making sure it was getting enough gas to keep us from stalling out. Lower and lower we came, the whir of the propeller behind our seats a constant background noise, until we were no more than a dozen feet above the ground. We touched down, bounced slightly up, and settled in again. Then I eased completely off the throttle and focused on the path, keeping us on line as we rumbled along the rough asphalt strip, slowing down and finally coming to a stop. I let out a big sigh of relief.

"Nice work," Herb said.

"Do you want me to taxi along to get us closer?"

"Closer, but not too close," he said. "I want to make sure your plane is out of harm's way if something explodes. We know the trucks contained weapons and ammunition, and there's always the potential for gas tanks to blow," Herb said.

"Then shouldn't we all just stay away until we know that there isn't going to be any explosion?"

"We don't have time to wait. We have to scavenge before they're in the water too long or consumed by secondary fires. There's a lot in those vehicles that we need."

"Okay, I see," I mumbled. I gave the plane more gas to taxi us along the strip.

"It's not going to be pleasant," Herb said. "I know it feels like stealing from the dead, but it's not like they're going to use those things anymore. Besides, anything we leave can easily fall into the hands of other people who can turn them against us."

"I understand . . . but they're all dead, right?"

"Anybody on that bridge is gone. It would be like falling

from a twenty-story building. Regardless, if they did somehow miraculously survive, they won't be surviving for long."

"What do you mean?" I asked.

"The injuries would be devastating. There's no way they can be saved. If we come across anybody who's alive, we'll have to, well, take action."

My stomach lurched. *Take action.* I knew what he meant. At least I thought I knew what he meant.

"I can't . . . I can't do that," I stammered.

"No one is asking you to. It's on me. I wouldn't leave a dog to die in pain."

"But we're not talking about dogs," I said.

"No, we're talking about men who were coming here to murder you and me and your mother and brother and sister and everybody who lived in our neighborhood. They were going to kill anybody who stood in their way, and then take everything, leaving those they didn't kill to ultimately die without food or the means to survive."

"I know. I know all of it. I know we had no choice."

"You saw what they were capable of."

It was impossible to get those thoughts and images out of my mind. I did know what they'd done. They'd overrun Olde Burnham, a nearby neighborhood whose residents had been on friendly terms with us, smashed through the walls, set buildings on fire, blown guards to pieces with rockets and grenades, executed prisoners by shooting them at point-blank range, killed innocent women and children in the crossfire, and then looted and plundered whatever was left.

"It's going to be a scene from hell over there," Herb said. He gestured toward the smoke.

"I've seen hell before," I said, thinking of Olde Burnham after the attack. "I've flown over it and landed in the middle."

"Seeing it once doesn't mean you need to see it again. Okay, this is close enough. Cut the power."

I reduced the throttle to nothing and we came to rest. Herb undid his harness and climbed out of the plane, his rifle in his hands. I did the same, removing my pistol from its holster. Just because no one survived the fall didn't mean there weren't other dangers lurking out here. There were always dangers.

Herb started walking toward the wreckage and motioned for me to follow. Pieces of the bridge—concrete, asphalt, metal—were strung out across the valley floor in a jagged line, starting on one side, crossing the river, and reaching over to the other wall of the valley. The cloud of dust and smoke started to dissipate before our eyes, the haze rising up, revealing more of the destruction, allowing us to see it more clearly. All that remained of the bridge were those two gigantic support columns, erect and defiant.

The debris was piled up, in places twenty or even thirty feet high, and the trucks themselves were scattered, broken, lying on their sides and rooftops. One still perched on its wheels, looking like it could just drive away. As we got closer I could see that its side was ripped open, with bodies intertwined, distorted into impossible positions.

It seemed incredible that all this had happened because of fertilizer and chemicals—from our kitchen cabinets and garages and ransacked supermarket shelves—that Herb had shown us how to combine to make explosives powerful enough to destroy a bridge, to take down all those trucks, to end all those lives.

"I've seen a lot of things in my time but nothing quite like this," Herb said as we closed in.

I swallowed hard. It was so awful and yet somehow mesmerizing at the same time.

"People talk about not being able to look away from a traffic accident, and this was like a hundred accidents all happening at once. You don't have to come any farther."

"I've come this far," I said.

"And this is far enough. I want you back in the plane and—"

"Look out!" I screamed. Up ahead a man climbed over the rim of the wreckage and he had a rifle. I was raising my pistol, but Herb instantly pushed my arm down. "They're our men, Adam! It's Brett."

My racing heart almost stopped. It *was* Brett, and right behind him another man and then a third—it was Todd, my best friend—followed by others I knew. There was Owen and Tim and Gavin and Mr. Gomez from down the street. I could have mistakenly shot them, or at least shot at them. I took a step back, stunned at how close I had come to pulling the trigger. Thank God Herb had stopped me in time.

"It happens all the time in extreme situations," Herb said. He put a hand on my shoulder. "You're on such an adrenaline high that you can't see straight."

Brett raised his hand in greeting but I ignored it.

"*You* saw," I said. "You saw enough to stop me from shooting."

"It's not the same for me. This isn't my first rodeo."

That was one name for it. I wondered what you could really call this? Was it a massacre, or a carnage, or a bloodbath, or . . . I stopped myself from going any further. It didn't need a name.

One by one the men appeared until there were at least a dozen. They'd come down the side of the valley—as my mother had ordered—and passed over some of the wreckage.

"Everyone, please gather around," Herb called out to them.

As others surrounded him I took a few steps back to the outside of the forming circle.

"We have won the battle," Herb said, and there was a chorus of cheers. "At least thus far." The cheering stopped. "There is so much more we still need to do, and we have to take care not to let one of our lives be taken by a dead man."

What did that even mean?

"We're going to go search the vehicles. We have to be aware of the rocks and rubble, the way the vehicles are perched—it is all unstable. We also have to watch for any weapons, like explosives that might be live. We're going to go through each truck, check each body, and take what will be of value to us."

I could see the looks of shock on faces. Strange how killing people was one thing but searching their bodies was another.

"There are obviously things like guns and ammunition, but I'm hoping for other weapons. I know we'll find things like RPGs—rocket-propelled grenades—but there might also be plastic explosives and other sophisticated weaponry. If you have any question about what something is, do not, I repeat, *do not* touch it. Step back and let me investigate further. Also, we'll take body armor, walkie-talkies, food, even shoes and boots."

"You want us to strip the bodies?" one of the men asked.

"They can keep their uniforms, but we'll take their boots

at least," Brett said. "They might be helpful to us at some point."

"I know this is going to be difficult," Herb added. "It's different when you look somebody in the eyes—even if those eyes are unseeing and the person is dead—but this has to be done."

"My men will do what has to be done," Brett said. His voice was calm. How could he seem so confident?

"Shouldn't we get more people to help?" another man asked.

"No, we want to minimize contact for others, limit exposure to what we're going to see," Herb explained. "You men have been on the front lines and you've seen more than other people. You're best able to handle this."

"Is there anybody who doesn't have the stomach for this?" Brett asked. He looked at the men who were with him—the ones he often led out on patrols. They shook their heads or mumbled that they could handle it. I wasn't sure if anybody had any choice but to agree.

I nodded, even though I knew that I wasn't feeling any more confident than most of the others.

"Here's how it's going to work," Herb said. "Brett is going to come with me. We're going to be the first in each truck to ensure that it's safe and to direct what needs to be done. Once we've cleared the truck, others will follow and remove the gear and the bodies."

"Why can't we just leave the bodies?" somebody asked.

"We can't allow them to simply decompose. It can contaminate the river downstream and spread diseases. We have to dispose of them," Herb said.

"We're going to bury them?"

I knew that wasn't the plan. So did Brett.

"We're going to have a big barbecue," Brett said.

I couldn't believe he was making a joke of it. Only a sick moron would find this funny. But maybe it was like laughing at a funeral, or maybe he was just trying to put people at ease in the middle of an awful situation.

Herb turned to me. "Adam, I want you back up in the air."

"I can handle this," I said. "You need all the help you can get."

"I know you can, but where I really need your help is up there," he said, pointing to the sky. "You have to get back up into the air to provide support and surveillance for us down here as well as for the neighborhood."

"But we got them!" Todd said.

"I hope we got *most* of them," Herb said. "We have to do a body count to find out how many men were in those trucks so we have an idea how many still remain alive."

"And you think that there could still be enough of them that they could be coming for us?" Owen asked.

"I hope it was a one-pronged attack, one group, but I'm not certain."

"If anybody is still stupid enough to attack us, then we'll take care of them," Brett said. "They'll be as dead as the rest."

Others nodded in agreement. He sounded forceful—and confident—and that was what people needed right now. That's the way Herb handled things, and Brett had learned from him.

"We need Adam up in the sky just in case," Herb said. "Forewarned is forearmed."

"Okay, sure, I'll get right up there. I've got two hours of fuel left. I could stay in the sky and keep watch overhead until I run low and then refuel and get back up in the air again."

"That would be excellent. I want you to make large circuits, making sure nobody else is coming along either of the two remaining bridges over the river to the north or south, and I also want you doing passes over the walls of the neighborhood. I want to eliminate the possibility there was a group sent wide to come at the neighborhood from another direction entirely."

"This is just a precaution, right?" I asked.

He nodded. "Just a precaution, but let's keep taking precautions. You need extra eyes, so I want somebody to go up with you."

"I could go," Todd offered.

I quickly looked over at him to see if he was joking—he had always said there was no way he'd ever go up with me in my flying lawn mower, as he called it—but he was dead serious.

"Good, then it's decided," Herb said. "Now we better get working. There's no time to waste."

2

Herb led the men off in one direction, and Todd and I headed in the other.

I nudged him as we walked along. "I thought you were never going to go up in my ultralight."

Todd shrugged. "Things change. I never thought I'd be searching bodies and stripping them out of their boots either. Up there is looking good."

We crunched through gravel and debris back to the plane. Carefully I grabbed the tail, picked it up, and started to spin the ultralight around, aiming it back in the direction I'd just landed.

"What are you doing?" Todd asked.

"The longest, straightest strip is that direction. It makes for an easier takeoff." I set the tail back down on the strip of asphalt. I climbed in and clipped on my harness.

Todd stood beside the plane.

"Are you getting in?"

"I'm just thinking. Is it better to search bodies or become one?"

I laughed. This sounded like the old Todd.

"Thanks for the vote of confidence. I have to get in the air. Jump in or go back and join them."

"I'm getting in," Todd said.

He climbed into the seat beside me, and the whole plane sagged under his weight. I reached over and grabbed his harness, clicking it into place.

"That should stop you from falling out," I explained.

"Great, now I feel *really* safe."

I handed him the helmet, which had an intercom wire that plugged into the console. "Put this on so we can talk."

Once we were situated I opened the fuel line and turned on the engine. It instantly came to life.

"Don't you wish your old car did that?"

"My car doesn't need to be that reliable. If it stalls out, we pull to the side of the road. If this stalls out, we fall from the sky."

I had the brakes on but could feel the force of the propeller behind the seats pushing us forward.

"Was that supposed to be reassuring?" Todd asked.

"Not so much reassuring as real. Here we go." I opened the throttle and we began to rumble along the path, picking up speed.

"Are we going to take off or drive all the way—"

The front wheels lifted and we soared up.

"We're going to fly. Hang on."

Out of the corner of my eye I saw Todd grab his seat with both hands. He was hanging on and leaning sideways, toward me. I increased the throttle so we were rapidly gaining height, then I turned slightly so I could watch Todd's expression. He looked scared. I didn't really want to do that to him—well, not too badly. I slowed our ascent.

"There's nothing to be worried about," I said.

"There are hundreds of feet ending in a sudden stop to be worried about. Can we fly lower?"

"We have to go a lot higher than this to see things. Besides, it's safer."

"How can higher be safer?" he demanded.

"If the engine stalled—"

"The engine could stall?"

"It never has. It's running well, and even if it did stall we could still glide to a landing. That's where height gives me more room to find a place."

"And more height to fall from."

"Look, it doesn't matter whether you fall from two hundred or two thousand feet, you're just as dead."

"Again, not reassuring."

"Again, not trying to be. Just keep your eyes open."

We were quickly coming up to the Dundas Street bridge across the river. A cluster of people stood at the edge, looking north, peering in the direction of the smoke and dust cloud in the sky. I wondered how far away the explosion would have been heard, how far the dust cloud was visible.

There were other people along the road, and in the distance I saw movement—an old truck was rolling down the pavement—but it looked like nothing we needed to be afraid of.

"This road is clear. Check in with Herb, and then I'm going to swing by the neighborhood."

After Todd radioed down the all clear, I banked to the right and I could see Todd grip the seat and tense up again. I eased off the turn, taking it slowly.

Down below were countless houses, surrounded by little

patches of grass, black ribbons of asphalt stretching out, schools and stores and offices. If it hadn't been for the abandoned cars littering the streets and the burned-out houses and buildings dotting the landscape here and there, I could have almost convinced myself that nothing was wrong.

"It looks so peaceful down there," I said over the intercom.

"I'm not sure how you can think it's peaceful," Todd said.

"I didn't say it *was* peaceful, just that it *looked* peaceful. Height and distance are deceptive."

"I wish it was all just deception, all just a trick. That I could close my eyes and open them again and it would be like it was. I'd be sitting beside you in your beautiful beat-up old car and us driving around, getting ready for a great summer and maybe finding a couple of girls to share it with."

"I have a girlfriend," I said.

"No, you don't understand, those couple of girls were for *me*. Then again, a couple might not be enough."

"You're right. The rate that girls break up with you, a couple would only get you through July at most," I joked.

"Strange how that happens," Todd said. "I think I'm an acquired taste, like a fine wine, and sometimes the ladies don't appreciate what they have until it's gone."

What a thought. Did any of us really appreciate something until it was gone?

I thought back to the lives we'd led just ten weeks ago. We had electricity, cell phones, fresh water, food, order, school, families, and a future that seemed certain and secure. Now we had *this*.

Then again, maybe I should appreciate what we had now

because it had almost been taken from us. We were only one blown-up bridge away from death, or worse. How strange to think there was something worse than death.

"There's our school about a mile up ahead," I said.

Todd gripped the side of the seat and tentatively looked over. "I can't see it."

"Follow the line of the road." I gestured with my hand. "See where it intersects with that other big divided street?"

"Yeah, I got it! I see the school and the police station across the road. You know, it does all look pretty normal."

"Normal just means what you're used to. It's starting to feel to me like this is the new normal, us needing to carry weapons, the neighborhood walled off, me flying this ultralight—"

"Hundreds of dead men at the bottom of the valley?" he asked.

That, too.

"I didn't want to admit it to anybody, but I couldn't be down there," Todd said. "The only reason I agreed to be here in your flying contraption was to get away from there. How pathetic is it that I'd rather risk death than face the dead?"

"It's not pathetic. I didn't want to be there either. I don't think either one of us will ever get to the point that that wouldn't bother us. That's just being human. It bothers everybody."

"Even Herb?" Todd asked.

"Even Herb. Some people just handle it better."

We were all alive because of Herb's ability to handle it better. He didn't just understand but was able to plan and then put his plans into action. He didn't just know what to do but was prepared to do it.

"Don't get me wrong," Todd said. "I'll try to do whatever we need to do to help us survive. It's that some things are just . . . just so . . . difficult."

"I get it," I said.

But Todd didn't even know the half of what had happened. So much of what I'd seen, so much of what I knew, I couldn't talk to anybody about except my mother and Herb—and the bits and pieces I gave to Lori. She was the only good thing that had come of all of this. That was one dream that had come true among the nightmares that surrounded us.

"You know if you ever need to talk, I'm here," I said.

"Most of the time you're *not* here. You're off on some mission with Herb or up here in your plane or lost inside your own head."

"Well, you're always welcome to come up here with me."

"I might take you up on that. It's not *too* terrifying."

We were now right over the school.

"So there's where it all started," Todd said.

"What do you mean?"

"Don't you remember? We were sitting in that computer lab working on my assignment when it hit." He paused. "It's unbelievable that it's only been ten weeks."

"Actually it's been slightly less than ten weeks. Sixty-six days," I said.

"Don't be so nitpicky. Right down there is where the virus started."

"It started *everywhere*, it hit *everywhere* around the world," I said. At least that's what Herb thought . . . what he picked up on the shortwave . . . what made sense. "We're all in this together."

"But that's where it started for *us*, for me and you. Right there. One minute my biggest worry was getting an assignment in, and the next, *poof*, no computers, no lights, and no cars. God, we had no idea how bad it was going to get."

"Nobody knew." Although Herb had suspected. But who could have really known that the entire world would be plunged into chaos in the blink of an eye?

Below us was the proof. No computers, no electricity, no water, no sanitation, no food distribution, gangs of armed people scrounging and fighting, just trying to survive. The same way we were trying to survive.

"The school looks pretty normal from up here," Todd said. "Even the cars in the parking lot make it look like a regular school day."

Those cars in the parking lot had been there from that first day, when the virus had rendered them undrivable. If we'd been low enough we'd have seen that the cars were vandalized, that equipment had been tossed through the school windows, lying on the ground where it fell.

"There's not much left of the police station, though," Todd said.

The station—my mother's old precinct house—had been abandoned and all the equipment moved into our neighborhood. People had attacked it, looking for something to help them. Finding nothing, they had destroyed it. It had been set on fire. The whole roof was gone, burned up. All that remained of the station were the bricks and stones and charred wood.

Herb had said that arson was an act of anger and that anger had been hurled against the station because people felt like they'd been abandoned by the police. Some people *had* been abandoned. A hard decision had to be made, and my mother had made it. They couldn't protect *anybody* if they tried to protect *everybody*. She and some of her officers had retreated into the confines of our neighborhood. There, they helped protect us, and the neighborhood helped protect them.

That was what had happened today at the bridge. That was just us trying to protect ourselves. Nothing more. Nothing less. We killed the men in the trucks because if we hadn't they would have killed us. I knew that. I had to just keep saying it to make me feel less like a murderer and more like a soldier.

"It's not normal and it's not peaceful down there, but I don't see anything that's a danger," I said to Todd.

"I'm glad. Herb had me scared."

"He never tries to scare people."

Todd looked over at me. Okay, maybe that wasn't strictly true. I tried again. "He never says things just to try to scare people. He wants to warn them, get them prepared. In fact, there's so much he never says to most people." I stopped myself. Now I was saying too much.

"I've always found it's easier to be ignorant."

I laughed. "I've noticed. It would be easier, but I don't think it would be better. I want to know what's going on."

"And do you really know?" Todd asked.

"Anybody who thinks he knows everything is stupid," I said. "Even Herb is only making guesses."

"Well, if he's the one who is really running the place, I hope his guesses are mostly right. Or we're in even worse trouble than I thought."

"The committee is in charge, and he's part of it. Really, in the end, maybe my mother has the most authority, although she and everybody else have learned to listen to what he has to say. But in the end, it's the committee that makes the decisions."

The committee was made up of my mother, as the police captain, along with Herb, Judge Roberts, Councilor Stevens, the fire chief, two engineers, a lawyer, Howie, who was one of my mother's officers in charge of the forces on the wall, and three other people in charge of various departments in the neighborhood, including Lori's father, Mr. Peterson, who was in charge of all the efforts to grow food.

I couldn't let the conversation distract me from what I was sent up here to do. I was now high enough to have a look along Highway 403, over its bridge and into the distance. There was nothing that could present danger. Well, immediate danger.

Now I could see our neighborhood. The perimeter was clearly visible. Inside the walls I could make out the lush green of crops growing, sprouting up in large patches that used to hold the school playing field and the electrical towers, in front yards and backyards, and along the walking paths. Sprinkled like diamonds among the fields were swimming pools, now used to store water for drinking and washing and irrigation—and flushing our toilets manually—along with the glass of dozens of little greenhouses that had been put together from windows and materials scavenged from the surrounding buildings and cars that had been destroyed or abandoned.

I came in low over the north wall. It seemed like everybody was out on the street, and as I passed they jumped up and down and waved. While I couldn't hear them over the noise of my engine, I could see them screaming out.

"It looks like a street party down there," Todd said.

"People are so relieved that they're out celebrating."

"Just get me on the ground—alive—and I'll join in that celebration."

"I have to bring us around so that we're landing into the wind," I explained.

I did a low, long, slow bank that would take us over the woods and the highway before coming back around to land from the north with the wind in our faces.

"I can't believe how many more tents there are down there in the woods," Todd said.

There were little flashes of red and yellow and orange canvas and nylon visible through the foliage of the trees south and west of our neighborhood. "They're springing up like mushrooms."

"I sure as heck wouldn't want to be camping out," Todd said.

"I don't know if anybody wants to camp as much as they don't have any choice. Maybe their homes have been destroyed or they think it's safer to be hidden among the trees."

"How can it be safer to be behind canvas instead of walls?"

"Walls only help if you can defend them. There are lots of people out there taking advantage of anybody who doesn't have a way to defend themselves, so they hide in the forest instead."

"I guess we're lucky to have what we have."

"Luck is only part of it," I agreed. "Hang on, we're going to come in now."

I'd made a full turn and we were coming back toward the neighborhood. I was going to land the ultralight right on my street.

"Didn't you once tell me that landing is one of the most dangerous times?" Todd asked.

"You heard me wrong. It isn't *one* of the most dangerous times. It's *the* most dangerous time."

"I'm okay with you keeping more of this stuff away from me. Feel free to offer reassuring lies at any time."

"Okay, there's nothing to be worried about. This is so simple that even you could land the plane. Is that better?"

"Much better."

We crossed back over the highway, dipping under the useless electrical wires linking the towers, and then dipped down lower and lower, so low I could see the guards on the walls. They waved wildly at us as we passed over.

"Isn't the ground coming up too fast?" Todd demanded as he braced himself.

"Of course not. It's not coming up at all. It's just that we're going down real fast."

We were now lower than the houses—fifteen feet, ten, five, and I looked up—there were people on the road! In all the excitement I'd forgotten to check the street! I went to pull up, but they scrambled out of the way and the road suddenly opened. The wheels touched down on the roadway with a bump and a big bounce. I hit the brakes hard and throttled back to an idle as we rolled along.

"We made it!" Todd screamed.

Not yet, I thought, as I hit the brakes even harder to bring us to a stop before we ran out of road. Finally we came to a stop. I killed the engine, and the roar of the motor was replaced by the roar of people all around rushing toward us. Todd tried to jump out, but he was held in place by his harness. He struggled with the buckle before I unclicked it for him and he jumped out and was mobbed by people—including his mother and father.

People offered me greetings, handshakes, and pats on the back, but I was only looking for a few people—my sister or brother, or— There she was. Lori pushed through the other people and wrapped her arms around me. No matter what had happened I knew it had all been right.

3

I stumbled out of the house and took a deep breath. The fresh air filled my lungs. It was good to get away from the committee meeting, which had just been suspended. It had been going on all morning. Three hours of details about yesterday's attack and its aftermath.

Finally Herb had asked for a break because, he said, there were other things we needed to consider and he wanted everyone to clear their head first. I didn't even want to think what those things could be, but I was just grateful when Judge Roberts agreed. It wasn't that I hadn't wanted to be there—there was no place I would rather be—but three hours was more than I could handle, or stomach. We all needed to stretch, have a drink, and use the facilities. I just wanted to get away, go for a walk or a run or maybe even jump in my plane and go for a flight. Maybe there was something even better I could do.

I strolled down the street. After moving from their farm to the neighborhood weeks ago, Lori and her parents had stayed with Herb for a while. Now they were living in what had been a vacant house at the end of the block. The real owners had been away when the virus hit and had never managed to get back to the neighborhood. That had been the case for so many people—including my father. He was a commercial pilot and had flown out the morning before it all happened, and had not made it home. Yet. I could only hope for him—not simply that he'd survived but that he'd be able to return. I just had to believe.

Lori's new house was right beside the park. A parcel had been corralled off for their small herd of dairy cows, and the garage had been converted to a chicken coop. When they'd moved here—forced to flee their farm—they'd brought the animals as well as all the farm equipment that could be trucked over. Now her father, the one farmer living in the middle of our gated suburb, directed all of our efforts to grow food. I didn't think we could even dream about surviving without his knowledge and equipment.

I turned up Lori's drive and was surprised to see her and Todd sitting on the front steps. I gave a weak little wave. Lori got up, rushed over, and gave me a hug.

"Just so you know," Todd said. "I think that Lori's been coming on to me a bit, but—"

"What?" She gave him a shove.

"It's a subtle thing," Todd said. "So subtle that you probably didn't notice, but I'm so in tune with the ways of women."

Both Lori and I laughed.

"But really, who can blame her when she has a choice between hamburger and prime rib?" he said, gesturing to me and then himself.

"Maybe I like hamburger." She kissed me.

"No accounting for taste, although I'm glad you admitted that I'm the prime rib," he joked.

"No question you are a prime something," I said, letting go of Lori to give him a shove myself.

"Oh, man," he said. "Why did I start talking about prime

rib and hamburger? Do you know what I'd give for a good burger?"

"A lot. So would I," I admitted.

"We should just be grateful for what we have," Lori said. "At least nobody in the neighborhood is going without."

"Maybe not completely without, but without enough," Todd said. "I think they should feed us according to size. I *need* more than other people."

I felt guilty. I *was* getting more than other people. We all shared in the community meals—a small breakfast and a large supper each day—but Herb had been giving my family some extras from the stock of canned goods he had stored in his basement. Although I had always thought there was more to Herb than him being some "old retired paper pusher"— his words—I had no idea just how much more there was. From the stockpile of food to the arsenal of weapons in his basement to his background working for the CIA, I was discovering surprises about him all the time. He was more than a neighbor; he'd been the primary reason we'd been able to survive.

"So is the committee meeting over?" Todd asked.

I was grateful for the distraction. I shook my head. "Just a break. We all needed one. All morning, it's been about the attack."

"Shouldn't it be simple? We blew up the bridge. They died. We won."

"There are a few more details."

"Like the final body count?" he asked.

"We didn't lose a person."

"I meant on the other side."

"I don't know if I should talk about it," I said.

"Come on, it isn't like I didn't see the results or what happened afterward," Todd said. "You can still see the smoke rising into the sky."

I turned around. There was a thin chimney of smoke visible on the horizon. I had to work to suppress a shudder.

After we'd refueled yesterday, Todd and I had gone back and done a number of big passes over the river valley. Even from up in the air we'd been able to see the growing pile of bodies. It was so much better to be high in the sky when the cremation had taken place, but of course even from that height there was still evidence of what was happening. Not just the smoke but the smell. There was a terrible odor—a combination of gas, burning plastics and materials, and of course the bodies themselves.

"Well?" Todd asked. "How many dead?"

I looked at Lori and she nodded ever so slightly, as if I was asking for her permission to talk about it. "Four hundred and eighty-three."

My friends were silent.

"Wow, I had no idea it would be that high," Todd finally said.

"It's probably more than that. Herb said he has no idea how many more bodies are hidden by the debris or have been washed downriver."

"I don't even know why they had to count," Lori said. "It just seems like they wanted to keep score or something, like it was a basketball game."

"If we know how many are dead, we have an idea of how many are left, how many we didn't kill," I explained.

"And?" Todd asked.

Now he was asking about something that I really shouldn't be talking about.

"Look, it's not like you're telling a bunch of strangers," Todd said. "Tell us and we'll keep it to ourselves."

I was too far in to turn back. "They think there could be well over a hundred who are still alive."

"But I thought you got all the trucks," Lori said.

"We got all the trucks but not the soldiers who stayed behind at their compound. They wouldn't have left it unguarded. That's why we had to count the bodies. As well, they had to be searched for valuables," I explained.

Lori shuddered.

"I know it sounds bad, but it had to be done. There were valuables. Lots and lots of weapons. A ton of ammunition, five RPG launchers, dozens of grenades, a hundred sets of body armor, a few more sets of long-range walkie-talkies, and close to three hundred guns," I said.

"But didn't all the soldiers have weapons?" Todd asked.

"All of them were armed, but not all the weapons could be recovered. A lot were damaged in the fall or in fires or trapped beneath debris or lost to the river. I think we did pretty well. We more than tripled the weapons and ammunition we had in stock."

"That's good . . . at least for us," Todd said.

"Better than good. Our survival depends on us having the weapons to defend ourselves."

"We have company," Todd said, and pointed behind me.

I spun around. Herb and Brett were standing at the end of the driveway. Herb waved and then motioned for me to come.

"I gotta get going." I gave Lori a kiss and started away.

"What about me?" Todd called out. I turned around. "Don't I get a kiss? Aren't I special? My mother always tells me I'm special!"

"No question you are *very* special."

I hurried after Herb and Brett, who had started walking back. I quickly caught up to them midconversation.

"Take a dozen men you know you can rely on and enough food and supplies and tents to camp out for the next twenty-four hours," Herb was saying.

"What's going on?" I asked.

"Your mother, the judge, and I had a short discussion and decided to send Brett and a crew to the far side of the bridge. Within the next twenty-four hours the people left in the compound might send a scouting party to find out what happened," Herb explained. "It's important that none of them go back to report."

"We'll get them," Brett said.

"*All* of them," Herb said. "Letting one get away is like letting them all get away."

"I understand. One way or another nobody is walking away."

There was that certainty again. I had never really felt comfortable around Brett, and I didn't even like him, but I believed he was a good protector. Brett would do whatever it took. I was just glad he was on our side.

"Do you want me to go up in the air to scout around as well?" I asked.

"You won't be able to pick up a small party from the air very well. Besides, I have something important to discuss with the committee, and I want you to be part of it."

Now I was even more curious. What was he going to talk about?

Brett gave Herb a little salute—and me a smirk—and headed off.

"We better get back inside," Herb said.

"Before we head in, could I ask you something?"

"Anything."

"The people on the bridge . . . did any of them live?"

"You know there were no survivors," he said.

"Did any of them live through the fall? Did you have to . . . have to . . . ?"

"Kill somebody?"

I nodded.

Herb looked at me closely before replying. "There were three men in one of the last trucks we checked. It was the closest to the edge of the bridge, and they didn't plunge nearly as far as the others. They were alive when Brett and I got there."

"And you killed them?"

"They were barely alive."

"And you killed them?" I repeated. I wasn't going to allow him not to answer.

"We didn't have to. They simply died."

"And if they hadn't?" I asked.

"If there had been hope, we would have called for the doctor. If not, I would have ended their suffering." He paused. "As we discussed."

"I couldn't," I said.

"I understand. That's not who you are. We all have roles to play. That's why you were up in the air and Brett was at my side."

That meant only one thing—he thought Brett could have pulled the trigger or at least been there when Herb did.

"Any more questions before we head in?" he asked.

There were lots of questions, but I didn't want any more answers. "I'm good."

"Let's call the meeting back to order," the judge said when we were back inside our living room.

Everybody took their seat. There was a sobering silence to the assembly, and I realized that I wasn't the only one nervously anticipating what Herb had to say next.

"Well, Herb, I guess the floor is yours," my mom said.

Herb took a sip from the glass of water in front of him before starting. I thought that was more about drama than hydration. Herb knew how to play an audience. I'd seen him do it again and again, and I wondered if I was ever part of those being played.

Finally he began. "I know we all feel good about the success we had yesterday. At least the partial success."

"Partial. It seems pretty complete to me," Mr. Gomez said.

"We have four hundred and eighty confirmed dead, but as you know we had their forces pegged at closer to six fifty," Herb said.

"But some are still buried under the rubble, and we did kill others when we attacked their base," Councilor Stevens said.

"Both are true, but those wouldn't total the missing one

hundred and seventy people. They still have a substantial force back at their compound. My best estimate is that they would have about a hundred men left."

"Still, we've taken out over eighty percent of their force," Judge Roberts said.

Herb turned to Dr. Morgan. "If you remove eighty percent of a malignant tumor, would you consider that a successful operation?"

"Of course not. It would be a failure."

"Because?"

"Well, while it would provide temporary relief, it would only buy time for the patient. The tumor would simply grow back."

Herb slowly got to his feet. Every eye was on him and it felt like nobody was even breathing. "If my understanding is correct, they are still a formidable force, equipped with more of the same weaponry that was in the trucks."

"I agree. Although we are now much better able to defend ourselves," my mother noted.

"From a frontal assault, yes, but they won't make the same mistake again. We are no more able to defend ourselves from a group of men coming out of the trees at night equipped with launchers and RPGs than we were before. They'd simply blow apart our outer walls."

"But they wouldn't be able to overwhelm us, take us over. We'd be able to defend ourselves," Howie said.

"Not without casualties. Again, I'm just making an estimate, but I would suspect that a sustained attack with RPGs would result in over a hundred of our people being killed and that those deaths would not simply be guards on the walls but innocents in their homes who would be hit by explosives."

"But after all that's happened, do you really think they'd attack?" Judge Roberts asked.

"Right now they're probably not fully aware of what happened. They've not had any radio contact with their men, and it's been almost a full day. They will be increasingly suspicious, but it could take a day or two before they risk sending out a team to investigate."

"Wouldn't they have seen the smoke?" I asked. "I know it was visible from a long way off . . . I've seen it from my plane when almost down by the lake."

"If they did see it, they would have only interpreted it as evidence of an attack on us by their soldiers. They have no reason to question the success of the attack."

"But once they do find out what happened, wouldn't that scare them away?" Howie asked. "Wouldn't they be afraid to face us?"

"Or they'd want revenge immediately," Herb countered. "Or they'd simply wait, gaining strength, regrowing like a tumor, preying on smaller, more vulnerable communities until they felt that they were strong enough to move against us once again. And this time they'd do it in a way that we might not be able to stop. Our element of surprise, which depends on their arrogance and overconfidence, would be gone."

"What are you proposing?" Judge Roberts asked.

The old spy paused, looking around the room. I leaned forward and noticed everyone else doing the same. There was a sense of dread, of anticipation, of fear. I could see it in people's eyes, I could almost smell it in the air.

"We have to finish the job we started," Herb said. "We have to attack them. There's nothing more dangerous than a wounded animal. We have to do to them what they were planning on doing to us. We have to destroy them."

"Destroy them?" the judge asked. "That makes us no better than them."

"We don't have any choice. As long as they're capable of launching an attack, they're a real and present danger, not only to us but to all others simply trying to live. They're predators who must be stopped. Either we go after them or they come after us. Not today, not tomorrow, and possibly not for months, but they'll be coming back at us. Of that I have no doubt."

"I thought it was over," Dr. Morgan said. "I guess I just wanted to believe that."

"We all wanted to believe that. But how do we tell our people? They're still out there on the streets celebrating the victory, their survival. You can't expect us to simply send people back out to risk their lives again," the councilor said.

"They trust us. They'd follow where we lead, do what we say. I know we can convince them," Herb said. He looked at my mom and she nodded grimly.

"Herb and I have had a discussion already," my mother said. "This isn't something we want or need, but he already has my approval."

Judge Roberts shook his head. "Even with that said, he still has to convince the rest of us. We can't simply march out and declare war on these people."

"War has already been declared. They declared it when they came to kill us," Herb said. "Look, I know what we all want to believe, what we all want to do, or more specifically *not* do, but by doing nothing we risk everything."

"Is it possible that we could negotiate with them, come to some understanding?" the judge asked.

"Yes, like a truce or a treaty?" Councilor Stevens said.

"We could, perhaps, assuming they simply didn't kill the members of the peace delegation we sent," Herb said. "But let's be realistic. We've all seen what they're capable of doing, what they would have done to us if they had gotten over that bridge. Even if they agree to a treaty, it would be nothing more than a blanket to cover them while they rearm, regroup, and plan how to destroy us. The only way to meet force is with greater force. Right now the advantage is ours. It won't be for long."

"How long do you think we have an advantage?" the councilor asked.

"It's all just guesses. Today we have the larger force, plus we have the momentum and the element of surprise. In a few days we lose surprise. In a week we lose momentum. In a few months they will undoubtedly have a larger force, perhaps one matching ours in size, and we will always have one distinct disadvantage. From what I've seen, these people don't care if they kill us. Our morality is a weakness."

"That's where I disagree with you, Herb," my mother said firmly. "It's our strength."

Herb's expression changed. For one of the first times, I saw him look flustered. "I wasn't implying it was wrong . . . please understand . . . I know we're doing what is right, but they don't suffer the same doubts around killing. Those pangs, those questions we're asking now, are what stops somebody from pulling the trigger for a split second, and in a split second you're dead. Ruthlessness is a weapon."

"I don't know the answer, but I know this all has to be discussed. We have to come to an agreement, we have to plan this," Judge Roberts said.

"With each hour that passes we lose the advantages we have. If I were in charge of the remaining enemy forces, once I knew what had happened, I'd either attack or take my remaining men, weapons, and resources and slip away," Herb explained.

"So you think it's possible that they might just run away and hide?" Howie said. "That they won't attack?"

"Perhaps not today, but by relocating to a new spot where we can't attack them, they're free to regroup and grow. It's no different from before, except for one thing. They'll be more determined to try to take what we have because they're that much more certain that it's worth taking."

"So you're saying by defending ourselves successfully, we've made ourselves more of a target?" the judge asked.

"Ironically, yes. Either we decide when and where to fight or they do. We have to be the ones who make those decisions first."

"And while I don't want this any more than the rest of you, the time has to be soon," my mother said.

"Within the next forty-eight hours is our window," Herb explained.

"And I bet you have a plan you are ready to talk to us about," the judge said.

I knew he was right. Herb was always playing chess—trying to stay a few moves ahead—not just with the enemy but with the people sitting around this table. He'd been thinking about this plan from the instant that bridge went down.

"The captain and I can present a comprehensive plan to this committee within an hour." He looked from person to person. "Well?"

"I'm not sure I should even be in on the discussion," Mr. Peterson said. "I'm a farmer, and that's all I am. I don't know about attacks and what needs to be done in situations like this."

"Me neither," Mr. Nicholas added. "As an engineer, I find all this well beyond my area of expertise. Can't we just leave this up to the captain and Herb, Howie, and the judge to decide?"

There was a nodding of heads and agreement from most of the others who weren't included in that group of names.

"No," my mother said, silencing them. "We can't. These decisions affect everybody, and we all have to have input."

"She's right," Herb agreed.

That surprised me. I thought Herb would have welcomed the opportunity to do things that way, without consultation or interference from more people.

"In an ideal world every member of this community would contribute to the decision because it will have dire, potentially fatal, impacts on them. We don't live in that ideal place, but all of you are the neighborhood's representatives. This has to be a collective decision because we will all have to live with the consequences. If we attack it is almost guaranteed that some of our people will die. We have to share in that responsibility," Herb said.

There was silence in the room as his words sank in. I think most of them would have relished washing their hands of the decision and then not being held responsible for what would happen—afraid of the consequences. Now they'd have to live with them, good or bad, successful or tragic.

"I just wish we could give them the opportunity to lay down their weapons," Judge Roberts said.

"They'd never do that," Herb said.

"How can you be certain?" Howie asked.

"The problem with a liar is that he doesn't believe anybody else is capable of telling the truth," Herb explained. "They'd think it was just a trick and that as soon as they surrendered their weapons we'd cut them down."

"We wouldn't do that," Judge Roberts said.

"But they *would*, and that's how they think everybody thinks. They're not going to simply walk away," Herb said.

"But if they did, would we let them?" I asked.

He didn't answer right away. He looked like he was struggling to come up with the right words. "It wouldn't be my decision to make."

"But if it was?" I wasn't going to let him get away without giving an answer.

He took a deep breath. "Those people have done evil and will be prepared to do evil again. If we let them walk away, then we're responsible for every action they take from that point on. Every death done by them would have been allowed by us. So, in answer to your question, I don't think they will surrender, but even if they did they shouldn't be allowed to leave . . . or live."

"And you think we should just kill them all?" my mother asked.

He looked straight at my mother. "Yes."

"But if we did, doesn't that just make us the same as them, putting a bullet into the head of an unarmed man?" Judge Roberts asked.

"It's not the same. They're prepared to kill innocents. I'm proposing that we kill the guilty to protect the innocent. Sometimes there are necessary evils that must be done. Does that make sense?"

I slowly nodded. There were many things that were necessary, but that didn't make them any less evil.

"But I know it's not going to come to that," Herb said. "They're not going to surrender. The only question on the table is simple: Do we attack them now or allow them to attack us later?"

I knew there was possibly going to be hours of discussion. I also knew what was going to happen in the end. For better or worse Herb—backed by my mother—would get what he wanted. All that remained was for everybody to be convinced in a way that would help them sleep afterward.

4

The next day, I was stuck at home looking after Danny and Rachel, my younger twin siblings. Around noon, while they were downstairs playing together, I was finally able to get outside to work on my car. Something was off with the timing and it was running rougher than usual. My 1979 Oldsmobile Omega was a junker, but that's what made it more valuable than a brand-new BMW, as I'd discovered the very first day of the crisis. Because it had no computers controlling any of its functions, it was unaffected by the virus. So it worked—but only as well as it always did, which wasn't saying much.

Yesterday, the meeting had continued for another two hours and then, just as I expected, after much debate, everybody came to an agreement with Herb's proposal. But by the time it had all been decided, it was too late to plan the attack for the next day. My mother and Herb and Howie had stayed up late putting it into place.

So today we would focus on preparation, and tomorrow would be the day of the attack. As usual, Herb got his way. Not only was the attack going to happen, but it was going to be a surprise assault, if we could pull it off.

Keeping the element of surprise had been the longest part

of the discussion. Most of the committee members—my mother included—had first wanted to try to negotiate with them, ask them to give up their weapons and flee. Herb had insisted that warning them was only going to give them time to react, not surrender. In the end he convinced people, one by one, including me, that you couldn't negotiate with monsters and murderers, until it was an argument almost exclusively between him and my mother.

Finally, she gave in. She said she knew the attack was going to happen. And she had to agree with Herb that losing the element of surprise was going to cost us lives.

Watching it all happen had confirmed what I already knew. While the committee made the final decisions, those decisions were driven by my mother and Herb. The two of them were the leaders, and as long as they led together we were okay. I didn't want to think what would have happened if they hadn't finally agreed.

As word about the plan spread throughout the neighborhood the mood shifted—again. We had gone from dread and fear two days ago to gratitude and relief, and now we were back where we'd started.

The lucky ones were those of us who had work to do. At least we could be distracted. For the rest, the waiting was hard.

At our house, Rachel and Danny were picking up on all the stress and had been fighting nonstop. They had always had a healthy rivalry, but this wasn't the usual brother-and-sister bickering. They had started saying really nasty things to each other until Rachel had broken down and started crying about Dad. That had gotten Danny crying, too, and because Mom was out, I had to work as hard as I could to offer them reassurance that Dad was fine. I hated lying to them, telling them things I couldn't possibly know were true. I just wished there was somebody to give me convincing lies.

Herb, my mother, Howie, and Brett were busy preparing the attack force. There were going to be 240 men and women from our neighborhood—forty of whom were being given weapons today for the first time and were receiving last-second training. It was risky because the newbies could shoot the wrong people, but Herb had said we needed to have twice as many people as the force we were going to attack.

Five people were being trained to use the RPGs. They'd be the ones who would be leading the attack, blasting through the perimeter walls and blowing up the barracks. Brett, of course, was one of them. There was nobody, except for Herb, that I would want beside me more than Brett when there were bullets flying around me. Not that I'd be beside him. Assuming the weather was right, I'd be in the air, watching and relaying information.

Part of me felt bad, almost guilty that I wasn't going to be with them on the ground, but I knew I'd still be in danger. Bullets could fly up as well as out. Besides, they needed my eyes in the sky. I was doing something that nobody else could do.

I heard horse hooves clattering on the pavement and looked up from my car engine. Two women and an older man were coming down the road, leading a horse-drawn farm wagon. They were the compost team. They gathered kitchen scraps produced by every household and then took them to a central location at the end of the parking lot at the school. The scraps were being composted and would be put back into the fields.

Sometimes they gathered other things. A call would go out asking for certain items like extra plywood, tools, snowblowers, lawn mowers, or rototillers. Any items that couldn't be delivered by the people to the shops were picked up and transported by horse cart.

It was encouraging to see people pulling together, working for the good of everybody. That was the way it was supposed to be. That was how we'd survive. That was the only way we *could* survive.

Beside almost every house that had southern exposure was a series of small wooden frames topped with a window attached by a hinge. These were tiny personal greenhouses that were growing a few plants. A few vegetables multiplied by hundreds and hundreds would make a difference in that fight to survive.

I looked over and caught sight of Herb walking up the street. I hadn't expected him to be out for a stroll. He waved and came over.

"You ready to go up tomorrow?" Herb asked, gesturing to my ultralight, which was parked in front of the garage, secured underneath an awning by guy lines to hooks on the driveway.

"The only thing that could stop me is the weather, but Mr. Peterson says he thinks it's going to be good."

"I have more trust in a farmer than I have in a weather forecaster on TV—not that we have TV anymore—so you should be good to go," Herb said.

"Are all the plans coming along okay?" I asked.

"It's fine, although I have something I need your help with," Herb said.

"So this wasn't a social visit."

"Nope."

"The winds are strong today, but I could go up and scout around if you want," I offered.

"This doesn't involve you going up in the air as much as going up to the mall. I'm planning to interview the prisoner."

A few weeks ago we'd captured a wounded member of our enemy, left for dead after they destroyed Olde Burnham and retreated back to their stronghold. He'd been brought back to our neighborhood, and Dr. Morgan had saved his life. Then Herb and I had tricked him into giving information that helped us with our victory at the bridge.

"How is he doing?" I asked.

"Recovering as well as possible, considering that he should be dead."

I felt a sense of relief. I had these terrible fears that once he'd served his purpose and given us the information, he was going to be allowed to die. Or worse.

"So what happens to him now?" I asked.

"I know a number of people who had loved ones killed in the other neighborhood who still think we should have just let him die," Herb said. "I have him under guard, not just to stop him from escaping but to stop anybody else from harming him."

"Do you really think that would happen?" I asked.

"What would you do if you thought he'd been responsible for killing a member of your family?"

I didn't need to think. "I guess it's the right thing to have him under protection."

"I don't know about right, but it's certainly wise. All along I thought he might have more information we could use. So, are you in?"

"Do you even need to ask?"

Dr. Morgan and the two nurses at the little clinic were busy, but it didn't look any busier than the times I'd been to the walk-in clinic before the power went out. There were two differences, though.

First, the clinic had three admitted patients in beds off to the side of the waiting room, where in normal times they would have gone to a hospital instead.

Second, there was an armed guard standing at the door leading to our prisoner's room. The guy with a gun was a jarring reminder not only of why we were there but also of how the world had evolved—or devolved. A few short weeks ago it was beyond belief that somebody would be standing in our mall, rifle on his shoulder, guarding a prisoner, two doors down from the supermarket and four away from the Baskin-Robbins.

Dr. Morgan saw us and came over.

"How is our patient doing?" Herb asked.

"Better, and we'll all be doing better once he's well enough to leave here."

"Is he causing problems?" Herb asked.

"Not directly, but he is a problem. We had another woman who showed up all agitated wanting to see him," Dr. Morgan said.

"She wasn't allowed in, was she?" Herb asked.

"Of course not. She was escorted out by the guard, but it's pretty disruptive and disturbing to all the patients when that happens."

"Has that happened often?" I asked.

"Three or four times. I understand those people are angry—that they need help, counseling, to get over what they experienced—but I have a clinic to run."

"We've got them help, but it isn't that simple," Herb said.

"I understand. I'm sorry if I implied it was, but I guess I just find it pretty disturbing myself," Dr. Morgan said.

"No apology necessary. We'll try to give them additional support. I just know that what they experienced, well, they'll never really get over. All we can do is help them cope. So when do you think he'll be ready to leave?" Herb asked.

"Two weeks, three at most, if there are no unforeseen downturns in his condition."

"So he's not out of the woods yet," Herb said.

"He should have died. Frankly, I was surprised he didn't die. It's not like I've had any experience with gunshot wounds before this."

"Let's hope it stays that way," Herb said. "Is it all right for us to go in and speak to him?"

"Of course. Take all the time you want. He's not due for his dressings to be changed for a couple of hours."

I followed Herb to the door. The guard was a retiree I recognized but didn't know by name. He gave Herb a little salute. I guess this wasn't how either of them was expecting to spend his golden years.

"We're going to interview our prisoner," Herb said. "Have you had a break, Stewart?"

Of course Herb knew his name. Herb seemed to know everybody's name.

"Straight duty, no breaks, since six this morning."

"Why don't you go down to the supermarket and explain to Ernie I sent you to have a coffee?" Herb suggested.

"Would that be all right?"

"I'm here, and so is Adam."

"Thanks, I won't be long."

"No need to hurry. We're not going anywhere for quite a while," Herb said.

I didn't like the sound of that.

Stewart gave another little salute and went off for his break.

We entered the room. The prisoner was handcuffed to the bed.

"Good afternoon, Quinn," Herb said.

Quinn. So he had a name—I'd always just thought of him as the prisoner. I guess that wasn't so bad. There were other names I could have called him.

"Afternoon."

"You don't mind me calling you by your first name, do you?" Herb asked.

"You can call me anything you want. You have the guns and the key to the handcuffs."

"I guess we do. Please call me Herb. And you remember my young friend, Adam?"

"I remember you both. I just didn't expect to see both the good cop and the bad cop at one time."

"And which one am I?" Herb asked.

The man laughed, which seemed to surprise even Herb.

"I've been told you're doing better. Are you pleased with your care?" Herb asked.

"As pleased as a turkey before Thanksgiving," he said.

"I'm not sure what you mean by that," Herb replied.

"The turkey that is being fattened up before the kill. Isn't that what you're doing with me?"

"Why would we be helping you to recover if we were simply going to kill you?" Herb asked.

"Probably because I still have some use. I don't assume you're here today to inquire about my health."

"Well, we are looking for some information that would be helpful," Herb said.

"And why should I help you?" Quinn asked.

"I guess the real question is why should you help us *again*?" Herb asked.

"I didn't tell you much of anything that would be useful, and I'm not going to be tricked again into giving anything more."

"Nobody is trying to trick you. I'm confused why you would be so loyal to people who abandoned you for dead, but even more I am wondering why you'd be loyal to people who no longer exist."

"Yeah, that's right, you killed them all."

"They say seeing is believing—I have something to show you." From his coat pocket Herb pulled out a stack of Polaroid snapshots and handed the photos to him. I moved around so I could see them. Almost instantly I regretted it. They were images taken of the carnage at the bridge. I wanted to avert my eyes, but I couldn't. The prisoner flipped through the pictures: the rubble at the bottom of the gully, the ripped-apart bodies, the crushed and shattered vehicles tossed about like toys.

"This could all just be fake," he said. His words didn't match the tremble in his voice or the look on his face. It was like all the blood had drained away. He knew it was real; he just didn't want to admit it.

"I guess I'm getting old," Herb said. "In my day that would have been proof enough. I guess what I'm going to ask will convince you that you should talk." Herb opened his jacket, revealing his pistol, then pulled out a piece of paper and unfolded it. "Does this look familiar?"

"So you know how our base is laid out."

Herb was holding a hand-drawn map showing a dozen or more buildings, the landing strip, and the perimeter fence. I recognized it but was surprised by the detail. Had somebody gone and scouted it out, or had Herb just remembered it from our flights over top?

"It would be helpful for us to know what is in each of these buildings," Herb said.

"If you've destroyed everybody, why don't you just walk in and find out yourself?" he asked.

"We haven't killed everybody. We counted close to five hundred bodies. As you are well aware, when they came out to attack us, they would have left behind a force to protect the base. Subtracting the bodies accounted for, that force would be around one hundred and twenty people, from the overall number you previously divulged."

I saw Quinn's expression flicker. Herb was giving a not-so-subtle message that Quinn had already betrayed his people and given us useful information.

"What I want to know is exactly what these buildings contain. I would prefer to spare the stocks of weapons and supplies that have been accumulated," Herb said.

"But you want to know which buildings contain the barracks because you don't plan on sparing those lives," Quinn said.

"No, I don't," Herb said. "Would you spare them? We need to strike quickly and kill as many people as possible."

"And you expect me to help you do that?"

"That would be most useful."

"I'm not helping you. I'm lots of things, but I'm not a traitor." He was becoming louder, more agitated. This wasn't working.

"To be a traitor is better than being a fool. They would kill you in a second to live. I think you should have loyalty to yourself."

"And what does that mean?"

"Your survival is dependent on our survival," Herb said.

"Are you going to kill me?"

"If that was our intent, it could be done like that," Herb said. He leaned forward and pinched the IV line leading into the man's arm. He then released it. "You're alive because we believe in life."

The man laughed. "And you're here to ask advice on how to kill my friends."

"You're a fool if you think any of those people are your friends. The only two friends you have are right here in this room with you. We're the reason you're alive, the reason you'll stay alive, and I'm here to ask for information that will help us live and, in doing so, help you live."

"And telling you would be like signing my own death certificate. Once I've told you, I have no more value. That's why you've kept me alive, isn't it?"

"That's not how we work," I said. "You have to believe me."

"I don't believe anything either of you two say. You're no different from us, no different from everybody else trying to survive. Maybe you're going to kill me, and maybe you're not, but I'm not going to tell you anything . . . not anything more!"

Herb let out a big sigh and slowly got to his feet. I went to do the same, but he placed an arm on my shoulder holding me in place.

"I understand what you're saying and feeling. Tell you what, I'm going to give you a few minutes to think—"

"A few minutes isn't going to make a difference!" Quinn spat out.

"Humor me. In the meantime, would you like a cup of coffee?"

Quinn didn't answer, but he looked interested. Cups of coffee were getting rarer and rarer, as supplies dwindled.

"I'll go and get us all a cup," Herb said. "Adam, I know how you take yours. Quinn, what would you like in yours?"

"Um, two sugars and black, please."

"Just like I take mine," Herb said.

That wasn't how Herb took his coffee, but I'd learned that Herb didn't say anything without a reason. He was trying to befriend Quinn by sharing something. How strange, offering a cup of coffee when a few seconds before we were discussing an attack and killing a hundred people.

"Adam, you are armed, correct?" Herb asked.

"Of course."

"Good, I'll be back in a few minutes."

Herb hustled out, leaving us alone. I suddenly felt very vulnerable despite the prisoner being cuffed to the bed and me being armed. I slid my chair slightly away from Quinn.

"Does he really think I'm going to sell out for a cup of coffee?" he asked.

"I think he just wants a coffee," I said.

"The coffee I'll take. Here, you might as well have these back." He went to hand me the photos and I hesitated before finally taking the stack.

"Is that the first time you saw those pictures?" he asked.

I nodded.

"I thought so. I could tell by your reaction."

"I didn't know it was that obvious," I said.

"You're not the only one watching. I guess you weren't there."

"I was there," I said. "I saw the bridge come down. I was the first one at the bottom—well, Herb and I."

"I'm surprised. If you saw the real thing, why did the pictures bother you so much?" he asked.

"I dropped Herb off and then took to the air again to provide cover."

"So you're the pilot of that plane, right?" he asked.

"It's my ultralight."

"I've seen you up in the air, right over our base."

"I've flown over it a few times."

"I was there. I got a shot off, but obviously I missed or we wouldn't be having this conversation. I guess you being in the air makes it all seem cleaner. From up there you don't see the faces of the victims."

"I've seen the faces of victims. I was there in the neighborhood that you attacked. I'm never going to forget what happened to our friends at Olde Burnham."

"And you're telling me you don't do anything different?"

"We don't. We're just trying to stay alive," I said.

"That's all we were doing, trying to stay alive."

"No it isn't. We mean no harm to anybody who doesn't try to harm us. We lived in peace with that neighborhood you destroyed, with all those people. We believe that working together we all have a better chance of surviving and—"

I stopped midsentence as the door opened and a woman appeared. She stood without saying anything, her eyes wild, her hair all askew, her clothing dirty. For a second I thought she was holding a portable drill or something in her hand and then I realized what it was. A pistol.

"I've come to kill you," she said.

5

I was frozen to my seat, but my mind started to race. Almost involuntarily my hand started to creep toward my gun, holstered at my side. I stopped myself. I couldn't possibly draw and fire before she did.

"I've been waiting for this," she said. Her voice was calm, but her eyes remained wild. Slowly she pulled up the gun and aimed it at Quinn. I leaned farther back in the chair.

"You, get away," she said, gesturing for me to get out of the line of fire. "I don't mean you any harm. It's him I came to kill."

I stumbled to my feet and staggered a few feet toward a far corner, putting distance between me and him—and her.

"I've come to kill the man who killed my family."

"Look, lady, I didn't kill anybody," Quinn pleaded. For somebody who said he wasn't afraid to die, he looked terrified.

"Maybe it wasn't you, but you were one of them!" Her voice was still calm. She looked almost peaceful. "Get out," she said to me. "Go."

I took a half step and then stopped. If I left, Quinn was dead. "I'm sorry, I don't know you," I said to the woman. "Do you know me?"

She nodded. "You're the son of the police chief; you fly that little plane. You're Adam."

"That's me . . . I'm sorry, I don't know your name."

"That isn't important."

"Sure it is."

She hesitated. "Paula."

I extended my hand to shake. "Hey, Paula, I'm pleased to meet you—"

"Don't come any closer, Adam," she ordered.

I drew back my hand. "Take it easy, Paula."

"I don't want to hurt you," she said. "I *really* don't want to hurt you."

"I appreciate that."

"You have to leave," she said.

Again she gave me the chance to walk away.

"He took everything. My husband and my children. And now I'm going to take all that he has left, his life."

"I was there at Olde Burnham," I said. "If it was my family, I'd want to do the same thing. I understand." I paused. "But I can't just leave. I can't let you do it."

"You think he deserves to live?" Suddenly her voice wasn't so calm, and for an instant she turned my way and the pistol was aimed at me. I felt a rush of panic and I had to fight to keep that fear from overwhelming me. She turned the gun back on Quinn.

"It's not for me to decide if he should live," I said. "Or for you either."

I stepped back into her line of fire. Behind me I heard the prisoner breathe in sharply. What was I doing?

"You'd risk your life to protect him?" Paula demanded.

I shook my head. "I'd risk my life for you, Paula. If you kill him, how would you live with yourself?"

"I wasn't planning on living. Do you think there's only one bullet in this gun?"

That should have been obvious to me. She wasn't leaving this room alive either. That was all part of the plan.

"Look, like I said, if I were you, I'd be feeling the same thing. Maybe it would be me standing there with a gun," I said. "I'd just hope that somebody was here to talk me out of it. If I'd lost everybody in my family like that I'd want to die, but I know that's not what they'd want. It's not what your family would want. You're all that's left. What do you think they'd want you to do?"

Her lower lip started to quiver.

"You need to honor them by living," I said.

"I don't want to live," she said, her voice practically a whisper. She started to cry.

"You have to keep going . . . for them. Besides, if you did kill this man you'd be no better than him, no better than his kind. We're better . . . *you're* better."

She lowered the pistol and started sobbing. As she dissolved, I rushed forward, taking the gun and holding her, stopping her from falling to the floor. At that same instant, Herb and Stewart rushed into the room, along with another guard. Stewart and the guard took Paula and led her from the room. Herb took the gun, and I felt my legs get rubbery and weak. I practically collapsed into the chair.

"That should never have happened," Herb said. "Adam, I'm so sorry."

"It's okay," I mumbled.

Quinn gasped. "That kid saved my life!" He turned directly to me, staring me in the eyes. "Why did you do that?"

I shook my head. "I couldn't let her kill you."

"If it was me, I would have walked away," he said.

"I doubt that, Quinn."

"I still don't believe it," he said. "You risked your life to save mine."

"It's not a big deal," I mumbled. The blood was still pulsing through me so strongly that I could hear my heart beating in my ears.

"You probably should have left," Herb said. "You shouldn't have risked your life for him."

"It's good that he did," Quinn said. "Give me those plans. I'm going to tell you what you need to know."

"Really?" I asked.

"I owe you that much."

Herb took the plans from the table and handed him a pen. "Just mark them in, label them. I want the doctor to look at Adam."

"I'm fine."

"No you're not. You're as white as a ghost. Come on."

He offered me a hand and I gladly took it. As he helped me to my feet, my legs were still shaking. All of me was shaking. We started to walk away.

"Adam!" Quinn called out. "I won't forget what you did, no matter what happens to me."

I nodded. "I don't think I'm going to forget today either."

Herb helped me out of the room. The woman—Paula— was on a bed off to the side. A nurse and Dr. Morgan were at her side, and as I watched they gave her a needle, probably something to calm her down. Herb led me over to a chair and sat me down.

"First off, I want you to know that you were in no danger," Herb said.

"No danger?"

"Her gun wasn't loaded." He held up her pistol and opened the breech to reveal that it was empty.

"How did you know?"

"Because I gave the gun to her."

"You what?" I demanded.

"I gave it to her. I gave her the gun."

"But, but, why? I don't understand."

"I'm so sorry I couldn't tell you. I knew that the prisoner wasn't willingly going to give us information, so I left to figure out what to do. And that's when I ran into her. I gave her the gun—I made sure it was empty and that she didn't have any other weapons—and I aimed her toward Quinn."

"It wasn't real?"

"It was real. To her and to him and to you."

"But why didn't you tell me what you were doing?"

"It all just happened. There wasn't time or the opportunity to explain it to you."

I felt myself filling with anger. "There was time. All you had to do was come back in, for just a minute, pull me out, tell me what you were doing. You could have done that."

"I couldn't risk it. I had to trick him."

"You tricked *me*."

"I had to have you react as if it were real."

"How would you know what I was going to do? I could have wet myself, run out, left her to kill him . . . or at least try to kill him. I could have pulled my gun and shot her. Did you even think of that?" I demanded.

"I thought of all of those things. It was a risk we had to take. Besides, you didn't do any of those things," he said.

"But I *could* have."

"No," he said. "You couldn't have. It isn't in you to just walk away. It isn't in you to try to shoot her. I know that. You did exactly what I expected you'd do."

"That doesn't change the fact that you lied to me."

"I didn't lie to you. I just didn't tell you right then, but I did tell you as soon as I could. I didn't have to do that," he said. "I could have kept it from you even now, but I didn't."

I got to my feet. The anger had stopped the shaking. My hands curled into fists, and I realized that I wanted to take a swing at Herb. But I couldn't do that either.

"You used me. You used her too," I said, gesturing to Paula. She was on the bed, silent, knocked out by whatever they had given her.

"I did, and that might be the best thing that could have happened to her. It might give her a little peace. And for you, I'm sorry, but I had to do it. If it makes you feel any better, it worked. Quinn is going to give us information that's going to save lives—well, at least the lives of our people."

I guess that's what mattered. I'd been tricked and my body was still surging with adrenaline, but I had to convince myself that was a small price to pay.

"If you want to take a swing at me, that's okay," Herb said. "I understand." He gestured to my balled-up hands.

"I don't want to punch you. Well, that's not the truth. I'm not *going* to punch you." Slowly, deliberately, I unclenched my fists.

"I just hope this doesn't mean you'll trust me any less in the future," Herb said. "Because you know I trust you even more now."

"What are you talking about?" I demanded.

"Because of what you did. You put your life on the line for *that* man. It just makes me realize what you'd be willing to do for the people of this neighborhood. With you this isn't just about empty words. You mean what you say; you believe in doing the right thing. That means a lot to me. Maybe more than I can express."

"Thanks. I guess that helps—" Then I had another thought. "You could just be playing me again right now, couldn't you?"

He gave a sad smile. "I could be, but I'm not." He paused. "At least I don't think I am. I've played so many games in my life that sometimes I'm not even sure anymore. What I am sure about is that we need people like me to help us survive. We also need people like you to help build something that matters once we do survive."

"I think we each need to be part of both. Don't sell yourself short," I said. "I know in the end you'll not just do what needs to be done, but you'll do the right thing."

"I know I'll do what needs to be done," Herb said. "I just hope the right thing doesn't get in the way."

I wasn't sure if I believed him or not. I didn't seem to know much for sure, but what I did know was that I needed to get away, and there was only one place—and one person—I wanted to be with. I'd find Lori. I didn't even know if I'd tell her what just happened, but being with her, sitting beside her, would make it all feel better.

6

Herb was beside me in the ultralight. We were cruising at slightly less than one hundred and twenty feet. Being up in the air, waiting for dawn to come, was eerie. As eerie as the fact that we were on our way to launch the attack. After not sleeping at all last night I needed to get my mind focused on what we were doing. I kept drifting back to yesterday and the way we'd fooled Quinn—the way Herb had tricked me. Knowing it was necessary and being okay with it were two different things. There was no room for my thoughts about that. I needed to keep us in the air and on target and on time. Our arrival had to be timed precisely.

Flying in the dark was new and unnerving. Last night, Lori and I had sat on her porch, holding hands and talking— while each of us wore a pair of night-vision goggles. I was trying to get used to them because I was told I'd be wearing them in this flight. How romantic, looking at my girlfriend in shades of green, a shadowy figure. Usually, looking deeply into her eyes meant something very different.

From the first time I'd laid eyes on her I knew how beautiful Lori was. Through school I'd learned that she was smart. Now over the past months I'd learned that she was smart in a whole different way. She understood what was going on, calmed me down, helped me understand. And behind those beautiful eyes she was strong, the sort of person I wanted beside me if things ever did go from bad to worse. But now I had other things to think about.

I could see just enough to make out landmarks below, and I was basically following a bright ribbon of road, using it for direction and the altimeter on my control panel to keep us at the right height.

We were heading for the compound, which was about thirty miles away. Ahead of us were over 240 of our people, evenly divided into four attack parties, aboard a number of trucks and cars. Each group was equipped with rifles, pistols, and an RPG launcher. Each group had departed at sundown the previous day, taking a different route, and had spent the night moving forward, getting in position, almost within sight of the compound but still away from where they could be seen by sentries on the walls or fences.

We'd be the first in. Hopefully we'd sweep in, do our business, and be gone before anybody had a chance to react and knock us out of the air.

"How soon will we be over the target?" Herb asked over the intercom.

"A few minutes. I just hope we time it right."

"So do I," Herb said.

The sun was still below the horizon, but the sky was already much lighter than when we had left the neighborhood.

Our plan was to arrive when there was just enough light to see our targets but not enough to become one ourselves. Our attack would be the signal for everything that followed.

I visualized the diagram that Herb had drawn and Quinn had labeled. There were a dozen buildings scattered across the compound. Those on the south and toward the center were used for supplies and storage. Five others were barracks, one hundred men per building. Four of them could be unoccupied, but more likely the remaining soldiers were scattered among the five buildings. If they were working on three shifts, then approximately eighty men would be asleep while forty would be on the perimeter walls. By now they had to know that something had gone terribly wrong with their attack on our neighborhood, but we hoped they wouldn't suspect just how bad it was. Regardless, Herb figured they'd be on high alert.

"You'll have to hold it steady," Herb said. "Be prepared for concussion waves depending on what the grenades ignite."

Herb had a bag on his lap that held a dozen grenades. He was going to drop three or four onto the barracks as we came over. With any luck Herb would be able to drop all of the grenades before we cleared the compound. Then, we'd come back over, stay high and clear as eyes in the sky, radioing down by walkie-talkie to the four squads, helping coordinate as they attacked from all sides.

We were flying almost due east. On the horizon a thin line of red light was emerging, getting bigger and thicker and glowing more brightly as I watched. I wanted to open the throttle up to get there sooner, but I knew I couldn't. We were going to come in low enough and slow enough to allow Herb to drop the grenades. I had to just hope there was still enough darkness to hide us, because they'd hear the sound of the engine coming. We were counting on them thinking it was from something on the ground and not the air.

"I see it," Herb said. He had his night-vision goggles down as well. "Straight ahead."

I saw it, too. The chain-link fence and stone wall were now visible. I pictured the compound layout and knew where I had to go. I banked sharply to the right so that we could fly the entire length of the compound. I needed to make a long pass right down the center, directly over the barracks. Inside those buildings were sleeping soldiers, bloodthirsty raiders who, we hoped, would never have a chance to wake up ever again.

We passed over the fence—and now we were above the compound—and nobody was shooting at us. We'd come in unseen, even if they could hear us. Our invisibility would probably only last a few seconds, but each second was like a golden gift of protection. I couldn't think about it. I focused on the building that I knew was the first of the barracks, with four more behind it.

"Lower," Herb said.

I was going to get him so low he could reach out and place the grenades onto the rooftop. I pushed down on the stick. "Here we go," I said, and felt my stomach rise as the plane dropped—and still no gunfire.

The first building was coming up fast. Herb pulled the pin and tossed down a grenade, then a second and a third. I swooped over the top of the building and then there was an explosion.

The ultralight bucked and we were bathed in bright light. *Ahhhhhh!* The brilliant flash nearly blinded me through the night-vision goggles, and with one hand I pushed them onto my forehead, holding the stick firm with the other. I pulled up on the stick as a second explosion sounded and then a third, each one hitting us with a shock wave.

Herb kept pulling pins and dropping grenades, one after

the other, with explosion after explosion detonating in our wake as we soared along the barracks rooftops. And then suddenly we passed by the last building and a few seconds later we cleared the perimeter fence and soared up and away and into the darkness. There was nothing but the steady roar of the engine and propeller. We'd gotten in and out without being fired on. We'd taken them completely by surprise.

"Come back around, hard, fast!" Herb yelled.

I hit the rudder pedals as hard as I could. We started to slide, and I heard the engine threatening to stall—I goosed the gas, opening the throttle up completely to regain the speed I'd lost.

I could now see the compound out of the corner of my eye—there were flames, pools of light, but there was no movement on the ground, no sounds of bullets or secondary explosions, no muzzle fire.

"It's deserted!" I screamed. "It's—"

My voice was overwhelmed by the noise of more blasts, one after the other lighting up the entire compound, the entire sky, with reds, oranges, and brilliant whites, and hundreds of muzzle flashes greeting the dawn, a steady barrage of shots. It was our four teams, attacking from all sides, precisely according to plan.

"Cease fire!" Herb yelled into the radio. "Cease fire! Cease fire!"

The explosions and the muzzle bursts continued. Hadn't they heard him?

Gunfire was streaming from all sides—and other voices screamed out over the radio, trying to stop the attack, bring things under control. Then the shots lessened until only a few scattered ones sounded out, and then total silence.

I brought us back around, the compound right in front of us, buildings on fire, the flickering light thrown out by the flames the only movement visible.

"Report in!" Herb ordered. "Report in . . . Is there anybody down there?"

"Negative, negative, it's deserted!" It was my mother's voice over the radio. "The fence has been breached, the walls aren't guarded!"

"It could be a trap," Herb warned.

"I'm going to send in Brett and his squad," Mom said.

"Good. Let's keep the larger forces outside, alert, keeping an eye on their flanks. Don't let anybody come up from behind."

"Roger that," my mother responded. "Do you really think it's a trap?"

"I don't know that it *isn't*. Keep watch."

As we came up over the compound again everything was much clearer. In those few short minutes, the sun had poked up over the horizon. Anxiously I scanned the ground for anything that could be dangerous. Three of the barracks were on fire at the center. All along the perimeter at different places the fences and walls had been breached, in some instances just blown to bits, the debris scattered behind. Outside the perimeter I caught glimpses of movement, sunlight reflecting off metal. I just hoped those were our people with our weapons.

"There's Brett's squad," Herb said. "To the right, coming through the gap in the wall at about ten-thirty."

Men were moving through the gap and starting to fan out across the compound, taking shelter as they moved, covering one another. We were too high for me to pick out which one was Brett, but I knew he'd be leading because he always was. No matter what the situation, he always put himself up front on point, taking the biggest risk, protecting the people he was leading. People respected him for that.

"There's an open stretch in the middle of the compound—that's where the Cessna landed. Do you want me to put down?" I asked.

"That's the last thing I want you to do. The place isn't secure yet," Herb said.

"But I don't see anything."

"There's lots you can't see that could kill us both. I want you to pull up and get elevation. We need to do a reconnaissance around the whole area to make sure that nothing is coming up from behind our squads."

"We wouldn't be able to see a man or two out there either, hidden among the houses."

"I'm not worried about a man or two. I'm worried about a hundred coming up in a coordinated ambush. That we'd see."

I pulled back on the stick, hit the rudder, and banked to start a circle around the perimeter.

The sun was now completely above the horizon. I turned slightly away from the glow as it came up over my right side. Five minutes ago the rising sun was something I feared, an enemy that would make me visible. Now it felt like a friend, showing me the dangers below. Of course that also made me just as visible to anybody on the ground with a high-powered rifle and a scope. Instinctively, I pushed back on the stick and we dropped down quickly.

"What's wrong?" Herb demanded. "Do you see something?"

"Nothing and nothing. Just a little evasive action to be careful."

"Careful is good. They could be out there. We might have just missed them. They could have heard or seen us coming and fled. If we see them, we can give chase," Herb said.

"Chase them? We'd send people after them?"

"People, yes, but us first. I still have four grenades. We could take out a truck or two, maybe twenty men."

"Or they could take us out."

"There's always that," Herb said.

"Shouldn't we just be grateful they're gone and not bother chasing them?"

"That's the last thing we should be grateful for."

"But we didn't have to fight. We didn't have anybody killed or hurt."

"Not now, but do you think it's good to have a hundred or so armed men out there doing harm, causing havoc, killing innocents, and possibly coming back at us at some point?"

"But they ran from us now, so wouldn't they be afraid to attack us?"

"Just because they're afraid now doesn't mean they can't rearm, gain strength, and come back at us again. The only certainty we could ever have of them never bothering us again is if we neutralize them once and for all."

Neutralize—such a polite word for *kill*.

"Okay," I said.

"Back home, the committee has to know that really this was far from successful, but for everybody else this has to be seen simply as another victory. They need to feel good about the positive and not worry about the future. Worry can be paralyzing."

"Or the truth can be liberating," I responded.

"Only as much truth as they can handle."

We circled around and Herb peered below with binoculars. He was looking down but also well into the distance. Would he be able to see them, driving away in their vehicles? And if he did would we go after them, just me and him, right now?

I was just grateful for seeing nothing except houses, stores, and a few seemingly deserted factories. Lost down there among all those buildings could easily be a hundred armed men, or a thousand, or ten thousand. But I couldn't let my mind get racing. It was only a hundred, and I was sure they were long gone, but it didn't matter if they were hiding or not, as long as they didn't attack our people.

We kept banking, executing a big circle around the compound. I wasn't seeing anything anywhere, not even the ordinary trickle of morning movement in the surrounding neighborhoods. No doubt the explosions and gunfire had kept people from chasing after water, food, and resources for a moment, but that moment was over.

I thought back to something Herb had said. "How much truth do you give me?" I asked.

"Truth is a tricky concept."

"No it isn't."

"Yes it is. Truth is subjective. Just because I think something will happen doesn't mean it will. There's no sense in bringing you into all of my nightmares and have you lose sleep as well."

"Sleep doesn't come easy right now, but I'd like to know," I said.

"Everything?"

"Everything."

"Really?" he asked. He turned to look at me and for a moment his eyes gleamed ferociously.

I swallowed. "Well, yes, I guess . . . sure."

"Look, Adam, I always tell your mother and you everything, just maybe not all at once, in the same instant."

"Like with the prisoner yesterday." I could feel the anger building up inside again.

"I know how much that bothered you," he said. "I didn't just withhold the truth but deliberately tricked you. You have my word that won't happen again."

"Unless you really have to."

He smiled. "Bring us around and let's see if we can land. I think the compound has been secured."

I was grateful to be breaking off the circle. I didn't want to find anybody or anything to chase. I just wanted to land.

7

By the time I'd come back around for the landing, the report from Brett's team had crackled over the radio. The compound was empty, deserted, and we had it completely secure.

I could see people—our people—surging through the gaps in the walls, swarming all over the grounds, and taking up positions along the perimeter. A big gate on the north side had been opened up, and all our vehicles were driving in. The rising smoke from the burning buildings was the wind sock I used to gauge the direction and strength of the wind. It also made the landing more difficult, since we were flying directly into the blowing smoke.

The runway was a wide pavement cutting through the middle of the compound. It was long enough to handle a Cessna, so it was far bigger than anything I needed. It was completely open. Herb had radioed down to make sure neither vehicles nor people crossed over until we landed.

I pushed forward on the stick, eased off on the throttle, and brought us in slow and low. We hit a patch of black billowing smoke and then descended beneath it, for a clear ride. We touched down so gently that for an instant I wasn't sure if we were even on the ground. I backed off the throttle and eased the brakes. There was no need to hit them hard because we had so much real estate ahead of us.

No sooner had we stopped and I'd killed the engine than we were surrounded by our people. We clicked off our harnesses, and practically before we could remove our helmets we were offered hands to help us from the ultralight.

When we were out, Herb looked my way. "I'm going to the main storehouse. Your mother is probably there already. Do you want to stay with your plane or come with me?"

"I'm coming with you." I knew from the interviews Herb had had with Quinn that the main storehouse was where they kept weapons, ammunition, some vehicles, and food. Now I was curious what, if anything, had been left behind.

We started off across the compound. It seemed chaotic, with people running around and shouting. I could tell Herb didn't like it, as he repeatedly tried to calm the situation, stopping folks to ask what they were doing, slowing them down. Our men and women seemed pumped, excited, almost like they were at a party, although it was a party where everybody had brought a weapon and many of them were wearing body armor. But as Herb walked and talked his way through, everyone did seem to calm down.

The storehouse was right beside the burning barracks in the middle of the compound. As we closed in I could feel the heat from the flames.

"Do you think they left much behind?" I asked.

"They would have moved the most valuable things, but there are probably things they either couldn't move or didn't have the time or the ability to move. I guess we'll find out soon enough."

My mother and I saw each other at the same instant.

"I'm glad you're okay!" I exclaimed.

"And you, too!" She wrapped her arm around me and we hugged through our body armor.

"Were there any casualties?" Herb asked, which surprised me.

"Two wounded," my mother said.

"But how could anybody be hurt?" I questioned. "Wasn't the compound deserted?"

"Friendly fire," my mother said.

"That's always a danger when you attack from more than one side at once," Herb said. "Will they be all right?"

"Dr. Morgan is already working on them. He didn't think that either was a life-threatening situation."

"Good. Excellent. So did they leave much behind?"

"Some bulk food, potatoes, and dozens of sacks of rice," she said.

Food—nothing was more important with so many mouths to feed.

"Unfortunately," she continued, "there are no weapons or trucks, but there is something that I know my son in particular will be really interested in."

"What is it?" I asked.

She smiled but didn't answer. Instead she motioned for us to follow her inside. I felt the hairs on the back of my neck rise up, but knew I was being a bit silly. Obviously, my mother wouldn't lead me into danger.

The building was practically empty, dimly lit, but I recognized the outline of a plane.

"A Cessna!" I exclaimed. "Are you kidding me?"

Herb gave a surprised laugh. "If they had another plane, why wasn't it up in the air after the first one went down?"

I thought back to the other plane, the one that had once tried to shoot me and Herb out of the sky. In the end they were the ones who crashed and burned.

"Maybe they didn't have another pilot," my mother suggested.

"Or maybe this one isn't flightworthy or doesn't even have an engine," I said.

"There's only one way to find out."

The plane was a vintage model, probably at least forty years old. That meant it didn't have computers and wouldn't have been affected by the virus. I pulled up the engine panel—there was indeed an engine, and it looked in pretty good shape. Of course, I couldn't tell whether it worked.

"Climb inside," my mother said. "We have to get it out of here. I'm afraid of the fire spreading from the other buildings."

"Even if the engine works, I don't know if I can taxi it out of here through those doors. They're not very wide."

"I'll take care of that. You get inside and I'll find some people to push you out," my mother said.

I slammed down the panel. There were blocks under the wheels and I pulled them free. They'd gotten it in here, so we'd be able to get it out—assuming they hadn't taken the wings off first and reassembled it inside. Maybe that was why it was still grounded.

I opened the cockpit door and climbed in. During my flight lessons over the last year I'd spent a whole lot more time in the passenger seat of a Cessna than in the pilot's seat, but I had taken the controls the last few times, getting ready to solo. I ran my hand along the instrument panel. It had a familiar look but with a slightly different arrangement from what I'd flown before. First off, it was mainly wooden and all of the dials were analog—sort of like the gauges on my car. That was what I expected from an older plane. Old was good in our new world. Of course it was very, very different from my ultralight and its open cockpit, and I had to think back to my time in the Cessna. It seemed like years instead of months.

I pulled back on the yoke and turned around to see the flaps on the tail—the elevators—rise up as they should. In flight this would cause the plane to gain altitude. I pushed the yoke forward, and the elevators dipped down, which would have pushed the nose down had we been airborne. I pulled it back and forth. It felt smooth. That didn't mean that the cables and levers weren't frayed or couldn't snap in a second but, still, potentially they were good.

I pushed the left rudder pedal and then the right. The rudder reacted properly. I could turn right and left—assuming the flaps on the wings, the ailerons, also worked. Still looking back I turned the wheel left and right. The flaps were sticky, but they moved.

There was a loud smash behind me and I jumped in my seat. Two men with sledgehammers were attacking the wall beside the door, making the opening larger. Good. The last thing I wanted to do was damage a wing before I got it outside and into the air. Actually, the last thing I wanted to do was get it up into the air and have the plane stall out or have a piece fall off.

Herb came in, accompanied by a dozen other men. He walked over to my door. I pushed down the window.

"Here are your friendly neighbors, ready to push you out," Herb called over the pounding hammers.

"Just give me a minute and keep everybody away from the prop."

"The engine works?" Herb asked.

"Let's find out."

I turned on the starter. The lights on the panel blinked on, and the indicators came to life. So we knew the battery worked. There was only one more step. I twisted the starter one more turn and got nothing, not even a click. The engine was silent.

I leaned back out the window. "No go. I'll need a push. Could you guys make sure to only hold on to the struts and push the solid parts of the wings? It's important not to touch the elevators or ailerons."

There were looks of confusion.

"The flaps. Don't touch the flaps. I'll show you."

I opened the door and jumped out. First things first. We had to turn it around and aim it toward the door, which was becoming wider with each crash of the sledgehammers. I showed them where to touch and where to avoid. Together we picked up the tail section and rotated the plane around to have its front facing straight out. I climbed back into the plane so I could control the brakes and signaled for them to start pushing. With this many men and this much muscle, the plane started forward.

We were just barely off line with the doorway. I depressed the right brake ever so slightly to shift us in the right direction. "Slow, no need for speed!" I yelled out the window.

The plane lurched to the side and we moved across the storehouse. The nose inched out through the doors. I swung my head left and right anxiously. It looked like there was room on both sides for the wings to pass through, but not with much to spare.

"Stop! Stop," I yelled as I stepped on both brakes. I needed to be certain there was space. A plane with banged-up wings either wasn't getting off the ground or was landing in a heap. I jumped down and went from one side to the other. The openings were jagged but bigger. There was a foot of clearance on the right and what looked like a few inches on the other.

"Okay, guys. Really slowly, let's do this."

They started pushing again, and I stood directly in front of the plane so I could guide it out.

"Slowly . . . slowly," I called out.

This was going to be even closer than I thought. The leading edge of the wing was almost there and just brushed by on the left. Now the wing was past, the plane was out and free! If I could get the engine to fire up, I had myself a Cessna!

"Push it away from the barracks!" Herb yelled. "Quick!"

The fire in the three buildings was even stronger now, the flames higher.

I jumped back into the cockpit, stepping on the left brake hard, and as they pushed, the Cessna spun around, away from the flames. Once it came right around, I let off the brake and the combined muscle moved us quickly down the runway. I looked over my shoulder as we put more and more distance behind us, until it felt like we were far enough away from the flames.

"This is good!" I yelled out the window. They stopped pushing and I coasted to a stop. I climbed out.

"We'll have two mechanics in your mom's squad look at the engine and see if it can be started," Herb said as he walked to my side.

"If they could get it running I could fly it home."

Herb shook his head. "Negative, son. I'm not prepared to risk your life until we've checked out everything from prop to tail. You should know better than anybody that just because the engine starts doesn't mean it won't quit midflight or that one of the cables might not snap or that a wing won't fall off."

Of course he was right. Putting it into the air right now wasn't smart. There might be a very good reason it was sitting in the storehouse instead of being up in the sky.

"But how will we get it back to the neighborhood if I don't fly it?" I asked.

"We'll get it there if we have to push it the whole way. Believe me, I'm not going to risk losing the most valuable thing we found here," Herb said reassuringly.

"Herb!" my mother called out. "Come with me. The compound isn't deserted. We think there are people in one of the buildings!"

8

Herb and my mother took off, and I ran to catch them.

"It's the building in the far south corner. We have it surrounded, and our people have taken cover," my mother said as she raced back to the building.

"Anything else?" Herb asked.

"I've got our sentries on the walls keeping their focus on the outside," she reported. "We don't want to be caught in the middle between one group attacking from the inside while a second coordinates an attack from the outside."

"Do you think that's what's happening?" I asked.

"I don't see any signs, but I guess I'm always suspicious when things aren't difficult," my mother said.

"This has all been too easy," Herb agreed.

We took a wide route around the burning barracks. Once past the buildings and free of the smoke, we could clearly see the building in question. It was surrounded by our vehicles, which were being used as cover a safe distance away. Behind them were about fifty of our men and women, weapons at the ready, aimed at the building. Bent over, trying to stay low, we came forward and took refuge behind a truck. No sooner had we gotten there than both Howie and Brett came over.

"Brief us," my mother said.

"Some of my men were doing a building-by-building search," Howie said. "They tried to approach this one, but then they heard movement and some voices and I ordered them to retreat to safety."

"Good thinking," my mother said.

"We set up the perimeter and that's all there is to tell," he added. "So what comes next?"

"I think we should establish contact and try to get them to surrender," Herb said.

My mother nodded. "Somebody get me a bullhorn," she ordered. Quickly one was handed to her.

"Howie, can you go around and try to position our people so there's less chance of us shooting each other in the cross-fire?" Herb directed. "I want to make sure that nobody fires unless they hear the order from the captain."

"Will do." Howie rushed off.

"Does that mean you don't think they're going to listen and surrender?" I asked.

"I think we have to be prepared. Your mom asking to speak to them might trigger a response that we don't want."

"If they don't respond, this might make them listen," Brett said, tapping the side of the RPG launcher he was carrying.

"I hope it doesn't come to that," my mother said.

"*They* better hope it doesn't," Brett said.

"It would be better for all of us."

Brett shrugged. "I was hoping to have a chance to use this thing, but either way they're coming out—walking and alive or dead and feet-first."

"Let's take it down a notch, son," Herb said to Brett.

My mother poked her head slightly above the cover of the car. "This is Captain Daley," she called out, her metallic amplified voice bouncing off the building. "You are surrounded. We want you to come out . . . hands up . . . no weapons. If you surrender you will not be harmed." She put down the bullhorn. "This sort of situation is usually handled by our SWAT team."

"Well, you made it sound like you've been through trouble like this before."

"Part of the job . . . one more thing to do. I have to give them a time limit."

She brought the bullhorn up again. "You have five minutes to respond. If you do not surrender within that time, we will be left with no choice but to come in by force."

"Perfect," Herb said.

"So now we wait," my mother said.

"If they don't react in five minutes, we give them one more warning—one more minute and then, well, we act," Herb said. "We've given them the choice and a chance. The rest is up to them."

"I'm timing it," Brett said.

I got the feeling that he wasn't hoping for the same thing as everybody else. He just wanted a chance to fire that portable cannon—no matter how many people could die because of it.

Herb brought his binoculars up and scanned the building. I didn't know what he hoped to see, but I was curious. I carefully peeked over the back of the truck at the building. It was no different from the rest of the buildings that filled the compound—dark, peeling paint, solid walls with a big sliding door at the front. There could have been other doors on other sides, but if a vehicle was going to come out, this was the place it was going to emerge.

"Maybe it would be better if we did something before the five minutes are up," Brett said. "You know, catch them by surprise."

"We wait," my mother said.

"It's just that if—"

"We wait," my mother barked.

He looked like he was going to argue.

"Stand down—*now*, officer."

He gave a disapproving scowl. "Yes, ma'am." Slowly, he took the grenade launcher from his shoulder. "I was just suggesting an alternative."

"Duly noted," my mother said. "Herb, do you see anything?"

"Nothing. No movement. No response."

"Could I borrow the binoculars?" I asked.

"Another pair of eyes, especially younger ones, can only help," he said. He removed them from around his neck and handed them to me. I brought them up to my eyes and adjusted the lenses as I tried to focus on the building. The binoculars were so powerful that it felt like I was seeing less and not more. All I could view was a small area of peeling paint. I slowly scanned along the front of the building, although I had no idea what I was hoping to see other than more peeling paint. Reaching one end of the building I started scanning back along, slightly higher up, still not sure what I expected to see, but what else was there to do to fill the seconds?

"That's four minutes," Brett said. "I don't think they're going to surrender."

I didn't think so either.

"I wonder if there's anybody even there to hear," Herb said. "Maybe our people simply heard somebody on the other side of the building."

"I guess that's a possibility. I might be making an ultimatum to an empty building," my mother said.

"That wouldn't be the worst thing," Herb said.

"Brett, I want you to get into position to take a shot," my mom ordered. "I want one round fired to take down the door."

"But not until you receive the order to fire from your captain," Herb added.

Mom was looking directly at Brett with her laser stare. I knew what it was like to be caught in those beams.

He looked slightly away.

"We're going to give them every chance . . . assuming I'm not talking to myself," she said.

Brett went to the back of the truck and steadied the RPG on the bed of the vehicle. He'd be ready to fire the second he was given the order.

"That's five minutes," Herb said.

My mother brought the bullhorn up again. "This is your final warning! If you don't come out immediately, you will be fired upon! You have one minute!"

"Do you hear something?" I questioned.

Herb shook his head. "Not me, but that doesn't mean much."

"I don't hear anything either," my mother said. "What do you think you hear?"

"It sounds like, I don't know, a rumbling noise . . . I'm just not sure."

"It could be the fire burning or the wind," Herb offered.

I turned my head to try to hear better. There was a sound, but I couldn't tell what it was or even if it was coming from the direction of the building.

"Brett, get ready to take the shot on my command," my mom said.

"Ready and waiting."

I put the binoculars back up. I just wished I could see through those walls. If only there was a window and somebody could get closer and have a look inside. Instead there was nothing but blocks, cement, and that one large sliding door—held shut by a rusty-looking little padlock!

"Wait!" I screamed. "There's a lock on the door! There's a padlock on the outside of the door!"

"Stand down!" my mother ordered.

Brett lowered the weapon.

"Everybody stand down," Herb said into the radio.

"It's right there." I handed him the binoculars. "Lower right—it's the same color as the building, so it's hard to see, but it's there."

It didn't take him long to focus. "I see it. This is a complication. If there are people in there, they can't get out."

"But why would people be locked in?" I questioned.

"I can only think of one reason and there's only one way to find out," Herb said. "We have to cut open the lock and have a look inside."

"Nobody can get closer without being in the open," my

mother said. "Maybe we could drive a car closer and use it for cover or—"

"I got this," Brett said. He had already placed the RPG launcher on the ground and picked up a tool from the bed of the truck. Before anybody could say anything he got up and sprinted toward the building, looking the part of an action hero again. He covered the open ground in just a few seconds and took cover against the solid blocks of the wall. He was right beside the big sliding door, close to the padlock. He pulled the tool up—bolt cutters.

"Have everybody lower their weapons," Herb said. "We can't afford anybody getting nervous."

My mother gave the orders over the radio.

Brett wielded the bolt cutters and then stood up, holding the broken lock in his hands. Then he motioned to let us know that he was going to slide open the door. Herb swung the rifle off his shoulder and took aim at the building to give Brett cover. Brett was now holding a pistol in one hand. He shoved the door, and it rolled wide open with a loud groan before coming to a stop. Complete silence as everybody watched and waited. There was nothing.

"Come out now with your hands up!" my mother called through the bullhorn.

I strained to see into the building, to peer through the darkness. Anybody was free to come out now. They had better come out now. But there was only the stillness. Had the whole thing just been a mistake?

Then there was a dull flash of movement, gray against the black, and a woman stepped into the light, her hands up. Then there was a second and a third, all in rumpled clothing.

More women followed, and then there were children, clinging to the women, hiding behind them. They kept coming into view and walking into the open. They looked faded, like ghosts drifting out of the darkness—terrified ghosts—with hands up and eyes wide open in shock and fear.

9

They sat in the shade of the building. There were forty-seven of them—thirty-one women and sixteen small children. They managed to explain that they had been locked in the building for what they thought was about thirty-six hours.

They had been kidnapped, abused, beaten, and practically starved to death. Now they just sat, almost motionless. I stared at them, sharing their silence. To kidnap and abuse them was despicable, but to lock them in to die of thirst and starvation was more evil than I could even imagine.

Herb walked over to me. "How are you doing?"

I shrugged. "I guess it's more important how they're doing."

"Dr. Morgan has examined them all. They're dehydrated and weak. It was pretty hot in there, and they'd been surviving on almost no food for weeks before being locked in."

"How could anybody do this? I just can't . . . can't . . ."

"The men who did this are—were—without any shred of humanity. They somehow knew we were coming and simply fled, taking with them everything of value."

"And the lives of these women and children didn't have any value to them?"

"They would have taken up space in the trucks that they probably used for more valuable merchandise."

"If they didn't want them, then why didn't they just let them go?" I asked.

"They didn't want to leave witnesses behind. They wanted them dead but didn't want to waste the bullets. If we had been two days later, there wouldn't have been any of them left alive. The building would have done the job of the bullets."

"I just keep thinking, What if we had fired the grenade gun?"

"Most of them would have been killed. Either in the initial explosion or in what would have happened next as the survivors came running out of the building. Our shooters would have cut them down. Thank goodness you saw the lock. They owe you their lives, and we owe you for preventing us from perpetrating a massacre."

"That was just luck, dumb luck."

"It was more than that. Do you recognize any of them?" Herb asked.

I shook my head. "Why would I?"

"Half a dozen of those women are from Olde Burnham, kidnapped when their neighborhood was overrun and their homes destroyed."

I felt ill. "Do they know about what happened? Do they know about their families?"

"They lived through it. Even if they don't know, well, they *know*. I guess the big question is what happens to them now."

"What do you mean?" I asked.

"It's almost noon. We can't stay here much longer to protect them. We have to get back to the neighborhood."

"But they're coming with us, aren't they?"

"Adam, you know we don't have the authority to bring them back into the neighborhood, or the supplies to feed them if they did come back with us. You know we can't just bring people in."

"But we took in the survivors from Olde Burnham. Aren't some of these women and kids just survivors?"

"I guess they are."

"Maybe they even have family members who survived and are waiting for them back in our neighborhood. Do you want to tell those people that we turned away people who could be their families? We have to take them."

Herb thought for a moment. "I suppose you're right. We should take any of those survivors who are from Olde Burham with us. It's not many—six or seven."

"And what about the rest?" I asked.

"We can leave them some extra food, some water containers, and—"

"And nobody to protect them, no weapons, or shelter. They don't have anything here!"

"They probably won't want to stay here, but they're alive and free to go where they want," Herb said.

"Leaving them behind is just leaving them to die a slow death," I said. "We're no better than the people who locked them in the building. Now *we'd* be the ones leaving them to die. The only difference is that we can pretend we're good people."

"We are good people."

"Not if we leave them here," I said.

"That doesn't change the fact that the committee has to

make the decision to let in more people. It's not for us to decide."

"I never thought you'd hide behind the committee," I snapped. "Besides, almost half the committee is here already. If that half agreed, we could take these people back and then let the whole committee decide."

"And if they decided not to let them in, what then?" Herb asked.

"Then they'd be no worse off than they are now. At least they'd be away from here."

"It's not that simple. You can walk by a piece of garbage on the ground, but once you pick it up you have a responsibility."

"These people aren't just pieces of garbage. We already have a responsibility," I argued.

"We have a bigger responsibility to the people who live in our neighborhood already, not to those who might need or want to live there."

"People will understand. Besides, we did find some food."

"Not enough to get that many people through any more than a few weeks. Do you think that the folks in our neighborhood will understand why we're not going to have enough food, why they are going to go hungrier, get weaker, why their children are going to be malnourished? Bringing this whole group along will potentially risk the lives of our people."

"If we bring them, then potentially people will die. Leave them behind and definitely these people will die. We'll do something, we'll get more food. We'll survive. Let's go and talk to my mother. She'll listen to us, she'll listen to *you*." I paused. "Besides, you couldn't really walk away from them, could you?"

"Adam, you know my history. You know some of what I've done. I have walked away before. I could do it again. We're doing that every day when we don't let the people walking by our walls into our neighborhood. We're all going to need to do it again before this is over. Time and time again. You know that."

"You're right. There will be times we have to walk away . . . but not this time. Not now. They're coming with us. We're going to convince the committee."

Herb smiled. "Let's go and talk to your mother. It might be right, but that doesn't mean it's the wise thing."

"Wise or not, I know my mother will agree and I hope the committee will come around as well."

"I'm sure you can convince them. The harder part will be having everybody else in the neighborhood believe that bringing in extra people was the right decision."

"People will understand."

"Forty-seven extra mouths is a lot of food. I guess we'll have to work on it. But right now, after we talk to your mother, I want you to fly back to the neighborhood in your ultralight. There are a lot of people anxiously waiting for the news you're going to bring them. Let them know we're all alive, that we won."

10

It had taken all of the day of the attack and most of the night, but the Cessna had been pushed back to the neighborhood. I'd heard them finally arrive with the plane, parking it at Herb's just before four in the morning. I had wanted to go out right then but knew it would be better to wait until first light.

I fell back into a restless sleep, waking just as the sky started to lighten. I strapped on my pistol and slipped out of the house. The plane sat on Herb's driveway, its wings extending well over the pavement onto his lawn on one side and our lawn on the other. With my ultralight tucked into the handmade hangar covering our driveway beside the lawn, it was like I was at an airport. And really, since I was using our street as my runway, it *was* a little airport. Of course, the Cessna couldn't take off or land from our street. It would need a much longer strip, assuming it could ever get into the air to begin with.

I ran my hand along the leading edge of the wings. It had a few little dimples, but it was mainly smooth and clean. This old plane had been kept in good shape. I mentally initiated the preflight checklist that I did before every one of my lessons, doing a visual inspection, manually testing to make sure things were operational.

Herb had made it clear—and my mother even clearer—that I wasn't going anywhere until it was completely checked out. But that was all just talk anyway if we couldn't get the engine running. Today our two mechanics would have a look at it. I would have felt more confident if they were airplane mechanics instead of car mechanics, but still, an engine was an engine.

I looked up and saw Brett coming down the street. He had a rifle slung over his shoulder.

"Looks like you've finally got yourself a real plane," he said.

"I already had a plane. Now I might have two. You must have gotten up early."

"I didn't go to bed. I knew I wouldn't be able to get to sleep."

"I know exactly what you mean. It's hard to sleep when there's so much going on in your head," I said.

"It's not my head, it's my blood. You get so pumped with adrenaline, and then when nothing happens there's no place for it to go."

"It almost sounds like you're disappointed there wasn't a battle."

"Well . . . I guess I am, but there will be other opportunities. I'd like to think we're not through with those bastards just yet," Brett said. "I'd like another shot at them."

"I'd like to never see them again."

"If not them, it'll be somebody else. Sooner or later somebody will end up in my rifle sights."

He had a slight smile on his face and a look of almost wonder in his eyes. It was like he was anticipating a battle to come.

"So what's the plan for the plane?" he asked.

"Today the mechanics are going to try to get the engine going. If they are successful, then Mr. Nicholas and I are going to go over it from top to bottom and see if we can put it into the air."

"You can't take off from here, can you?" Brett asked.

"Nope. The street isn't long enough. I'd taxi it up to the hill and use Erin Mills Parkway as my strip. It's straight and clear and would easily handle a takeoff and hopefully a landing."

"You don't know if you can land it?"

"I can land it. It's just that the final test to see if it can really fly is flying it. Until then, well, we don't know for sure. One way or another it's coming down. It would just be nice if it was a landing I could walk away from."

"You know, I don't want to fly with you, but getting up there for the first time in a machine you're not sure about— it's a bit of a high, isn't it?"

"I'd rather know that it was airworthy," I said.

"Come on, admit it! The first time you took up your ultra-light, wasn't it a wicked buzz?"

"Well, yeah, I guess." What I *wasn't* going to admit was that most of the rush hit me when I realized I hadn't checked the fuel before going up and was feeling the sheer terror that I was going to run out of gas and crash. I'd never told anybody about that.

"Is that what you felt when you ran toward that building yesterday?" I asked.

"It is a rush. I get one whenever I go outside the walls, especially at night." He slapped me on the back. "Maybe I should go up with you in your ultralight one of these times, just for the high."

"Don't you get enough of that already?" I asked.

"It's addictive, man. You just want more and more. Do you get tired of flying?"

"Nah, of course not, but it's not the same. I take precautions, do the preflight checks, and know my equipment. I don't just go running toward a building I think is filled with people with weapons."

He laughed. "That was crazy, like a jolt of electricity surging through my veins."

"I still can't believe you just ran in like that. What were you thinking?"

"That's the whole thing, man. I wasn't *thinking*, I was *feeling*. Like I said, it's a rush."

We stood there in silence, watching as the horse-drawn cart passed by the end of the street. How strange that the sight of horses in the neighborhood was the new normal. So much was new. All of the front lawns turned over, crops popping up through the soil. Two men and a woman walked by, rifles slung over their shoulders. And, of course, the ultralight and Cessna sitting in front of my house and Herb's.

"Have you ever gone hunting?" Brett asked out of left field.

"Target shooting, but never hunting."

"You'd mentioned to me once that there were deer down in the ravine," he said.

"Yup. There used to be a big herd, but it's hard to know if there are any still there now," I said. "Probably lots of people would have the same idea."

"Only one way to find out," Brett said. "We need to go and

try to find them. I've seen bows and arrows hanging in your garage. We could use those."

"You've done bow hunting before, right?" I asked. I remembered him saying something about it.

"It's the only real way to hunt."

"It does seem like more of a challenge, more of a fair fight," I said.

"It's more than that. It's just more . . . more real, more *intense*. You're right there."

I didn't really care about any of that. I was just thinking about how much meat was on a deer, how many mouths it could feed, and how we now had extra mouths to feed. Why hadn't I thought of this before?

"Let's have a look at those bows," Brett said. He gave me a slap on the back. "This could be fun, buddy!"

"What could be fun?"

Lori. I turned around. She was wearing shorts and a T-shirt—was it one I hadn't seen before? Something was different.

"Good morning," I said.

"Good morning to you." She gave me a little hug. Somehow it seemed awkward in front of Brett.

"I like your hair," Brett said. "It makes you look older."

Hair! That was it—she'd had her hair done. And I hadn't said anything.

"You're up awfully early." I thought it was best to change the subject.

"Cows don't sleep in. They need to be milked. So what's going to be fun?"

"Brett and I are going out to see if we can get a deer. We're going to go bow hunting."

"Wouldn't you have better luck with a gun than a bow?" she asked.

"Luck has nothing to do with it," Brett said. "Besides, we'll take our guns along."

That was just smart. It didn't make sense to go outside the neighborhood armed with only bows and arrows.

"You're obviously busy now, but those cows need to be milked twice a day so there will be other opportunities to help if you really want to," she said to me.

"Then I will, for sure."

"It'll be nice to have help and company." She paused. "Thanks for *that*, at least."

I knew what she meant. This was back to the hair and me not saying anything.

"I was going to say something about your hair, really . . . It looks good." I paused. "But you *always* look good."

Lori smiled, but before I could say anything more Brett cut in.

"So enough gabbing. Let me get cleaned up at your place, and then we can go get us some meat."

"Can I grab breakfast first?" I asked.

"No, it's always better to go hunting on an empty stomach. It gives you a little more incentive." He turned to Lori. "And I'll see *you* later."

———————

By the time we had both gotten ready and gathered the bows and arrows, the shift change on the wall was in process. New guards were now in place, while others were either lingering or making their way home. A lot of the people on the walls weren't the usual guards, who were still resting or sleeping from yesterday's raid.

Up ahead I saw Mrs. Julian walking with her dog, Bubbles, a little white poodle with a bright pink sweater. Until a few days ago I only knew Mrs. Julian as poodle owner, but she'd filled in on the security team and Bubbles was a guard dog. He was certainly a lot different from the German shepherds and Labs that some people had on patrol, but I'd been told he was good at alerting the guards to outside noises. I guess that made sense. If I was that little, I would be super-aware of what was happening around me.

"Good morning," I said as we came up to her. I dropped to one knee and gave Bubbles a scratch behind the ear.

"Nice sweater," Brett said.

"Bubbles is old and he gets cold easily, even in the summer," Mrs. Julian explained. "It was a bit chilly last night for him."

"Thanks for being out here," I said.

"Just doing my part, although I'm not sure what good I'd be if there was a problem," she said.

"As long as you can alert people, you're doing your job," Brett said. "That's why they have people with guns out here."

"And I'm so glad I am not one of them!" she said.

I think we all agreed with that.

"I'm just so thrilled that everybody came back fine," she continued. "Is it true that you brought back prisoners?"

"Not prisoners," I said. "Survivors. People *they* had imprisoned. Women and children."

"Oh, my goodness, that's awful . . . not that you rescued

them but that they were being held prisoner. I don't think I even want to hear anything more. It's too disturbing. I should get home and give Bubbles his breakfast. I just wish I had more of his special food."

"I heard that one of the scavenging parties just brought in a lot of dog food," I said. "Bags and bags of it."

"That won't please Bubbles. He simply *refuses* to eat kibble. He's *very* fussy."

I saw a flash of disgust cross Brett's face.

"We better get going," I said. "And Bubbles does look hungry. Take care."

She and Bubbles walked in one direction, and we headed in the other.

"If she isn't careful, little Bubbles there might just become somebody's meal," Brett said.

"At least he's earning his keep."

"I feel so much safer knowing that she and her dog are on duty," Brett said sarcastically.

"I guess the extra eyes and ears are what matters," I said, although I didn't really disagree with him. "Maybe you should have complimented her hair."

Brett looked confused.

"Like you did with Lori."

"Oh, I get it," he said. "Big difference. One is an older woman with a poodle, and the other is young and, well, has it going on."

"Hey," I said sharply.

"Don't take it personal. I was just telling her what she wanted to hear," Brett said. "Young people want to look older, and older people want to be seen as younger."

Actually that did make sense.

"It's the same way a smart woman likes to be told she's pretty and a pretty woman wants to be seen as smart. Stick around with me and I'll give you the benefit of my years of experience with the ladies."

"Just stay clear of Lori."

Brett smirked at my look. "Don't worry, I'll leave her alone. I respect your stuff."

"She's not my stuff."

"I thought you two were going out."

"We're going out, but that doesn't make her my property."

He laughed. "Whatever you say. I just know that I'm pretty protective of what's mine, that's all. Nobody touches something that belongs to me."

There was a tone in his voice and a look in his eyes that made me realize all over again he wasn't somebody you'd want to cross.

I almost said that she didn't belong to me, but I figured there was no point in pushing this fight further. He didn't get it, or maybe he thought I didn't get it. Either way, though, he needed to keep his eyes and thoughts somewhere else besides on Lori. She wasn't mine, but she certainly wasn't his.

More people joined us out in the street. Two little girls—who couldn't have been more than eight or nine—were up ahead of us, water containers in hand, on their way to the creek.

We were going to cross the creek and head out of the neighborhood into the woods that bordered us on the west and went all the way to the Credit River down in the valley.

At that point, there was a band of brush and wilderness that extended right down to the lake in one direction and up into the country in the other. That's where the deer lived. It was the perfect place for them. There were lots of things to eat and cover from the winter weather, and because of the local bylaws it was illegal for anybody to fire off a gun, so they had long been completely safe from hunting. Usually their only danger was being hit by cars. Now they didn't have to worry about cars that much, but nobody was going to be enforcing a ban on hunting.

My mother had told me that before any of this started the only time she'd ever fired her service weapon off the practice range was one time when she was new on the force and had to shoot an injured deer that had been hit by a car. Twenty years later, it still bothered her. Probably shooting a deer today wouldn't trouble her at all if it meant food for the neighborhood.

Brett and I walked along the perimeter fence, which looked strong in some places but flimsy in others. It offered a line between us and them, the inside from the outside. Of course, that protection was just an illusion to an RPG. I couldn't help but think about our enemy out there, maybe a hundred strong, fully armed, dangerous and angry, and ruthless.

"This looks like a good place to get over," Brett said. He climbed up onto a little perch that normally would hold a sentry and dropped his bow and quiver of arrows over the side and then jumped to join them. I followed but stood for a minute scanning the woods. I knew I looked a little paranoid, but maybe that wasn't such a bad thing.

"Are you waiting for an invitation?" Brett asked.

"Just checking things out. Better safe than sorry."

We started walking.

Being outside the neighborhood felt a little strange. Sure, I'd been away—a lot farther than anybody else had—but that was in the air. There was a safety that height and distance offered. Not just from real dangers but from seeing real things. The illusion of normal was stronger the higher up I got.

Following the slope down to the little creek, we came to an open spot where later on in the day more people would gather to collect water. It was so early that the flow was still high, but not so high that it covered the rocks, which formed stepping-stones across the creek. I jumped from rock to rock and reached the other side in four steps. Brett was right behind me.

"You know where we're going, right?" he asked.

"I used to play down here all the time. We had a fort in the bushes over here."

"Then lead the way."

The little trail went away from the creek and into the woods. Instinctively I slipped my free right hand under my jacket, placing it on the butt of my pistol. I needed more than a bow and some arrows to keep me feeling safe.

"Do you think we'll run into anybody out here?" I asked.

"We can handle whatever or whoever we do run into."

He spoke with such certainty. I didn't think he had any doubts. Through all of this, Brett had seemed to be getting more confident as everything else was becoming more and more unsure. He seemed to be thriving amid the chaos. There was something about him that reminded me of Herb and then other parts that seemed so different. Was it just the age difference?

"Hey, buddy, you seem a little distracted," Brett said.

"I guess I can't get yesterday out of my head. I keep picturing those women and kids walking out of the building."

"It was strange."

"I just don't know how they could have done that, locked them up to die."

"Yeah, pretty awful, but you almost have to admire them for what they did," Brett said.

I skidded to a stop. "Admire them? You *admire* them for trying to kill those helpless women and children?"

"Look, of course I know it's wrong."

" 'Wrong' is shoplifting at a store or not paying all your income tax. That was inhuman, barbaric, monstrous, and—"

"Okay, maybe 'wrong' wasn't exactly the right word."

"And maybe 'admire' wasn't the right word either," I suggested.

"Look, I'm not so good with words. That's why I'm a cop instead of a poet."

"My mother is good with words."

"I said *cop*, not *captain*."

"My mother is a cop." I knew she hated that word. She was a law enforcement officer.

"Your mother *was* a cop, but now she's a captain. Big difference. Being a captain is being half administrator and half politician. I wouldn't take that job if they offered it to me."

"I don't think there's any danger they're going to offer it to a *rookie*," I snapped.

"I may be a rookie, but I think I've proved to everybody just what I'm capable of doing!"

He showed a flash of anger. His face was suddenly red and his nostrils flaring. He looked like he wanted to take a swing at me. I didn't want to fight him and maybe I was angry, too, but he was right—he had proved himself and he didn't deserve me crapping on him.

"Look, I'm sorry. You've shown your stuff—I crossed the line," I apologized. "We could probably use another dozen rookies if they were like you."

"Hey, I'm sorry, too. I guess I met you at least halfway in crossing that line. I didn't mean anything about your mother. She is my captain, too."

His angry expression was gone as quickly as it came, like a summer storm blowing away. He smiled and offered me his hand, and we shook.

"Thanks, and to be honest, out here, you're one of the people I'd like to have at my side. And I think everybody feels that way," I said.

"You know, kid, you're high on that list, too. Herb has a lot of faith in you, and I have complete faith in him. No offense to your mother, and believe me I don't want to start anything, but he's the guy who should be running the place."

"He plays a pretty big role in influencing the committee. People talk and he listens."

"If they'd listened faster, we wouldn't have found an empty compound," Brett said.

I knew Herb had wanted to move sooner, but still, maybe it was better they did get away. If we'd gotten there earlier, maybe one or both of us wouldn't be here to have a conversation.

"Herb is pretty good at convincing people to do things. He says that words are like weapons," I said.

"Still, if it comes down to a fight, I'd rather have a loaded gun than a big vocabulary."

"I think Herb has both."

"Tell you what, if we run into trouble today, you talk and I'll aim. But back to what I was saying, it's not that I admire what they did but that they're prepared to do whatever it takes to survive."

"If it comes to that I'd rather not survive."

"You better be careful or you might get your wish," Brett said. "There are going to be more times ahead when hard decisions have to be made, and I'm not sure if our group can make them. Sometimes being kind can get you killed."

I felt like arguing, but I knew what he was saying was right. It was the same sort of thing Herb had been talking to me about.

We continued to move through the trees. We were almost all the way to the river and well away from the neighborhood now—from the safety of the wall. Although the trees and thick brush did provide a level of cover and protection, it also helped to have Brett here with me.

"Doesn't it feel good to be out here?" Brett asked.

"I'd rather be up in the air, but this does feel pretty good."

"I'd like to spend more time here. I'm going to ask Herb and your mom for permission to set up a special unit, you know, the guys I really trust, to go out, especially at night and scout around to see if we can—"

Brett stopped suddenly and froze in place. He held up a finger to his lips to silence me and then pointed. For an instant I didn't see, and then they came into focus. There were deer—three, no four, of them down the steep slope of the ravine.

11

Two of the deer were drinking from the river and the other two were on alert, looking around, but I didn't think they'd seen us or they would have reacted.

"I'm going downwind. You go the other way and drive them toward me," he whispered, gesturing with his hands where he wanted me to go and where he was going to go.

I nodded.

"Give me time to get into position, then make a lot of noise to drive them forward. I don't think they'll come up the slope or go into the river."

Brett moved off to the left, quickly disappearing behind a stand of trees and brush. I tried to follow his movement, but he soon disappeared from view. I couldn't even hear him. I was amazed at how quietly he moved for somebody that big. I certainly didn't hear him—but did the deer?

I turned my focus back to them. All four were females and around the same size. They hadn't moved, but now all of them were looking around anxiously. Had they heard Brett? Did they smell me? Were they going to sprint away?

Two went back to sipping from the river and the other two started eating, nibbling on the new-grown grass at the edge of the water.

Slowly I bent down until I was hidden behind the bushes. Keeping low, I followed the path around, trying to walk softly. I didn't want them to hear me—at least not yet. If they heard me now, it would be just as likely they'd run away from Brett as they would toward him, and that was assuming he was even in position yet.

The path branched and I took the route to the left, leading down into the ravine, to the river's edge. The slope was steep, and despite holding on to trees with one hand I stumbled and made a lot of noise—certainly enough for the deer to hear something. I hoped at this point it didn't matter. I was supposed to be loud. I picked up my pace, letting gravity pull me quickly downhill until I hit the river, and then I made a sharp turn to the left, toward where the deer were—or at least where they *had* been.

I crashed through the woods, now deliberately making noise, crunching down the underbrush. I wanted the deer not just to hear me but to think a whole pack of wolves was coming toward them. That would panic the bunch and push them toward Brett. That is, unless they went straight up the steep slope or even jumped into the river and started swimming to the other side.

I ran along the path and then skidded to a stop—this was the spot where the deer had been, but they were gone. A gun went off and I startled. The deer must have run by Brett, who at least had taken a shot at one. But wasn't he going to use the bow and arrow? More shots rang out. Wait, I thought, they sounded different from one another. They weren't coming from one gun. There was another shot and a *whizz* as a bullet tore by me. I dropped to the ground and scurried to take shelter behind an old log.

What was happening? Did Brett have a backup gun? Was he firing two weapons? Had a bullet that missed the deer almost hit me?

Before I could think what to do next, I heard the distinct sound of somebody coming down the path toward me. I pulled the bow off my shoulder, dropped it, and drew my pistol, holding it in front of me like a shield. Three of the deer came charging toward me, and the first leaped over me and the log I was hiding behind. I tumbled backward, discharging my gun, and one of the deer staggered and fell to the ground as the other two ran off—I'd hit it!

I jumped up. Another adrenaline burst overcame both my fear and my logic. I charged up the path, practically tripping over Brett, who was huddled down beside a tree. I scrambled over on all fours until I was right beside him, protected by the same tree.

"What happened?" I gasped.

"I took a shot at the deer and I got it," Brett said.

For a second I thought he meant the deer I knew I had shot, but he was pointing up the hill in the direction he'd just come from. Had he shot a deer as well? I was going to mention the deer I'd hit—the one back down the path that he knew nothing about—when he said something more pressing.

"But then I got distracted," he continued. "There was somebody shooting at me. Do you see anybody?"

"I can't see anything, but I heard the shots. Let's get out of here."

"We have to sit tight and wait until I know where the shots came from. Besides, I'm not going anywhere without that deer."

I didn't want to wait. I wanted to run away as fast as my legs could carry me, although right now I wasn't sure they could carry me very far because they were shaking so bad.

"There, do you see him?" Brett asked.

I did. It was a man—no, two, and they were working their way down the steep slope. They were both carrying rifles. "We aren't outnumbered but we're outgunned, especially from this distance," Brett said.

"I don't think they see us here or they wouldn't be coming down like that," I said.

"They must think I've fled. They have rifles, so we have to let them get closer to even up the odds."

Here I was hiding behind a tree from two armed men who had taken a shot at Brett and we were calculating just how to get the advantage over these men so that we could take a shot at them.

Is this what it had all come to?

They got closer—they were coming quickly and carelessly, making lots of noise, talking, even laughing. But what was wrong with their voices?

"It's just a couple of kids," Brett said.

The two of them ran over to the deer Brett had shot. They were whooping and cheering in high-pitched kid voices, and one of them was female and only one of them had a rifle. The girl was holding some sort of spear or club.

Brett jumped to his feet. "Drop the weapon!" he screamed as he ran toward them. The two kids stumbled backward, tripping and falling over, letting their weapons fall to the ground. Brett continued toward them, his gun out, screaming as he ran. I got up and ran after him. The two kids were huddled on the ground with Brett standing over them, his pistol in one hand and their rifle in the other.

"Why did you try to shoot me?" Brett screamed, his gun pointed right at them.

The two kids—a boy about thirteen and girl who wasn't that much older than Danny and Rachel—were both in tears.

I held my hands up. "It's okay," I said. "It's all going to be okay." I stepped forward, placing myself between Brett and the two kids. "How about if we all just calm down." I turned around to face Brett. "They're just a couple of kids, and you have their rifle . . . Please lower your pistol—you're only pointing at me right now."

Brett hesitated—he had a look of complete rage on his face—and then his expression softened and he lowered the gun. I let out a big sigh of relief.

"What are your names?" I asked.

They didn't answer. They looked terrified—too scared to talk.

"Look, we're not going to hurt you. I'm Adam, and this is my friend Brett. What are your names?"

"Penny," the girl said between her sobs. "And this is my brother, Leonard."

"Good to meet you. You weren't shooting at us, were you?" I asked.

"No," the boy said, shaking his head. "We were just shooting at the deer. We didn't even know you were here."

"Are you saying you didn't hear me fire my gun?" Brett asked.

"I heard something, but I thought it was just an echo of

my gun, bouncing off the other side of the ravine when I hit the deer."

"*You* hit it?" Brett questioned. "*I* shot the deer."

"It was right in my sight. I shot it," the boy said. "It's *our* deer."

"Kid, you're crazy. I shot it, and there's no way I'm letting you have our kill," Brett said.

Brett was back to looking angry and scary. I needed to calm this down again.

"Look," I said. "I don't know who shot *this* deer, but I know who shot the other."

Brett looked suitably surprised.

"I shot one, back there, down the path, so there's two," I explained. "We could take one and these guys can take one."

Brett smiled at me. "Good work, buddy." He paused and his expression changed. "Or *we* could take two. After all, we have the guns. What are they going to do, cry some more?"

"We're not taking both," I said. "We're not. Fair is fair."

"Fair is that you shot one and I shot the other and both deer are ours."

"You didn't shoot it—I shot it!" Leonard yelled. He was angry but still brushing back tears. I had to give the kid credit. At his age I just would have run away as fast as my legs could carry me.

"Shut up or I'll—"

"Just stop!" I yelled, interrupting Brett. "Let's just talk. I don't think anybody will argue that I shot the second deer. It's ours, right?"

Everybody nodded.

"And since the other might have been shot by both of you, how about if we split that second deer?"

"Split it?" the boy asked.

"You get half and we get half."

"That would be good," Penny said. "Half would be good. There'd be enough for us to eat for a long time."

"But they'd have even more than us," Leonard complained.

"You should just be grateful we give you anything," Brett snapped. "We have hundreds of people to feed."

"Yeah, hundreds," the boy snickered.

"We do. We're trying to feed everybody in our neighborhood. It's just the other side of Sawmill Creek."

"Behind the wall?" Penny asked.

"That's us," I said. "How many of you are there?"

"There are five of us in our family," Penny said.

"So you don't need as much," I reasoned. "It would even go bad before you could eat a whole deer."

"But we can trade meat to other people for things we need," Leonard said.

"You'd be in a much better position to argue that if you had a gun," Brett snapped.

"And besides half the deer, we'll also give you back your rifle," I said. Brett looked like he was going to object. "It's their gun, and we don't take anything from anybody."

He laughed. "Like the scavenging teams don't take anything?"

"Scavenging isn't stealing." I felt like I was dealing with three kids. I turned back to the two who really were children. "Where do you two live?"

Neither answered.

"Look, I just want to know how far you're going to have to carry the meat."

"It's not that far. We're living in the middle of the—"

"We can carry the meat," Leonard said, cutting off his sister. "Don't worry about us."

"I am a little worried," I said. "Okay, you know where we live. Tomorrow at noon you have to come to the fence and tell them you've come to see me, Adam."

"Why would we do that?" Leonard questioned.

"So you can pick up your share of the meat."

"What?"

"We're going to take the two deer with us, have them butchered, and you'll get your share of the meat tomorrow."

"Do you think we're stupid?" the boy questioned.

"Look, I'm not trying to trick you," I said. "There's no way to divide it out here. We'll have it done back at the grocery store and package half of it for you. What do you think?"

"I think you're not going to give us anything."

"Look, Leonard, if I wanted to take it all we could take it all," I said.

"You *are* taking it all," he snapped.

"And I'm giving it back to you. Tomorrow. You have to trust me."

"Yeah, right, like I should—"

"I trust him," Penny said.

"Good. You come tomorrow. I'll even tell the sentries to expect you."

"And what about our gun?" Leonard asked. "Are you going to give us back that tomorrow, too?"

"No, you get that today."

"There's no way I'm giving them back the gun so that they can shoot at us as we walk away," Brett said. "Now you must be thinking that we're stupid, too."

"Nobody is going to shoot anybody," I said. "I want the

two of you to walk up there to the top of the ravine and have a seat. We're going to leave the rifle right here in this tree and the bullets right over there by that big rock. You wait right up there until we've left with the deer. Deal?"

Leonard didn't answer.

"Look, the alternative is we just take the rifle with us," I said. "How about we shake on this one instead?" I held out my hand.

Reluctantly, Leonard held out his hand and we shook.

"You're really going to give us the meat?" Leonard said. "You're not just tricking us?"

"I don't need to trick you," I said. "If I wanted to I could just take it all. I gave you my word and I'm going to keep my word," I said. "Tomorrow around noon the meat will be waiting for you."

"Thanks. We really do need the food . . . We don't have much left," Leonard said.

"It's not easy anywhere right now, but I'm sure this will help some."

"And I really wasn't trying to shoot anybody," he said. "I wouldn't do that. I didn't see either of you."

"I believe you," I said—even if Brett didn't.

"We're just trying to get by, and that deer, our rifle—we need those to get by," Leonard said.

"I know. Now you two go up there and wait. Just sit down at the top where I can see you."

Penny took her brother's hand and they started toward the hill. We watched as they struggled up the slope.

"That was pretty smart," Brett said. "We get the meat without having to make a scene."

I took the rifle from him. "I'm going to keep my word." I

took the bullets out of the rifle and then hung it by the handle on a low-lying branch.

"No, seriously."

"Seriously. We'll take what's ours, but we can't be stealing, especially not from a couple of kids," I said.

"Kids who took a shot at us."

"He didn't see us."

"I don't believe that," Brett said.

"Did you see them before they fired?" I questioned.

"Well . . . no."

"I think it was the same for them. He took a shot at a deer—maybe he even hit it," I said.

"I shot it."

"I guess we'll tell when they butcher it," I said. "It'll be easy to know for sure if they find a twenty-two-caliber bullet from their rifle or a forty-five slug from your gun."

Brett didn't look so confident all of a sudden.

"How about if we just get the two deer back and worry about that later?" I said. "Maybe we should get some help."

"We can do it. Come here."

We walked over to the deer carcass. It was on its side, head at a strange angle, eyes open, an entrance wound on the side. "This one isn't big. It can't weigh much more than a hundred and fifty pounds." He lifted it up and wrapped it around my shoulders, the front legs dangling over one side of my head, the back legs over the other. I sagged under the weight.

"Now show me where the second one is," he said.

12

I stumbled under the weight of the deer carcass once again but managed to regain my balance before I fell flat on my face. I heard Brett chuckle. I was struggling, but he didn't seem to be having any problem with the weight on his back. He wasn't just big but also strong. I could have kidded myself into thinking I was having more problems because my deer was the larger of the two, but I knew it wasn't. If anything, it was smaller, which of course meant my kill—the one Brett was carrying—was larger. That should have given me some satisfaction, although it was hard to feel any satisfaction struggling uphill, through the brush, with a dead deer around my neck and its blood dripping down my side. At first when I felt the trickles I thought it was because I was sweating like a pig, but when I looked I was pretty sure I didn't sweat red.

"How you doing, buddy?" Brett asked.

I wished he'd quit calling me that. I mumbled out an answer. I needed my air for walking, not talking.

His words had sounded concerned, but I didn't think he really was. If anything he was hoping I'd drop it—and his hope was close to reality. If I could just hold on a little bit longer, we could make it without having that happen. I knew the neighborhood was just ahead, the fences almost in sight.

"Makes you think it would have been better if we'd field-dressed the deer before we took them," he said.

"What?"

"Butchered them in the woods. If you were serious about giving the kids their share, then you would have only had to carry half of it. I could have done it with my knife."

"I was serious . . . I am serious about giving them their share," I puffed. My legs were shaking even worse than before.

"*We* should be keeping all the meat," he said.

"We're not keeping it."

"It really isn't your decision to make," he said.

"It *is* my decision."

"No it's not. You're the one who keeps talking about the committee making the decisions, so shouldn't they make this one?"

"I gave the kid my word."

"You didn't have the right to *give* him *anything*, especially not the meat."

He had a point. It would be up to the committee, but I'd talk to Herb and my mother first. If I could convince them, I could convince the committee.

"Look, I know you just want to do what you think is fair, but it's like I said, sometimes you have to do what's right for yourself, not necessarily what's right for other people," Brett said. "Besides, bringing in those captives means we have almost fifty more mouths to feed. This is at least a few meals in that direction."

"You're right, the committee will have to decide. I'm not in charge of anything . . . except what's going to happen to the one deer. You can keep all of the second, but I'm giving them half of what I shot. I'm going to ask the committee to let me keep my word."

We broke through the brush, and the creek was right in front of us. A few kids were standing on the rocks, collecting water. Behind them was the fence. A couple of sentries, rifles in hand, were watching over them.

One of the kids saw us, and he pointed. Others stopped and watched as we approached. Brett went down the slope and stepped onto the first big rock in the little creek. He then lifted the deer up over his head like it was a trophy. People cheered. He was like a conquering hero returning home. I just stood there, watching, my legs shaking, my back aching. Brett waved for me to join him.

I started down the little slope, and once gravity got ahold of me I almost tumbled over. Falling flat on my face wasn't the entrance I was hoping for. The kids surrounded me as well, and then the two sentries came off the wall and out the gate to help pull the deer off my neck. I felt so light, I was practically floating. I wasn't sure they should have left their posts to help, but I was just grateful that they had.

"Please, could you take them up to the grocery store?" I huffed, still struggling to get my breath. "Give them to Ernie and tell him I'll be up in a while."

Four men carrying the two deer started off. They were as excited as the kids at the creek.

"Time for a well-earned breakfast," Brett said. "I've worked up such an appetite that even that porridge will taste good today."

"I'm hungry, but I don't think anything could make that porridge taste good. It's like eating glue," I said.

"Believe me, sprinkle in a little venison and it will taste really good."

I nodded. "First, I want to get changed out of these clothes and into something that doesn't have blood on it."

"Maybe you should wear it like a badge of honor. We did good out there. We could do even more good with me going out over the fence each night. No telling what things I can scavenge out there. Be sure to tell that to the committee the next time they meet."

"Like I said, the committee makes the decisions."

"Then tell your mother, or better yet, we should both tell Herb. That should be enough."

Actually, he was right, that might be enough.

———————

After I'd cleaned up and eaten some porridge—which actually did taste better than usual—I headed up to the store. My mother was already gone, so I couldn't talk to her about what I had promised to do with the deer, but I did tell Rachel and Danny. Rachel thought it was nice that I was going to share it. Danny thought it was stupid. It didn't matter what either of them thought. I'd have to talk to Herb, and I was in luck. As I walked up Herb came out of the grocery store, saw me, and waved me over.

"Congratulations on the kills," Herb said. "When I said we needed more food, I had no idea that you'd go out and get some right away."

"It was more of an accident than anything else. The thing practically ran me over and I shot it in self-defense."

"Brett's been telling a different story about the one he popped," Herb said.

No surprise there. "I guess that's assuming he was the person who shot it."

Herb gave me a confused look. "The way he's telling it, there's no question he shot it. Do you think it was the boy he mentioned?"

"Yeah, it could be. I guess you heard the story." I just wondered how Brett had told it and how slanted his version of the truth was.

"I did," Herb said.

I was waiting for him to say something more—something about my promise, but he didn't.

"Let's go inside and talk to Ernie. He's just finishing butchering the second deer. Was Brett carrying his service weapon?" Herb asked.

"Yeah, and the kid had a rifle, a twenty-two."

"Not much of a rifle. It would be hard to take a deer down with one shot from that gun," Herb said.

"I only shot my deer once," I said.

"And you have a bigger-caliber pistol and were practically on top of it."

"Maybe he shot it more than once or maybe Brett shot it, too."

"That's a possibility."

The front door of the grocery store was guarded. We hadn't had any problems with pilfering so far, but there was no point in taking a chance. People were surviving on a lot less than they were used to. Discussions about food seemed to be a chief topic of conversation.

We passed by the guard on our way in and walked down one of the aisles. How many times had I walked down these aisles—or been in the little seat in the cart when I was a kid? I'd spent my whole life shopping here. It was the same, but different now. Not just the man with a gun out front, or the boarded-up windows, or the dimness as we walked, but things like the completely empty freezer cases and the big tables that used to hold piles of fresh fruit and vegetables. At least the regular shelves still contained canned goods and boxes and bags. They weren't full, but they were far from empty. This grocery store used to draw customers from the areas all around us, but now it was just for our little neighborhood. We'd also caught a lucky break. There were two delivery trucks—transports filled with groceries bound for other stores—that were there when it all went down. Those trucks were the only reasons so much food still remained. Being smart was necessary. Being lucky didn't hurt either.

"How long can all of this food last?" I asked.

"It depends. If people eat the way they normally do, then we'll run completely out of food in another six weeks or so."

"That's long enough for us to harvest what we're growing," I said.

"I'm afraid we're going to have to tighten the rationing even more," Herb replied.

"Because of the extra people?" I asked.

"That's a contributing factor, but it was going to happen anyway."

"People aren't going to be happy about that."

"Better to live unhappy than not live at all. With a little luck and things like these deer, we'll get through until harvest."

"And then we'll be okay," I said.

"Then we'll be okay for longer, but how long is debatable. At this time we still don't know if we can produce enough food to feed this many people for a full year until the harvests come due next fall."

"It still bothers me to think it could go on that long, for more than a year," I said as we walked past an untouched shelf display of lightbulbs.

"'Pray for the best, plan for the worst' is the wisest advice I can give anybody. In this case the best still might have us falling short."

Was he softening me up, preparing me for not being able to keep my promise to Leonard? Is that what he was shaping this conversation toward?

"I'm feeling guilty about all the extra people coming into the neighborhood," I said.

"Don't ever feel guilty for suggesting the moral thing to do. I've thought a lot about it. It would have damaged us in a whole different way to simply drive away and leave them behind."

We pushed through a door and went into the back of the store. I was relieved to see that more food was piled on the shelves at the back. I heard the sound of sawing and wondering what they were building—until I saw that it wasn't wood. Ernie was cutting through the deer with a big hand saw. He was wearing a white apron that was smeared with so much blood it looked more red than white.

"So how's it going, Ernie?" Herb asked.

"Pretty good. Do you realize that one of these deer can form the base meat for a meal that can feed the entire neighborhood?"

"That is excellent," Herb said.

"So right here we have two meals."

Or a meal and a half, depending on what was decided. Herb didn't say anything, and I was afraid to ask.

"Hey, Ernie, we were wondering if you found the bullets that killed the deer," Herb said.

"Nobody wants lead in their venison stew. Right there on the counter I dug that forty-five out of one of them."

That could be Brett's bullet—or mine.

"It was a clean hit, right through the heart. The deer probably was dead before it knew it had been hit."

"And the second one?" Herb asked.

"You'll find that slug in the bowl, too."

Herb picked up a metal bowl and removed a bullet. "Twenty-two caliber."

"So the kid did shoot it!" I exclaimed.

"Was there another bullet in it, a forty-five?" Herb asked Ernie.

"Nope, that was the only one."

"Then Brett didn't even hit it," I said.

"He could have," Herb said. "It might have been a through and through, or Ernie might have even missed it—no offense."

"None taken," Ernie said. "It gets a little messy in there, so I could miss a bullet."

"Even coroners doing an autopsy can miss a round. There are lots of places for a bullet to hide."

"At least we know that the kid did hit it," I said. "He deserves his share of the deer . . . right?" This was the moment of truth—what was Herb going to say?

"Not only deserves it but will get it," Herb said. "The committee members I spoke to had no problem with your decision."

"Doesn't this have to be decided by the whole committee?" I asked.

"Some things are better dealt with outside the committee. You made a promise, and you'll keep it."

"Thanks. I guess that maybe I should have checked before I made that promise."

"Again, don't feel bad for doing the right thing. There's not a lot of that going on out there. When are you going to deliver the meat?"

"He's coming tomorrow to pick it up," I said.

"Unless he's a very strong kid, he's not going to be able to carry it all."

"I could help him."

"It's a nice offer, but you should never go out by yourself. You need to bring at least one other person with you, and that person should be armed, as should you. Why don't you ask Brett?"

"I'm not sure he'd be happy about helping deliver the meat. I think it would be better to bring Todd along, if that's all right."

It was fine with Herb, who asked Ernie to have half of one of the deer packaged the next day so that I could take it to Leonard.

"You seem to be pretty good at this. Have you ever dressed a deer before?" Herb asked.

"Never, but it's really no different from a cow. Of course, it's been a lot of different animals that have gone into the stew pot over the past few weeks."

I wasn't sure I wanted to know, but I had to ask. "What sort of animals are we talking about?" I asked.

Ernie and Herb exchanged a look.

"Are you sure you want to know?" Ernie asked.

I paused. "I guess so."

"You have to keep the information quiet," Herb said. "Some people might not understand."

"He's right," Ernie added. "What happens back here, stays back here. Sort of like Vegas but without the shows or gambling . . . and lots more blood."

"I'll keep it to myself," I promised.

"Have you noticed there aren't as many squirrels in the neighborhood?" Herb asked.

"I've noticed. That's not so bad. What else?"

"There's a problem with abandoned pets. Packs of wild dogs can be a problem," Herb said. "We've had them killed both to reduce the threat and to provide food."

"So I've eaten dog meat?"

"Dogs and cats," Ernie said. "I've got to tell you, it didn't feel right butchering them. I'm not sure how people would feel knowing that they've been eating domestic animals."

"Not good." I thought of Mrs. Julian and her little Bubbles. "But we're not eating pets from the neighborhood, right?"

"I don't think people are going to give up their pets no matter how hungry they are," Ernie said.

"You're right," Herb said. "People would rather go without than have their pets go hungry. That's why it was so important that the scavenging teams brought back dog food. Those pets need to be fed even if nobody is going to eat them. Stray dogs are another matter."

"Besides, in lots of countries people regularly eat dog meat, and horse meat," Ernie said. "It's just what you get used to."

"I don't think Lori is going to let anybody harm her horses," I said.

"They won't," Herb said. "Those horses are working for their keep. As are the cows producing milk and the chickens laying eggs. Using them for an ongoing supply of milk and eggs rather than a one-time supply of meat is a smarter use of these resources." Herb paused. "You know I was stationed in countries where horse and dog were standard menu items. They didn't taste bad at all," Herb said.

I thought about it. "Maybe it's best I don't know exactly what's in every stew. Dog, cat, or squirrel . . . What exactly does squirrel taste like?"

"Like rat."

"I don't think I could ever do that," I said.

"Have you ever been really, really thirsty?" Herb asked.

"Sure."

"And do you remember how good the water tasted when you finally took a drink?"

"Of course."

"When you don't have anything else to eat, well, almost anything can taste like prime rib. You do what you have to do to survive."

"So at some point we might be eating rats?" I asked.

"I hope it doesn't come to that," Herb said.

"But we have mixed in raccoon, opossum, and whatever else can be caught or trapped," Ernie added.

"We're beggars, and beggars can't be choosers," Herb said.

"I guess I should try to get another deer," I said. "But first I better make sure Leonard gets his share of this one."

13

"I appreciate the help," Leonard said.

"It's no problem, little man," Todd said. "It's just good to get outside the neighborhood. It was starting to feel like those fences were prison walls."

Both Todd and Lori had volunteered to go with me to help Leonard take back his share of the deer, but I'd only brought Todd. In one way it would have been nice to have Lori along because it would have meant spending time with her, but I still felt it was better to have her stay safe and sound inside the walls. I just told her that we didn't need her help to carry the things. Still, I think she knew the real reason. She seemed a little annoyed with me, but she didn't say anything. I guess better annoyed than in danger.

"I can breathe out here. It does feel nice to be outside the walls," Todd added.

"I wish we had walls," Leonard said.

"Well, I guess it's a good thing," Todd acknowledged.

The load wasn't heavy divided between the three of us. It was all packaged and bagged just like we were coming home from the grocery store—which, in fact, we were. Take away the rifles being carried by Leonard and Todd and the pistol strapped to my side, and this would have been a normal walk home. Then again, when did I ever walk through the forest with grocery bags?

It had certainly been a very different experience from my trip through the woods yesterday with a dead deer around my neck and blood dripping down my side. There was still some venison in the bags I was carrying, but it was less than a quarter deer. Leonard had agreed to take the rest in canned meat, canned vegetables, packages of pasta, and some of the chloride tablets. Venison could only go so far, and all those other things were almost impossible to get—at least outside the walls—so he was happy with that trade.

"You really don't have to go all the way," Leonard said.

"Not much choice, little buddy," Todd said. "How would you have gotten it all to your home without us helping?"

"I figured I was going to make a few trips. I could still do that. You could just leave it here and I could do it," he offered.

"I don't think we want to just leave it in the forest," I said. "Somebody else or even an animal could get it."

"I won't be gone that long," Leonard said. "It isn't far, really; you could just leave it."

"If it isn't that far, then we might as well take it all the way," Todd said.

"You've already come this far—it's okay, really," Leonard said.

I was starting to think this wasn't really about him being polite about us helping him but had more to do with a reluctance to have us go to his home.

"Hold up," I said, and we all stopped. "Look, Leonard, if you really want, we can just wait right here. You can take your load home and then come back and we'll stay to make sure nobody or nothing takes anything."

"That doesn't make sense," Todd said. "Why wouldn't we just carry it instead of waiting around?"

I looked at Leonard. "I understand if you're feeling nervous about showing us where you live. We don't have to go there if you don't want us to. You know we aren't going to harm you or your family. Is that what you're worried about?"

He didn't answer.

"Leonard," Todd said. "We are not going to do anything. Adam is the nicest person I've ever met. He always keeps his word about everything."

"But it's your choice," I said. "Do you want us to wait here or come with you?"

"I guess you can come with me. I'd like you to meet my mother and my grandfather."

Leonard walked forward.

We followed him down the path. It was narrow with thornbushes sprouting on both sides. There should have been a way around this patch, so there had to be a reason why he was going straight through it. I heard a noise and turned.

There was a woman standing in a clearing behind the bushes, and she had a rifle pointed right at us.

Instinctively, my hand started to move toward my pistol.

"Don't even think about it," she said. "Put your hands up, both of you."

I hesitated for an instant.

"Now!" she ordered.

"Better do what she says," I heard Todd say from behind me.

I started to raise my hands when Leonard pushed past me. "They're with me, Auntie Mary."

"You weren't supposed to bring them here. You know that!" she yelled.

"They're my friends."

"Your friends are carrying weapons," she said.

"Everybody who's got any brains is carrying weapons," Leonard called back. "Could you stop aiming that rifle at us?"

I expected her to do what Leonard asked, but instead she pulled the rifle up so that she was looking down the barrel, right at us, right at me! In response I raised my hands a little higher, trying to somehow appease her.

"Look, there's no need for this. We'll leave the supplies . . . even our weapons if you want. Let's not do anything we'll all regret."

"Come on, Auntie Mary," Leonard said.

The rifle remained aimed above Leonard's head and right at my chest. I was wearing body armor—so was Todd—but would that stop a rifle shot at such close range?

I saw a glimpse of movement behind Leonard's aunt and couldn't believe my eyes. Leonard seemed too distressed to notice anything at the moment. "You know," I called out to his aunt, to keep her attention focused on me. "I really don't want to cause any trouble at all. I was just wondering if—"

Silently, Lori appeared out of nowhere directly behind our opponent. She placed a pistol against the back of the woman's head. Then she leaned in close and said something, and the rifle lowered. Then it was in Lori's other hand.

"Don't hurt her!" Leonard yelled. "Please don't hurt her!"

"Nobody is going to hurt anybody," I said, my voice

sounding hoarse and hesitant. I walked over as Lori, still holding both weapons, backed away from the woman.

"Hello, I'm Adam," I said, offering Leonard's humiliated aunt my hand.

She didn't respond. Her expression was blank. Not hostile, not friendly, just neutral. Leonard came to her side.

"I thought we had a deal," I said to Leonard.

"We did . . . We do."

"Did that deal involve us being threatened with a rifle?" Todd asked. "Because I wouldn't have agreed to that deal."

"I'm sorry. I didn't know she was going to do this, honestly. My aunt has been through a lot . . . She doesn't really trust people."

It wasn't just the words he was saying but the way he'd reacted to things that made me believe him. He had seemed as surprised as we had been.

"Are there any more surprises we need to know about?" I asked.

"None . . . Well, I don't think so."

I couldn't help but laugh, and that lessened the tension for everybody.

"Do you still want us to come to your camp?" I asked.

"I'd like that. Please."

"You and your aunt should lead, then."

Leonard gave her one of the bags, then took her by the hand and pulled her down the path. They squeezed by Todd, who looked both confused and amused. He shrugged. "I guess as long as she didn't shoot us it's all good." He turned around and started after them.

"What are you doing out here?" I asked Lori while the others walked ahead.

"Apparently saving your bacon."

"I was trying to talk my way out of it."

"I saw how that was working." She strapped on the rifle and took some of the load I was carrying.

"No, seriously, why are you out here?" I asked again.

"I thought you could use some backup, and I guess I was right. Are we going with them, or are we going to play twenty questions?"

"Going with them."

Lori went down the path and I stumbled after her.

"I guess I should have invited you to come along in the first place," I said.

"You guess? It seems pretty certain right now. You know, I'm not helpless."

"I don't think you're helpless . . . just special . . . too special to put at risk."

"I know that was supposed to be a compliment, but I'm just as capable as you out here, probably more so with a gun."

"I didn't say anything about that."

"I was raised on a farm and spent a lot of time playing in the woods, so it probably would have been better if I went out and you stayed inside the fence."

"Look, I'm sorry. I won't do that again, I promise."

She reached over and took my hand. "Apology accepted."

"Thanks. And thanks for saving our bacon."

She laughed. "You're welcome. Just be more gracious the next time it happens."

We hurried to catch up to the rest. They were still in sight and hadn't gone far, although falling back might even have been better. I didn't want any more surprises.

The path opened up into a small clearing where there were two tents, one orange and the other bluish—no, the bluish one wasn't a tent but two tarps, one tied between trees for a roof and the other as a lean-to. I'd seen tents sprouting up in other places outside the neighborhood, but I'd never talked to anybody who was living in one. The orange tent was old and sagging, and it looked like a rip in the side had been sewn up. Sitting at a picnic bench beneath the tarp was Leonard's sister, Penny, a woman who I guessed was their mother, and an older man—I assumed he was the grandfather.

Leonard led us into the clearing and everybody got up. Auntie Mary walked off to the side and stood there, staring at us. I tried to keep an eye on her in case she went looking for another weapon. She made me nervous.

"This is Adam," Leonard said.

I placed my bags and the rifle on the ground beside the ones the others had been carrying. I shook hands with the grandfather. "Pleased to meet you, sir."

"Likewise, son. You can call me Sheldon."

"And this is my mother," Leonard said.

"I'm Amy. Glad to meet you, Adam."

"Did you get it all?" Auntie Mary called out from across the clearing to Leonard. "Did you get what you'd been promised?"

"I didn't get all the deer, but—"

"Why not? We need that meat!" Her expression changed from blank to angry.

I was almost reassured by the anger.

"There's more here than just the deer meat," Leonard said.

"They gave me canned goods and bags of pasta and some stuff to make the water fit for drinking."

"That's wonderful," Amy said. "I was a little worried about how we were going to keep all that meat fresh long enough to eat it. Thank you."

"You're welcome."

"Would you like to stay for a cup of tea?" she asked.

"We don't want to take your supplies," I said.

"You brought us enough in return. Besides, we have plenty. It's brewed from local chicory," she said.

"My grandfather knows all about using natural ingredients," Leonard said.

"There are hundreds of plants that can be used for foods," Sheldon said. "Everything from reeds to pine cone seeds can be eaten or brewed or chewed on." He paused. "Although, unfortunately, there's no easy way to replace cane sugar. There's honey, but that's hard to come by."

I bent down, reached into one of the bags, and rummaged around. "Then I guess you could use this." It was a small bag of sugar that had been included as part of the exchange for the deer meat.

"Then you have to join us," Sheldon said. "Please, have a seat."

"We really have to get back soon," I said. "People will get worried if we're gone too long."

"I can understand that," Amy said. "There are lots of reasons to be worried, but we'd be grateful for the company and the conversation."

"Well, I guess we could stay for a bit."

Todd and Lori took a seat on both sides of Penny. She

looked happy to have them join her. I sat down on the other bench, sideways so that I could face Leonard's mother but still keep one eye on his aunt.

"You don't have to worry," Amy said quietly. "She won't hurt you." She gestured to the aunt.

"She had that rifle pointed at us," I said. "Lori took it away from her."

"She's had a rough time. She was in the city when it all happened. She's just scared."

"I guess we're all a little scared," Lori said. "It's okay."

"I've heard stories about the city," I said. "It got pretty bad, pretty fast."

"I won't be sharing my sister's story, but it was pretty bad for her. And then when she did get home, she was forced out by the fire."

"Is that why you're out here?" Todd asked. "There was a fire?"

"The whole complex went up."

Leonard's grandfather returned and set down mugs of steaming tea in front of us.

"There have been a lot of accidental fires," I said.

"There was nothing accidental about this fire," Sheldon said. "It was deliberate. A bunch of fools set one townhouse on fire, and it spread to every unit. No fire department to put it out or police to stop it from happening to begin with."

"Adam's mother is—" Todd began.

"Really upset about all of this," I said, cutting him off and giving him an evil eye. What was the point in telling them that my mother was the person responsible for there being no police to help them outside our walls?

"I lived on a farm. We had to leave it, too," Lori said. "There were groups of armed people who forced us to go."

"That's why we're better off out here in the woods, away from people, on our own," the grandfather said. "You three are dressed for trouble. I've never seen anybody except riot police wearing body armor."

"We were lucky enough to get us a few sets," I said, downplaying what we had. "We wouldn't want to be out here without it."

"Probably smart. That's why we're staying in the woods," Sheldon said. "There are people living all through these woods."

"I've seen flashes of color as I fly over," I said.

"Fly?" Amy said.

"Is that you up there in that little plane?" Sheldon asked.

"That's me."

"Pretty amazing. You must be just about the only thing in the skies," he said.

"He is now that we shot down that Cessna," Todd said.

There were shocked looks from all of them. I wished Todd had kept his mouth shut. Now I had to say something.

"It was self-defense," I explained. "They were trying to shoot me down."

"They were going to kill all of us," Todd said. "But we took care of them."

Again, I wanted to reach out and give him a slap. Instead I shot him a dirty look that he didn't seem to see.

"We had no choice," I said. "They had already wiped out an entire neighborhood and they were coming to destroy us."

"But you have lots of people, walls, and weapons—I see them poking over the walls. How many of them could there have been to be a threat to you?"

"There were hundreds of them," I said, "and they had more weapons, better weapons that our walls couldn't have stopped."

"But we stopped them at the bridge. You should have seen it!" Todd exclaimed.

"The Burnham Bridge?" Amy asked.

I nodded.

"I wondered what that was all about," Sheldon said. "We heard the explosion and saw the clouds, so we went to investigate. So you people did that?"

"Again, it wasn't what we wanted to do, but they were coming to attack us. There was no choice."

"I saw the trucks at the bottom among the rubble," he said. "How many died?"

"There were over—"

"More than any of us would have liked," I said, again cutting Todd off. "We were only doing what we had to so we could survive . . . It's hard to explain."

"No it isn't, son. A few months ago it would have been impossible, but now . . . well . . . if you threatened my family, I'd have no hesitation shooting you."

"Have you had to shoot anyone?" Todd asked.

"The forest has been enough protection. The people around here living in tents have agreed to help protect each other, and we're hidden. So far that's been enough."

"That's okay for now, but what about in the winter?" Todd asked. "You can't live in tents then."

"I'm sure this will all be taken care of long before that," Amy said. She hesitated. "Unless you know something we don't know." There was worry in her voice.

"We don't know anything for sure," I said. "Nobody does. We're all just trying to do the best we can, the way you've been doing."

"We've been watching your neighborhood since the wall started going up. How many people are working together inside there?"

"I'm not sure." I knew, but I wasn't going to say anything. I stood up. "We should be going." Todd and Lori got to their feet. Todd was still holding the mug and tipped it back to finish off his tea.

"And thanks for the tea," Todd said.

"You're welcome to come back for another cup, anytime," Leonard's mother said.

"Thanks, Amy. We appreciate that offer," I said.

"Not as much as we all appreciate the food you brought," she said.

"Really, we just brought you the food you deserved. We were just being fair."

"Acts of fairness and kindness mean even more now," she said. "Could you do me one more favor?"

"Of course."

"If you do hear anything about what's going on out there, could you share it with us?"

"Definitely. And I was wondering if I could share one other thing with you," Todd said. "I have this tent—it's pretty big, and it's not like we're using it—you could have it if you'd like."

"Thanks for the offer, but we'll be okay."

"But, Mom, this one leaks," Penny said.

"I'm pretty sure mine doesn't leak," Todd said. "How about if you just borrow it, then? You can return it when you don't need it any longer."

Amy smiled. "I think we'd be wrong to turn down such a generous offer. Thank you."

"Just have Leonard come up tomorrow. I'll have it left with the guards at the fence where we met today."

"When do you want me there?" Leonard asked.

"Anytime after noon."

We said our goodbyes and started off.

"That was nice of you," I said to Todd.

"You're not the only nice guy," he said. "Besides, they need our help and it's not like I was planning on going camping myself." He paused. "Now if I could just learn to keep my mouth shut about other details we'd all be fine."

14

I tried to sit quietly at the back of our dining room while the committee members all settled into their seats. I knew I should just consider myself lucky that they allowed me to listen in, because it meant that I knew everything going on. Then again, I wished I hadn't learned about the dog and cat meat in the meals, so maybe knowing everything wasn't always a good thing.

Herb settled into a seat at the side. Judge Roberts always sat at the front, flanked by Councilor Stevens and my mother. Officially, they were the three people most in charge, but Herb should have been seated up there. Maybe Brett was right and Herb should have been the only one sitting at the front.

"There are more issues than usual on the agenda tonight, so we might as well get started," Judge Roberts said, calling the meeting to order.

I'd been at—or listening in on—enough of these meetings to know that the day-to-day stuff would happen first and the new developments would wait until the end of the meeting. I knew it was all important, but some parts were of much more interest to me than others.

The school was continuing to operate, even though it was

summer, with all students in grades one through eight attending a half day five days a week. There had been talk about extending the program right through high school, but now there was a greater need for the older students to be working in the fields or guarding the walls than sitting in classrooms. I guess the least of our worries was that we were all going to miss a year or fall behind. Survival trumped education, and I guess in many ways we were getting a whole different type of education.

Dr. Morgan reported on an outbreak of chicken pox—nothing that wasn't to be expected or that his team couldn't handle. I was glad to hear that both men injured by friendly fire during our attack on the compound were coming along nicely and that one had been released from the clinic already. Also, almost ready for release was our prisoner, Quinn.

Herb offered reassurances that Quinn wouldn't stay in the hospital but gave no specifics about where he'd go from there. Some members asked whether they should set something up as a jail or just release him, expelling him from the neighborhood. Or, they went on, would there be a more final answer? That opened up a whole discussion about what was going to become of Quinn. Finally, the committee agreed to put off a decision until he was completely back to health.

Mr. Nicholas gave a report on some water projects. His daily tests showed that the river water was still potable, if boiled or treated with chlorine; that our wells were producing water; and that the pools were filled to the top from the rainwater collection after the last storm. His crew had been working out a way to block off the sewers and start to store water under the roads. If water was the most important thing to keeping us alive, we had plenty of life in us.

The hair salon was operating—I knew that from Lori's hairstyle experiment—along with the vet's office. And the bakery had started making bread again, using wood to fire the oven. Ernie talked about the community meal and received lots of compliments about the tasty stews he'd been serving.

Mr. Peterson had nothing but positives to say about the crops and their growth. Two new greenhouses had been assembled from scavenged windows and car windshields, and they were both ready to be seeded with some fall vegetables. Another snowblower had been converted to a small rototiller to help with that process, and four more lawn mowers had been remade into noisy little go-carts that were helping to patrol the neighborhood. None of those contained the motor I was most interested in. I shifted impatiently, wanting to hear about the Cessna, but didn't dare interrupt.

"I'm a little concerned about the general mood out there," Councilor Stevens said. "Is it just my imagination or are people more on edge?"

"It's not your imagination," my mother said. "My officers have had to deal with a number of what we'd normally call domestic disputes or disturbances involving neighbors."

"I would have thought with the threat removed that people would have been happier," she said.

"No, it's often the other way around," Herb explained. "When there is an external crisis people pull together, put away minor issues. And then when the crisis is resolved, all those small issues that have been festering boil over."

"So far, we've kept the boiling-over to a minimum and nobody has been hurt," my mother said. "Although we had a funny incident the other day when a husband and wife over on Wheelwright Crescent got in a domestic and were chasing each other up and down the street while actually brandishing frying pans. My officer thought he was watching a cartoon."

There was plenty of laughter over this.

"It's just that it gets more complicated when there are more weapons readily available," my mom added. "What people have seen and experienced somehow seems to devalue life."

"You'd think it would make life more valuable," Mr. Peterson said. "Isn't something more valuable when there's a threat to take it away?"

"That makes sense," my mother said, "but when you've witnessed so much death and trauma, then these things become more the accepted norm. People aren't shocked the same way."

"Lordy. I hope we can stay ahead of this," Judge Roberts said. "There are more than enough external threats without violence being an internal worry. Okay, I'd like to turn now to an item that I know is of importance to all, but of particular interest to Adam, who's being so quiet over there."

I perked up at the sound of my name.

"Can we hear about the condition of the Cessna?" Judge Roberts asked.

"Structurally it appears to be in good shape," Mr. Nicholas said. "The issue is with the engine. There is significant damage, and we're trying to modify certain car parts to make it run."

"Are modified car parts going to be safe?" my mother asked.

I knew that was more the mother talking than the police captain.

"An engine is an engine more or less," Mr. Nicholas said. "Don't worry—I'm going to personally certify it before your son takes it up. In fact, I'll be so confident that I'm going to request that I go up as the copilot on that flight . . . if that's all right with Adam."

"I can take you up, but I think it's better if I go by myself that first trip. From a weight perspective, it's better." And better that two people don't die, I thought to myself, if the car parts should have stayed in cars.

"Okay, then the second flight."

"I think we all understand the importance of having that plane in the air," Herb said. "It would give us greater range as well as more air support, and if we can train another pilot, potentially more eyes and weapons in the air. In the meantime, it's been very reassuring to have Adam up every day for a scouting flight to provide information about what's outside our walls."

"Always with somebody else with him for security," my mother added.

"Always," Herb agreed. "Often, me. I'm also asking that we continue the ground patrols outside the neighborhood with particular emphasis on the two remaining bridges across the river."

"I'll make sure that happens," Howie said. "It's getting more dangerous out there. It's not just that there's more desperation and deprivation, but we're hearing reports that the roving gangs who prey on others have become larger, more violent, and better armed. So I'd like permission for the patrols to be increased in size."

"That's wise," Herb agreed. "We want to make sure your

patrols are big enough and well enough armed that they aren't even considered a target. Those new go-carts can be used in that capacity."

"I also want to make sure they arrive behind the safety of our walls well before nightfall," Howie added. "It's a different world out there when it's dark."

"Which leads me to another thing I wanted to mention," Herb said. "We do need to know about what is happening after dark. Brett has offered to lead a small patrol over the walls at night on a regular basis."

"I can't think of a better person to lead those patrols," Judge Roberts said, and others voiced agreement.

My mother didn't say anything and her face remained neutral. I knew from little snippets of conversations we'd had that she had doubts about Brett. But, really, who else would be crazy enough to want to go outside the walls after dark?

Herb surprised me by asking my opinion. "You've been spending some time with Brett lately. Do you think it's a good idea?"

"We're lucky to have him on our side," I said. "I know the men he's gone out with before say they'd follow him anywhere."

From the nod of his head, Herb seemed to be pleased with my response. "I'll let him know he can select his patrol and start immediately," Herb said. "There is a great deal of information that can be gathered through those patrols. What is happening now under cover of night is an indication of what will eventually happen during the day. And while Brett is outside the walls we need to make sure our guards on the walls double their vigilance."

"I'll make a point of talking to each guard individually," Howie said. "I know there's potential for a letdown when the job starts to become routine."

In the beginning it had mainly been men on the walls. Now it was almost a fifty-fifty split, since more women had been trained. Herb said he had a lot of faith in the women— less testosterone and more level heads, he said. Besides, many of them were out there protecting their children and it was never smart to come between a momma bear and her cubs.

"Please remind the sentries that there are still over a hundred heavily armed and very angry men who survived our attack and could materialize on our doorstep any night," Herb said.

"I think we all have to remember that," my mother said. "The sentries on the wall, the patrols going out during the day, Brett with his men at night, and of course my son in the air."

I had been waiting for that last part.

"I'll keep my people focused," Howie said. "I know the danger is real for them, but the most difficult part, the part that's having the greatest impact on them, isn't the fear of attack but having to watch innocent people walk past each day . . . families . . . women and children . . . It's hard to know that they can't do anything. It's really bothering some of them."

"When it stops bothering them is when we should be worried," Judge Roberts said. "It's only human. I wish we could do more."

"We all do," Councilor Stevens said.

"We've noticed that more people are setting up tents, making camp, in areas surrounding our walls," Howie said.

"Are they any threat?" Judge Roberts asked.

I thought about Leonard and his family. They weren't right by the walls, but I hoped that nobody saw them as a danger to us and tried to clear them away.

"No threat that we can see," Howie said, and I felt relieved. "I think they just feel safer in the shadow of our walls. We're getting more people just lingering on the outside within sight of our guards. My guards want to know whether, if there was a problem, they could go out and offer assistance."

Everybody looked at Herb.

"Captain, what do you think?" he asked, and the attention shifted to my mother.

"We might have to intervene, but it has to be done in a coordinated way, with approval. We can't have people just running out on their own without support or in scattered numbers. If we go out, it has to be in force."

"Caution is best," Herb agreed. "After all, we don't have the resources to help everybody. Or, I should mention, the resources to bring anybody else into the neighborhood."

He'd said that to everybody, but it seemed like it was directed at me.

"Speaking of which, how are our newest members doing?" Judge Roberts asked.

"Some have settled into some vacant houses over on Trapper Crescent, and others have been taken in by other folks," Councilor Stevens replied.

"Good to know they've been welcomed," Judge Roberts noted. "And psychologically how are they doing?"

"There has been a whole range of responses," Dr. Morgan replied. "Most of the children have already started attending classes, and some of the women are helping in the fields and preparing meals. We also had a very tearful reunion when one of the men who was originally rescued from Olde Burnham was reunited with his wife and son."

"I assume others are not doing as well," Herb said.

Dr. Morgan shook his head. "They went through a pretty horrific time. All will recover physically, but mentally there are some who will never be the same."

Some people looked down at the table or floor as if they couldn't even make eye contact with Dr. Morgan. I'd heard the stories—I guess we all had.

"I think this is the time for me to mention the food situation," Ernie said. "I know it sounds a little insensitive, but all my calculations have had to change with forty-seven new people to feed."

Now it was my time to look down at the floor.

"There will be shortfalls. I'm almost afraid to suggest it, but I think we have to do more than just talk about reducing the daily rations of food."

"That would have a negative impact on the mood and morale of the entire neighborhood," Judge Roberts said.

"And I know that food, or rather lack of food, has been a source of tension leading to some of the disputes we've been settling," my mother added.

"I know, but we can't get soup from a stone," Ernie said.

"Then maybe we have to get more soup," Herb said. "What if we tie the larger patrols in with the scavenging crews and see if we can find more food?"

"I'd even offer to lead that," Howie said.

"I'd appreciate you being part of that—your leadership would be such a positive—but if people don't object, I'd like to go out on the first few," Herb said.

"I wouldn't object," Howie offered. "I'd feel safer knowing that you were with me."

"We all can endorse that," Judge Roberts said.

"I don't think we even need to go far," Herb said. "We might take a little trip to the mall down the road."

"We'll leave that to your discretion. Now, if there are no more items in need of immediate attention, I suggest we adjourn for a few minutes, stretch our legs, and get something to drink."

15

We rumbled through the neighborhood on our way out. It had taken less than twenty-four hours for Herb's suggestion to become a reality. No surprise there. First in line was the open-bed truck with three men in the cab and another half dozen in the back—all of them armed. Howie and Brett were among them, which was reassuring.

The truck pulled one of the hay wagons from the farm, rigged up with a special harness. The wagon and the bed of the truck were our grocery carts. It was good to have the wagon and everything it could carry, but it was really slowing us down. It was old and wooden and rickety, and if they tried to pull it too fast it might just fall to pieces. We weren't going to be running from trouble pulling that behind us.

We had been given a grocery list: nails, cement, fertilizer, windows, and anything else that looked good. It was a strange list, even stranger when you thought that we were authorized to use force to get what we needed, armed to protect ourselves, and the "anything else that looked good" didn't involve impulse purchases at the check-out line. My hope was that we could find some food. I felt like all of those extra mouths that we'd brought in were on my head.

I was second in line with my car, Todd in the backseat and

Herb beside me. Along with us, simply for security, were four other members of the security team, all armed, all riding on newly constructed go-carts. All of us were wearing body armor as well. We were a formidable force—one I wouldn't mess with. I just hoped other people thought the same.

"Lots of activity at the school," Todd said as we passed by.

"You give teachers a job to do, and they get organized. The school is running extremely well," Herb said. "It's also allowed the parents of the children to be freed up to do other things around the neighborhood."

"I'm good with school as long as they don't try to rope me in," Todd added.

"It's not a reform school," Herb said.

"I don't think I've ever heard you crack a joke," Todd said.

"Who said I was joking?" Herb asked.

I thought Todd was wrong about school. I would have loved to have things back the way they were. We should all be wishing we were back in class. Would that ever happen again?

"Besides," Herb said, "it's not only that those kids need to be educated but also that we need to establish a sense of order, of normalcy."

"Come on, none of this is normal," Todd said.

"Not normal, but a *sense* of normal. In a normal world, kids go to school or day care and their parents go off to work," Herb said.

"Well, if a bunch of us going out to scavenge and steal from other communities is a normal job, then I guess this is all just a usual day," Todd said.

"The hope is to make it as normal as possible," Herb said. "And that's why the dentist is filling teeth and doing examinations, the doctors are seeing patients at the walk-in clinic, and the salon is open to cut hair."

"But all those things need to be done as well," I said.

"They do, but there's a basic human need for things to be normal and predictable," Herb said.

"The strangest thing for me is still the group supper," Todd said. "An intimate dinner with sixteen hundred people each night isn't any part of normal that I've ever heard of. I still don't know how they're doing it."

"Ernie has plenty of help with that meal," Herb said. "There is a whole crew that is cutting, chopping, cooking, and serving."

Each night everybody gathered at the school in three shifts for the one big meal served to all. It was amazing to see it being prepared. There were always at least fifty people who helped chop and mix and cook. They used a series of small stoves—they were called buddy burners—and I'd learned about them in Boy Scouts. They were used for most of the cooking. When the weather was good and the sun was out they used solar cookers assembled from pieces of corrugated card-board and aluminum foil with a window on the top to keep the heat in. There had to be a hundred of them that lined the south wall of the school where they could best harvest the sun. Using those meant no wood or fuel was consumed. I was continually amazed at how something could come from nothing.

Politely, people lined up, had food put on their plates, and then went to one of the classrooms to eat. Nobody was going hungry, but the amounts weren't as much as most people were used to and there wasn't a lot of variety. At least now the first crops had come in and there was some fresh lettuce, peas, and spinach. A stew didn't need much meat if it had fresh vegetables. Some strawberry plants had produced fruit, and some black raspberries had been gathered from the ravine. None of it was much, but together it was enough to keep us going.

There was a whole lot of grumbling, though, and it was probably going to get worse before it got better. The other part we didn't know was how tough it was going to be to even keep this amount of food flowing. We had to just hope we found enough to keep us fed until the big harvest in the fall.

We came up to the guard post at the intersection. The armed guards saw us approaching and opened up the big gates to let us pass. The truck pulling the wagon eased through the gap and turned to the right, toward the mall. Two of the go-carts followed right behind and then roared off, taking the lead to scout what was up ahead.

"Stop here for a second," Herb said.

I halted right in the gap and the guards came over to our open windows. I recognized them both.

"Tony, Ralph, how are things going?" Herb asked.

"I worked the whole night," Tony said. "It was quiet, but it looked like it had potential for trouble."

"Yeah, around midnight one group rolled by in a big beaten-up old church bus," Ralph added. "They slowed down and gave us a long look before they decided to keep going."

"We were pretty glad about that. There had to be a dozen of them, and they had automatic weapons . . . I could see gun barrels out the windows."

"As long as they can see easier prey they won't target us," Herb said. "Marauding gangs are no different from a pack of hyenas or jackals—they'll try to pick on the soft targets, the easy score, places and people who look like they can't or won't fight back."

"We'd put up a fight," Ralph said. "Believe me, nobody is getting past us."

Tony nodded. "Listen, Herb. I had a thought about something that would make the neighborhood easier to defend."

"Tell me," Herb said.

"We could do something about the fences on the other side of the street," Tony said.

Herb looked across the road at the high walls, which had been identical to the ones on our side of the street before we'd made ours taller and stronger. They had been put up by the city alongside the road as a sound and sight barrier, and were made of interlocking cement slabs stacked on top of each other, strong and high. On our side of the street they made great boundaries to protect us. On the other side of the street they were something for somebody to hide behind and take shots at people on our side.

"Well, we've contemplated that, but there are people still living over there, aren't there?"

"A lot of the houses have been abandoned, but I know there are some residents," Ralph answered.

"I'm not sure we can justify taking down their walls to make ours safer," Herb explained.

I know Herb had already had some conversations with the people who still lived there in the shadow of our neighborhood. They hadn't been able to organize themselves enough to provide adequate security or to start planning for the future. Instead they lived side by side with the few remaining neighbors, not working together, relying on the illusion that being close to us would provide some safety.

"I guess I understand," Tony said.

"I gotta tell you, and this may sound strange, but it's not the armed punks passing by that trouble me," Ralph said, still leaning into the car to talk. "It's people like that." He pointed to a man and woman. She was holding the hands of two kids: a little boy who couldn't have been any more than eight or nine and a girl who was maybe two years older. The father was pulling a kid's wagon loaded down with things.

"I hear you, brother. I just wish we could do something for them," Tony said.

"You're both good men, but I want you to be good sentries. Remember, just because something or somebody looks innocent doesn't mean it is that way. Try not to let your guard down. I've seen experienced soldiers who did that and found themselves dead. There are places and times when I've come across twelve-year-olds who would kill you just as soon as look at you."

"I've heard about things like that . . . child soldiers."

"But I can't imagine that happening here," Ralph said.

"Could you imagine *any* of this happening here?" Herb asked.

Ralph shook his head.

"All right, gentleman, we have to get going. There's safety in numbers both here and out there." He motioned for me to go.

I put the car into gear and we edged out through the gap. The guards waved goodbye. I hung the turn and hurried after the rest of our group. The two other go-carts roared off to catch up with the lead truck and wagon.

We quickly caught up to the family that had passed by the gate. The parents eyed us carefully and the little girl pressed in behind her mother to hide from us. In that half second I saw fear in her expression. The little girl was afraid of us—they were *all* afraid of us. I couldn't help but wonder about that look in her eyes, which made me think not of my little sister but of my own father, who was still out there, somewhere, even more alone than this family, far from home.

I had tried hard not to think about him much. It made me feel guilty that he wasn't in my thoughts more, but feeling guilty was better than being frozen with fear for him, wondering how he was doing, and if he was even still alive.

I pulled us in tight behind the farm wagon and then realized that I didn't like the idea of having my view blocked, so I backed off a little.

We crossed Erin Mills Parkway and then rumbled into the parking lot of the mall. We passed by row after row of abandoned cars. The car owners had all come innocently to shop at the mall seventy-odd days ago. Many of the vehicles now had obvious signs of vandalism—smashed windows, trunks open, and doors ripped right off. Several had been set on fire. Our scavenging parties had already been here and drained each vehicle of its last ounce of gas.

Some people were walking through the parking lot, but they fled as they saw us coming. I didn't blame them: We were a large, well-organized posse carrying weapons.

We pulled to a stop by the main doors, or at least where the main doors had been before they were smashed and ripped apart. Inside was darkness. We gathered by the opening.

"I want to make sure that we all follow the rules," Howie said.

The rules were simple. We were going to be scavenging, taking things, but we weren't simply going to be stealing. We were to mark every item; every single thing had to be logged in a notebook and given to the procurement committee. We had to record the date, the location it was taken from, any damage that was done, and who had taken it. It was what we had done with the cars, with everything that had been taken. Some people, like Brett, thought it was a stupid waste of time, but it was our attempt to do things the right way. Today I just figured we were wasting our time in a different way. After ten weeks, what of value could possibly remain in those stores?

"I want four people to stay out here and guard the vehicles," Howie said. He pointed at four of the team. "The rest, come with me."

Todd moved in right behind Howie. I hesitated. It might have been better to stay out here with the vehicles, but that wasn't an option. Instead I went over to Herb, who was standing by Brett.

"I want you to be on the six," Herb was saying to Brett.

"Understood."

Herb started walking, while Brett remained behind. He would bring up the rear, protecting the back of the line. Being "on the six" meant being the last in line. I fell in beside Herb. The smashed glass, all in little cubes on the ground, crunched noisily under our feet. It was a strange sensation, almost like walking through snow that was crusted over.

Herb stopped at the directory listing the stores in the mall. He studied it, running his finger along the lines and then finding the corresponding store. Typical Herb—nothing done without a plan.

The mall was deserted and destroyed. Storefronts, windows, and doors no longer existed. Metal grilles had been torn down and were either lying on the ground or had been pried up or twisted into grotesque statues. There were no lights, of course, and the farther we got into the interior, the dimmer it became. It wasn't dark, just dim. There was enough light coming in through the skylights—which hadn't been smashed—to allow us to see and move. Could we find anything of use in here? Hadn't hundreds and hundreds of people already been through here?

The men up ahead were fanning out on both sides, staying close to the stores themselves, looking into each as we passed. Herb stayed right in the middle, as did I. Brett was still in the back, walking carefully, fanning his rifle from side to side and then spinning around to see behind him.

We all had to be careful as we walked because the floor was littered with debris. Some of the merchandise from the stores had only made it this far. There were some clothes, broken racks, empty suitcases, bent golf clubs, deflated soccer balls, and gutted TVs and electronics everywhere. It was almost as if the looters had blamed the electronics for what was happening and had taken their anger out on them. Completely illogical, but somehow, on some level, I understood. It felt like technology had betrayed us and that the only way to react to the betrayal was to rage against it.

A big fountain lay ahead, silent, its pool of water bad smelling and algae stained. The little gardens had all been ripped out, and the trees—some of which had soared up almost to the skylights—had been torn down. What was the point in any of that? I understood the electronics, but why take it out on innocent vegetation?

I looked into each store as we passed. I should have been looking for people, but instead I was absorbed by what I saw—or didn't see—inside. The stores were destroyed, their contents looted. What remained was in piles on the floor, racks knocked over, nothing much standing.

We came up to the electronics store, the place where the TVs had come from. The metal grates had been taken down and were in a pile in the middle of the mall. Inside, though, it was different. It was stripped clean, the entire store emptied out down to the fixtures. There was nothing left.

How stupid. At a time without electricity, without the Internet, without anything that would allow them to work, those items had still been targeted as being valuable. Right now they were nothing more than deadweight. Forget TVs and computers; go for food or water or chlorine tablets.

Herb had known right from the beginning what would be valuable and had traded money—which was now useless—for things we'd need. He figured he had enough chlorine to last him for decades. Now I hoped he had enough to take care of sixteen hundred people for as long as this all lasted.

I heard voices echoing up through the empty mall and turned my head to try to pick them up. I caught sight of two or three men coming our way. They skidded to a stop when they saw us, turned, and ran away, disappearing around the corner. I could still hear them running long after I couldn't see them anymore.

"That's good that they're gone," I said.

"Unless they've gone to get reinforcements," Herb said.

That wasn't reassuring.

"We'll keep an eye out," he said. "There's nothing here that we can't handle."

"Are you saying that to make me feel better or because it's the truth?" I asked.

"It is the truth and it should make you feel better."

Up ahead Howie and three of the men disappeared into one of the stores. Two others fanned out, taking spots against the base of another fountain, protected from anything coming. We came up to the store where our men had vanished inside. It was the discount pet food store. Like the other stores, it had obviously been looted—windows and doors shattered, metal grates pushed up and broken, the cash register lying open on the floor, racks knocked over, and bags of dog food ripped open. Food pellets that were scattered across the floor crunched noisily beneath their feet as they came out. Howie and each of the men had big bags of dry dog food on their shoulders.

"There are still a few in the back," Howie said. "I guess looters don't care much about dog food."

"That works for us," Herb said. "Get as much of it as there is. I want you to send back for more help to carry things."

"There's not that much," Howie said.

"Other things. I want the soil taken out of all the mall gardens. It's excellent soil, treated, highly fertilized."

"That will take some manpower," Howie said.

"I also want people up on the roof. Those skylights are still intact, and we can build a greenhouse or two just from them."

"I'll get Mr. Nicholas and some members of the engineering team out here to work on that. Anything else?" Howie asked.

"That's still to be determined, but from what I've seen I should have had us here sooner. Adam and I are going to go exploring a little further . . . if that's okay with you."

"You're the boss," Howie said.

"Adam, I guess I should have asked—do you want to come along or stay here and lug dog food?"

"I'll come along. I've got your back," I said.

"Actually, I'm going to ask Brett to cover both of us. He's coming, too."

"Oh . . . okay." I should have been glad to have him along—safety in numbers—but still, didn't Herb think I could cover him? I guess I couldn't blame him. I'd rather have Brett—the living, breathing action hero—on my six instead of me.

We walked out of the store. Herb motioned for Brett to follow and then for one of the others to take up the position Brett had been guarding.

"Where are we going?" I asked.

"The sporting goods store," Herb replied.

I wanted to ask him if he planned on picking up some soccer balls, but I knew that if Herb wanted to go there, then there was a good reason—sort of like with how he'd gotten the chlorine tablets at the pool store the very first day this had all started.

Herb took his pistol out of the holster, holding it hanging down by his leg. I quickly did the same thing. Brett was behind us, his rifle out, swinging it from side to side. With each pass it was briefly aimed at us. That was unnerving. *Everything* was unnerving.

I looked in each store as we passed—the jewelry store, Everything for a Dollar with its sign smashed, a florist, a hair salon. It didn't matter what type of store it was before, because now they were all gone. Same broken glass, twisted grates, piles of debris. What did Herb hope to find at the sporting goods store that would be any better?

I heard more voices coming from ahead, and the hair on the back of my neck stood on end. I looked over at Herb. He nodded. He'd noticed as well. At least the voices sounded like they were far away, and the store was just up ahead, wasn't it? I was feeling disoriented. I'd been in this mall dozens—no, hundreds—of times, but it was all so different now. I was walking through a nightmare instead of a shopping center.

The sporting goods store came up on our right. The front window was gone, but the metal grating was still in place, although some of the bars had been forced apart far enough to allow people to go inside—and come back out with merchandise. There didn't appear to be much left on the shelves, which had been pushed over and formed a jumbled pile in the middle of the store. Herb squeezed through one of the openings in the grate and went in. I didn't need an invitation. I followed right behind, instantly feeling safer in the smaller space. Brett came up to the grate but didn't come inside. He and I made eye contact—he gave me a smile, a nod, and a thumbs-up.

"Adam, come on back here!" Herb called out.

I scaled the junk layering the floor. Overturned racks, random clothing, soccer shin pads, and empty display cases. If we were here for soccer balls I couldn't see any. I came to Herb's side.

"Didn't this store sell archery equipment?" he asked.

"Yeah, this is where we bought our equipment."

"Where did they keep all the bows and arrows?"

"They had equipment right over there," I said, pointing to where a display case and rack holding bows used to be. It was gone, along with any hint of bows or arrows.

"And did they have a storage area?

"No room, but they did keep a lot of equipment locked in the bottom of a display case."

I looked around and spotted the case. The whole glass top had disappeared, and the bows and hunting knives were all gone. The big wooden case was now sitting on its side. I knelt down beside it. The bottom section was still intact. I went to pull open the drawer, but it wouldn't budge.

"It's locked," I said.

"I think I just might have the key right here," Herb said. "Hold this."

He handed me his gun and then reached into his pocket and pulled out a little piece of metal. "It's called a pick," he said. He pulled his glasses out of his other pocket and then knelt down in front of the case and inserted the little metal pick into the lock.

"That's a pretty interesting thing to know how to do," I said.

"You live long enough and you learn a thing or two."

"My grandmother was eighty-three when she died, and I'm pretty sure she didn't know how to pick a lock," I said.

"You never know what people know or don't know. Before all this, did you ever think I could pick a lock?"

"I'm starting to think you have a whole collection of skills you don't talk about," I said.

There was a click, and Herb pulled out the drawer. It was filled with hunting knives, some bows, a couple of crossbows, and more arrows than I could count.

"I think these might be helpful," Herb said. He removed one of the crossbows and handed it to me. "Beautiful, isn't it?"

I nodded.

"Have you ever fired a crossbow before?"

"Just bows and arrows—the ones you've seen in my garage."

"The crossbow superseded the bow. It was a major development in warfare that was as significant as the first firearms," Herb said. "At short range the crossbow is as accurate and deadly as a small-caliber firearm, and it has a very distinct advantage." He reached into the drawer and pulled out a crossbow bolt. "It has reusable ammunition. Let's get all of these into the vehicles and back to the neighborhood."

I felt a sense of relief as the guards closed the gate to our neighborhood, sealing us safely inside. The backseat of my car was filled with archery equipment. The truck and the wagon were still back at the mall and were practically overflowing with scavenged items. Aside from the dog food, the soil, and the skylights, there were hundreds of bags of fertilizer our men had found at the garden center; some camping equipment; and some hand tools, shovels, nails, and screws from the hardware store.

The things in my car—the crossbows and bolts—were going to be stored in Herb's basement. All the extra weapons and ammunition that weren't being carried by the guards were secured, under lock and key, with an armed guard watching them if Herb wasn't home. I wasn't sure crossbows and bolts were in the same category as the firearms, but I guess it was best to have them in one location and I was glad that location was with Herb. This was a good day of scavenging. I just wished we'd found some food that wasn't meant for dogs.

16

I listened in on the conversation between Danny and Rachel as they ate lunch—stale crackers with peanut butter that had come from the seemingly endless supply in Herb's stash. I didn't have an appetite today, or maybe I just was sick of eating the same food all the time. I sipped a glass of water that had a faint chemical taste from the chlorine tabs. The twins continued to haul water up from the river and put it into a big drum that sat in our kitchen. Chlorine was added according to a specific ratio, and the treated water was drawn from the drum as needed for drinking. On days when it rained it was just collected in a rain barrel as it fell. It didn't need to be chlorinated and tasted so sweet, so natural. Rainwater was the best-tasting thing in the world.

The twins were both upset, along with almost all the young kids, that school had been extended into the summer instead of ending when it normally did.

"It isn't fair," Danny complained. "It's getting too hot to sit inside a classroom."

"My legs keep sticking to the chair," Rachel chimed in. "Why can't we just have a summer vacation like we always used to?"

They knew as well as anybody else that normal wasn't normal anymore. They were just grumpy.

There was a simple way for me to end their complaining, but it wasn't up to me to tell them. For now, school might have been extended into the summer, but in the fall it was going to start much later than usual. In September and October even the kids would be busy working all day in the fields with the harvest. It had been agreed by the committee to keep this plan from everyone right now for the sake of morale. People didn't need reminding that nobody knew when our nightmare was going to be over.

According to Herb, people needed to know just enough to keep them moving forward but not enough to paralyze them with fear or dismay. There wasn't going to be a magic solution to save us all, but we still needed to hope, to believe in miracles. I knew the only answers were going to come from the people inside these walls. My hope was in them—in us. It would probably be easier if I believed in miracles, too.

While I was listening to Danny and Rachel, I could also hear the wind outside, which was getting stronger. Just to put something in my stomach, I grabbed a peanut-butter cracker from Danny, ignoring his protest, and headed out to check on my ultralight. I wanted to make sure it was safely lashed to the ground.

As I was bending down to recheck the ropes holding it in place, I heard the clip-clopping of horse hooves on the pavement. I looked up and saw Lori riding up on one horse, holding the reins of a second, leading it behind her.

She came to a stop right beside me.

"Howdy, pardner," I said. "You're out for a little ride, I see."

"That's the plan. What are you up to today?" she asked.

"I'm supposed to go up on a surveillance flight, but if the winds keep up this strong I'm grounded."

"Then this is perfect timing. Are you interested in joining me?"

"I'd like to, but I better stay close. If the winds do die down, I'll want to get into the air quickly."

The truth was, I hated riding horseback. Hated the smell, the awkward jouncing, and the way I never felt nearly as in control as at the wheel of my car or the controls of my ultralight.

"Don't worry about it," Lori said. "I'm sure I can find *somebody* who would be interested in going for a ride with me. Maybe Todd or Rachel or even Brett."

"I know Rachel would be interested, but how about I join you this time?" I said. "Let me just tell the twins that I'm going and that I'll be back soon."

I wanted them to know I was gone and for Lori to know I would only be a sec. I ran to the door, yelled at them, and they yelled back an "Okay!"

Lori was waiting.

She gave me a smile and handed me the reins. Awkwardly I climbed up onto the horse's back. I hadn't ridden much and felt a little nervous, but I wasn't going to let her see that. Lori started off and I gave my horse a bit of a kick with both heels to get it moving. I bumped up and down as he trotted along. What a ridiculous way to travel. I slowed down when we were right beside Lori. Her mount was taller and bigger, and it felt a little weird looking up to her. Then again, I didn't really want the bigger horse. If it was up to me I would have ridden one short enough that my feet were dragging along the ground.

"I love riding," she said.

"Yeah, it's awesome." I tried to sound enthusiastic but obviously didn't do as well as I'd hoped.

"But it's not as much fun as flying a plane," Lori guessed.

"Not even close—" I stopped myself. "Not as much fun for me, but I know it is for you . . . and lots of other people."

"You don't have to come with me."

"That's what makes it fun for me," I said.

"So you'd never ride on your own?"

"I understand why you like it—it's kind of cool—but I guess I just like to know that when I push or pull or turn the controls on my plane it does exactly what I want it to do," I said.

"And you like that predictability, that sense of control?"

"Exactly," I said.

"Well, you're never going to get that completely with a horse—or with a girlfriend."

This had taken a turn I hadn't predicted or had control over, which I guess proved her point. "It's very different. I'd never want to control a girlfriend, and I hope she'd never toss me to the ground and break my neck—although there's probably still the danger that she'd break my heart."

I was relieved to see her smile. "I don't think you have to worry about either," she said. "We have hours until it gets dark, so why don't we ride down by the ravine? We could even go see Leonard and his family."

"It's pretty far, so I'm not sure that's a great idea, especially just the two of us."

"I think I've shown I can take care of myself . . . and you as well," she said.

"No offense meant. It's just that more is always better. Three is better than two, and four is better than three," I said.

"I guess we could get a third horse and ask Brett to come along, if that would make you feel safer," she said.

That was the last thing I wanted, but it would be safer. "I'm sure he would come if we asked him. He likes being outside the wall."

"He probably would, but to be honest he gives me the creeps," she said.

I smiled, not just because that was how she felt but because that was how I felt sometimes.

"I guess he's starting to remind me of a vampire—you know, the way he's always dressed in black and only seems to come out when the sun is going down," she explained.

"Since he's started those night patrols, he needs to sleep during the day," I explained.

Brett had chosen nine people to be on the night patrol with him, the first of which was the night after we "shopped" at the mall. At dusk, dressed in black and armed to the teeth, they slipped over the fence and disappeared into the dark. I had to admit that I almost envied them, going out there like heroes in an action movie. Then I reminded myself it was no movie. People died out there. It was better to fly over it during the day than wade through it at night.

At one point it looked like Brett might want Todd to be part of his squad. Thank goodness Todd had a good excuse to say no. He was needed to continue to work on the walls with his father.

As it was, most of the people Brett selected to be part of his team were relatively young. A couple guys I knew pretty well. Owen and Tim were a few years ahead of us at school; I'd played football with Owen one year before he graduated. He was a pretty good guy and I liked him. Tim lived on our street, and Todd had dated his younger sister for almost two months. That was a record for Todd, and when it ended badly I thought Todd and Tim were going to come to blows. Thank goodness Rachel was just a kid. Todd was my best friend, but him ever dating any sister of mine was way out of the question.

"I understand why they dress that way to go out at night, but it still makes him and his little army of Goths creepy," Lori said.

I laughed. "I don't think any of them would be impressed by being called Goths, but they might like being called vampires. I just know I wouldn't want to go out there."

"Neither would I."

"But you have to give the guy credit," I said.

"When did you start defending him? You've *never* even liked him."

I'd tried to keep that to myself, but Lori was always able to read me even when I didn't say anything. "It's not that I don't like him." That was a lie. "It's just that somebody has to do it."

"I get the feeling he gets off on doing it," she said. "That he likes sneaking around out there in the dark and causing trouble."

"He told me that he likes the rush of danger, so I guess that's how he's getting his rush."

"That still doesn't make it any less creepy," she said.

"He's not just causing trouble, he's getting information. They've also been scavenging while they're out there. Two nights ago they brought back some tools and a bunch of light-bulbs they found."

We came up to the gate at the northeast corner of the neighborhood.

"Nice afternoon for a ride," one of the guards said.

"How's it looking out there?" I asked.

"There's still some activity out on the 403, but it's pretty calm."

"Can you please open the gate?" I asked. "We're going to go out for a short ride."

"You know we're not supposed to just let people out," one of them said. "But I guess it's okay because it's you, Adam." He hesitated. "You have a weapon, right?"

"Yes." My pistol was always with me.

"And I have this." Lori reached down and pulled up the butt of a rifle, which was inside a bag tied to the side of her horse.

"Besides, we're not going to go far." I turned to Lori. "You agree that we're not going to visit Leonard and his family. We're going to stay in sight of the walls."

She nodded, although she didn't look too happy about it.

The two men opened the gate and let us out. I heard them close it behind us. I would have preferred it to stay open but couldn't really say that. Lori led, and I reluctantly followed.

Lori took a deep breath. "The air out here is better. Can you feel it?"

"Not really, but it does feel better up there," I said pointing to the sky. "Do you want to come with me when I go on patrol tomorrow?"

"That would be wonderful . . . except you're probably not going tomorrow. It's going to rain."

I looked at the sky. There was hardly a cloud in it, but then I remembered about her father.

"Your father's prediction?"

She nodded. "He's hardly ever wrong."

"Well, if not tomorrow, the next day. Would that be good?"

Lori didn't answer. She was staring back, her eyes wide open. I turned around in the saddle to see flames. The condominium on the southwest corner of Burnham Drive and Erin Mills, just outside our western boundaries, was on fire. Bright orange flames had shattered the windows of one of the units and were licking up the side of the building.

"Come with me!" Lori yelled, and started galloping off.

I pulled on one rein and pointed my horse toward hers, dug in my heels, and chased after her. My horse was moving at a full gallop, bouncing me up and down, moving way too fast for me to be comfortable, but Lori was still pulling away from me.

"Open the gate!" I screamed as we approached the gate we'd only just come out. "Open the gate!"

The gate opened and we charged in—Lori first and me pulling up the rear.

It was obvious that we weren't the only people who'd noticed the fire. All around us people were coming out of their houses, pointing, standing in groups or walking or running toward the corner of our neighborhood that was closest to the burning building. The flames were bright, lighting up the whole top of the building, making it almost glow.

"Slow down!" Lori yelled out.

I pulled at my horse's reins and brought it under control.

"It's not good for their legs to run on the pavement, and they could even slip and fall," she explained.

We slowed to a walk. We came up close to the wall at the top of the neighborhood, and Lori stopped and climbed off her horse. I did the same.

"I don't want to get any closer. Horses get spooked easily, especially by crowds of people and fire," she explained.

We tied their reins to a tree and continued on foot. There were already dozens and dozens of people standing around, staring, and pointing, and the crowd was growing quickly.

The building wasn't tall—only fifteen stories—but it was the tallest thing around the neighborhood. Herb had mentioned to me that he was troubled by its presence. He didn't like anything that held the high ground.

Lori looked around. "Shouldn't we do something?"

"What can we do? It's not like we can call the fire department."

"But don't we have some firemen here in the neighborhood?"

"We do, but they don't have any equipment or a truck or any way of pumping water to put it out."

"Shouldn't somebody go and rescue the people?" someone else in the crowd asked.

"Most of the units are already empty," I replied. I'd heard that bit of information while the committee was talking.

More and more people arrived, some on the run, attracted by the fire. It was amazing how fast the fire was spreading. Thick, dark billowing clouds rose up, staining the sky. This was quickly going from bad to worse.

There was a loud crash—a gigantic pane of glass shattered—and people in the crowd shrieked in surprise.

"I can feel the heat," Lori said.

I could feel it as well. The sound of a car coming up fast behind us made me turn back, and I caught sight of my old sedan. It skidded to a stop, and my mother and Herb both jumped out at the same time. They were instantly surrounded, people asking questions and pointing at the flames. I spotted Howie with a number of guards, the fire captain, and Brett. I guess there had been enough ruckus to wake him and get him out here. I pulled Lori over to them to hear the discussion.

"Just let me go over with a couple of my men and—"

"And do what?" Herb questioned, cutting off the fire captain. "You have no equipment, no vehicle, and no water."

"But we still have skills. We know how to rescue people, perform CPR, and care for the injured."

"Or get injured or killed yourself," Herb added.

"It's just hard to stand here and watch a building go up in flames, not to try to rescue people."

"I understand your feelings, but you have to understand that we don't know what caused this fire, what other dangers are out there," Herb said. "Even under normal circumstances a fire department wouldn't go in if there was a sniper."

"There's a sniper?" the captain asked. "That's ridiculous."

"There are definitely people out there with guns," Herb said. "We can't just—"

"I could go over," Brett interjected. "I'd be just as happy to let the whole thing burn to the ground, but if you needed it, my team could provide security."

My mother gave a subtle nod.

"Okay, fine," Herb said. "Get your firefighters together. Brett, put together a security detail."

"Is there anything I can do?" I asked.

"We're going to have you sit this one out," Herb said.

I couldn't help feeling a little disappointed, but I could see my mother relax.

"I'd like you to go home and watch the twins," she said. "You could get Lori home at the same time."

"I'm going to stay here," Lori said.

"Is it all right if I stay, too?" I asked. "The kids will be okay for at least a while without me."

"Well, okay," my mother said. "But as long as you're staying here I'm going to put you both on guard duty."

"Don't you have enough guards?"

"I'm going to put more sentries out all along the walls. This is going to potentially draw more attention to the neighborhood. I want to be ready," she explained.

"That's wise," Herb said. "You might want to put some on the far wall as well. If somebody was going to attack, this would be a smart diversion."

I hadn't thought of that. Probably nobody would have except Herb.

"Howie, I'd like you to arrange all of that, the extra guards," she said.

"As good as done, Cap," he said, and hurried off.

My mother and Herb rushed off as well and it was just Lori and me again—alone with a few hundred other people, watching as a whole condominium tower went up in flames.

17

As predicted by Lori's father, it started to rain in the middle of the night. I woke up to hear it rattling against the window. Lori and I had stayed longer at the wall until I persuaded her to walk back with me so I could watch the twins and she could take care of the horses. I lay in bed, listening to the rain hit the windowpanes. At the very least, the rain would help put out the fire—it would also fill rain barrels and swimming pools, helping keep our water supply steady.

As soon as the sky started lightening, I got dressed and went out to see the results of the fire. The umbrella I was holding didn't seem to give much protection from the blowing rain. As I got closer to the wall, the smell of fire was thick and wisps of smoke floated through the air. I could see the top floors of the condo had blackened, with gaping holes where windows used to be, but smoke was still coming out of the openings. Despite the early hour and the rain still falling, there were other people lining the wall, looking out at it. I wondered if I'd find Lori up here.

I scanned the crowd and saw her standing on the ledge of the wall closest to the condo, staring out intently.

I came up behind her. "Good morning."

She smiled sadly. "Not particularly good for them," she said, gesturing out to the building.

"I know." I climbed up beside her and took her hand.

Even from this distance we could see a lot of people—men, women, and children—standing in the rain, partially sheltered by the building or under the thin cover of trees. Thank goodness they were far enough away that I couldn't make out the faces or expressions. The loss was hard enough at this distance without being able to see them as individuals.

"I wonder how it started," Lori said.

I shook my head. "Probably somebody cooking inside or using a candle for light."

I really wanted to believe that it had been an accident that spread, but in the middle of the night, in the darkest corner of my mind I couldn't help but wonder—did Herb do this? I'd heard him talking more than once about how he was worried that the building was there, offering a vantage for anybody looking into our neighborhood and now, suddenly, it wasn't going to be there anymore. Still, there was no way that Herb would have set the fire. I knew that.

"What's going to happen to those people now?" Lori asked.

"Some of them might be able to go back into their units after this," I offered, although I didn't necessarily believe that.

"And some probably can't. Where are they going to go?" she asked.

"Maybe some of the people in the other units will take them in."

"Or maybe they're too selfish to take them in, you know, the way we're too selfish to take anybody else in here," she said.

I didn't know what to say. It wasn't selfishness—it was survival. We couldn't take in everybody.

"It just seems so wrong, standing here doing nothing. We should go out and see if we can help."

"We can't go out without permission."

"I don't need permission. Besides, it's not like there's anything to worry about out there."

She was so wrong about that. Desperate people with no food, no shelter, no hope were probably the most dangerous people in the world. They had nothing to lose.

"I'm going over there," Lori said.

Before I could say another word she climbed over the wall and jumped down to the other side. Without thinking, I hopped over and went after her.

We ran across the grassy boulevard and onto the street. There were a number of guards posted along the way and I was surprised to see Todd among them.

"What's going on?" I asked him.

"There were a few deaths, and lots of injuries. Mostly it's sprains, a couple of broken bones that happened when people jumped out of lower-level windows, and a whole bunch of people with smoke inhalation. Dr. Morgan set up a sort of hospital in the lobby of the building."

"I guess it could have been worse," Lori said.

"Worse is what's going to happen next," Todd said. "Most of the building isn't going to be fit to be—"

There was a loud smash, and all three of us jumped and

spun around. A whole bay window had tumbled down and shattered on the ground.

"Stuff keeps crashing down," Todd explained. "It's been doing that all night."

"That could have killed somebody."

"Not could . . . *did*. That was one of the deaths. The kid couldn't have been any more than ten. At least it was fast. He probably didn't even know what hit him."

Lori flinched. I didn't. That troubled me.

"Then this is as close as we should go," I said to Lori, hoping to get her back inside the neighborhood.

"You can go around if you want a closer look," Todd offered. "Nothing has fallen off the other side of the building."

"Thanks," Lori said.

I would have thanked him if he'd kept his mouth shut. Some things didn't change.

"Are my mother and Herb over there?" I asked.

"I've seen them both. Check in the lobby. That's where they set up a control center."

We hurried off, coming up on the building through the woods where the crowd of people was clustered. They were dressed, or partially dressed, in a variety of clothes and pajamas, some with shoes, some with slippers, some in bare feet, hair all messy, some with smudges on their faces, all with expressions of grief, concern, or fear.

Lori stopped and bent down beside a little girl and her mother.

"You know, I have a teddy bear just like that," she said, pointing to the one the little girl was clutching. "What's its name?"

"Snowball," the little girl said.

"That is such a pretty name. My bear was named Sammy the Bear."

"This is a *girl* bear," the little girl said.

Lori laughed. "I can see that. Maybe someday your Snowball can meet my Sammy."

The little girl smiled. So did her mother. Then she started crying and the little girl did, too. I was just happy that neither the bear nor Lori started to cry—or for that matter, me.

"I'm sorry," the woman sobbed. "It's just that after all of this . . . all that we've been through . . . We have no place to go . . . We're burned out."

"Maybe we can help," Lori said.

I looked at her. What was she going to say? She knew we couldn't bring them into the neighborhood.

"Would it help if you had a big tent?" Lori asked.

I let out a sigh of relief.

"It isn't much, but it would get you out of the rain, at least for now. It would be like camping."

"I like camping," the little girl said.

"There are already a number of people camping in the woods, by the wall," Lori said. "Right by the creek so they can get water."

"I've seen them. That's where we get our water, too, but we don't have anything," the woman said. "No clothes, or blankets. I don't even have shoes," she said, pointing to her bare feet.

"I'm sure I can find all of those for you." Lori turned to me. "We can at least do that, *right*?"

What could I say? That wasn't a question as much as a challenge. I nodded.

"But it's not just us," the woman said. "There are at least three dozen families burned out."

"Then I guess we need three dozen tents," Lori replied. "There must be that many tents in the neighborhood."

"I have a few sleeping bags in our basement," I offered.

"And I'll bring you some of my clothes and shoes . . . You look like about my size." She then said to the little girl, "And I'll also bring Sammy. Would it be all right if he comes and sleeps with you? He loves camping!"

The little girl sniffled back her tears. "He could come," she said. "I'd take care of him."

"I know you will," Lori said.

"Thank you. Thank you so much," the woman said, also sniffling back her tears. She gave Lori a big hug.

It made me feel selfish for wanting to stay behind the wall.

"Could you do me a favor?" Lori asked the woman. "Would you find out how many tents we need and try to get a list of what else is necessary? I'm going inside, and when I come back you can give me the list."

"I'll do that." The woman turned to me. "Your girlfriend is an angel."

"Yes, she is." I handed the woman my umbrella.

We started toward the building again. "Remember that," Lori said. "What an angel I am."

I pointed up at the building. "So you don't become a real angel, how about we stop, look up, and then run for the door together, just in case something does fall from this side, okay?"

"Okay."

It looked solid enough up there and I didn't see any

shattered glass on the ground, but it was always better to be extra careful.

"Okay, let's go."

Still holding hands we raced across the opening and under the concrete awning over the entrance. We skidded to a stop and Brett was standing right there. He offered some slow, sarcastic applause.

"So you finally made it," he said to me. "I guess that signifies that it's finally safe."

"I guess it is if you've done your job correctly," I replied.

"I've done my job. In fact, it's so safe your mother came over."

I took two steps toward him. "What did you say?"

"I'm just joking around," he said. "Don't be so sensitive. I'm sorry if I offended you by talking about your big mama." He laughed. "Are you going to tell on me?"

I didn't answer, but that thought *had* popped into my mind.

"Your *captain* can take care of herself . . . rookie," I said.

Brett chuckled. "Are you going to call me that every time you're annoyed with me?" He paused. "But I guess I understand. I wouldn't want anybody to say anything about my mother . . . or my girlfriend either."

He gave Lori a long look, and then turned his gaze directly at me, daring me to say something. I didn't know what to say, but I wasn't going to look away. We stood there, a few strides apart, staring each other down.

"I'm going inside," Lori said. "And you should come with me." She grabbed me by the hand and dragged me through the shattered front doors of the building. Part of me was angry she'd done that. Part was just relieved.

"Like I said before, he's creepy," Lori said.

Just inside the door, injured people lay on makeshift beds or sat against the walls. The air was foul and held a visible film of smoke. Herb was talking to one of the doctors but finished up and came over to us.

"I didn't expect to see you two here this early," Herb said.

"I didn't expect to be here."

"I made him bring me," Lori said. "Is there anything I can do to help?"

"Please, feel free to ask around," Herb said.

She walked away and immediately went up to a woman sitting against the wall.

"How bad is it?" I asked Herb.

"Better than I expected, although worse than I would have liked."

"What does that mean?"

He motioned for me to follow him and we stopped at an empty section of the lobby.

"None of our people were killed or injured," he said.

"That *is* good, but lots of other people were killed, right?"

"That's bad, but that's not the worst thing. By coming here we've become responsible for these people."

"Do mean you're bringing them into the neighborhood?"

"You know we don't have the resources to do that. But the doctors have brought over medicine and bandages. The firefighters and two nurses have been administering first aid. Some of the women have even brought over blankets and pillows. I have no idea where these people are even going to go, but they can't come into the neighborhood."

"They could sleep in tents," I said.

"Tents?" Herb gave me one of those piercing looks. "Is that a suggestion or a plan?"

"Sort of a plan. We offered some tents, some clothing and blankets, even some sleeping bags. Just things that we can scavenge from the neighborhood that aren't needed."

"You can never know what we might need someday," Herb said. "Still, that might be the smart compromise. But remember, you can offer them nothing else."

"Nothing else." I paused. "They could probably pitch those tents in the woods beside the creek, right by our wall."

"People are already doing that, so a few more tents won't matter," Herb said.

I was glad that wasn't an issue.

"Now, why don't you take that young lady of yours back inside the neighborhood and start scrounging for tents and clothes and blankets."

18

Four days later, Lori, Todd, and I visited the growing tent city outside our wall.

"Do you think it's ever going to stop raining?" Lori asked as the three of us stomped through the forest.

"It's such bad timing," I said. "They're burned out of their homes and they get four straight days of rain."

"We're only thirty-six days short of having to build an ark and gather up two of everything," Todd said.

"That could really be a problem since I don't think there is another one of you on the planet," I joked.

"That is such a sweet compliment!" Todd said. "Are you trying to win me over? Lori, you might want to be a little bit worried here. I've always suspected that he had a thing for me."

"I'm not too worried," she said.

"You have nothing to be worried about," I assured her, giving Todd a little slug on the shoulder and hitting my knuckles against his body armor.

Up ahead a little cluster of tents peeked through the trees and brush. There were more than four dozen of them—the people who were already living in the trees joined by the people from the burned-out condos. The tents were different sizes and colors, all in varying states of disrepair. Some of the tents surrounded a little fire smoldering in the rain. Four men and a woman sat around under umbrellas. Two of the men had weapons visible. Normally the sight of those would have me reaching for my own weapons, but I knew we really didn't have to be worried about them. They were desperate but grateful.

They saw us, and all five smiled and waved. Lori had been here what seemed like a hundred times over the past few days, bringing supplies, helping them set up tents and their campsite, and just offering to assist in any way she could.

I'd come with her a few times. With the rain I was grounded anyway. But I'd made a point of keeping my distance from the people. Sure, I could help set up a tent, but I didn't want to get to know them. I couldn't let it get too personal.

I remember reading somewhere about how the Inuit never named their sled dogs because it wasn't good to name something you might have to eat. Not that we were going to eat anyone, but there was no telling what might eventually have to happen. If things ever got bad for them, we wouldn't be able to do anything more than watch from behind the walls.

Lori tapped on the side of the tent. "Can we come in?" she asked.

The flap opened and Madison—the little girl she'd first met—poked out her head. She practically bowled Lori over with her hug and then dragged her inside. I pulled the flap back, bent over, and stuck my head in.

"The place is looking pretty good," Lori said.

"Thanks to you," Madison's mother, Elyse, said. "You really are an angel."

Herb and the committee were fine with the tents staying, but nobody could give them any food, or medicine, or supplies of any kind without permission, and nobody from the apartments was to be offered a place in the neighborhood or even allowed in for a visit. As well, the sentries and guards had been told that under no circumstances were they to enter the forest to offer security to the tent dwellers. They may have been camped within the shadows of our walls, but those walls offered no security or support for them.

I saw Lori slyly pass something to Madison. I pretended not to see, but she saw me *not* see her. I knew what it was—food. Lori and Elyse spoke and Madison clung to Lori's leg. They were both friendly enough to me, but I think they sensed my distance. Distance was protection. It was the difference between walking through some place and flying five hundred feet above. I wanted to get back into the air and away from the realities on the ground. I hoped that tomorrow I could get back up there and away from here.

I waited for the conversation to end. They hugged goodbye, and we exchanged polite nods and farewells.

"I'll be back tomorrow," Lori said.

"Aren't you coming up with me for my next flight if it's not raining?" I asked.

"Even if it's not raining I'm not going to be up in the air all day, am I?" she replied.

"Not all day."

"Then I'll be back tomorrow, rain or shine."

She and Madison hugged again, and I stepped completely out of the tent while they continued to talk inside, practically bumping into Todd. He and I walked over to a tarp strung between four trees. It offered some protection from the rain.

"Don't even pretend," Todd said.

"What are you talking about?"

"Don't even pretend that you have any free will. If she wants you back here with her tomorrow, you'll be here."

"I can't very well let her come by herself."

"Yeah, right, like she needs your protection to come out here. The girl is handier with a gun than you are."

We'd both seen her taking shooting practice with the people being trained, and there wasn't much question about that. Lori knew how to shoot.

"You are *so* easy to read," Todd said.

"Me? *I'm* easy to read? What about *you*?"

"So what am I thinking about right now?" he asked.

I smirked. "You're thinking about food."

"Clever. You know I'm always thinking about food. The question is, what *kind* of food am I thinking of?"

"Pizza."

"Okay, what kind of pizza?" he asked, and I couldn't help but laugh.

Food was on almost everybody's mind most of the time. The scavenging teams were bringing back some food, other items were being harvested, collection teams were out gathering things like crab apples and other edible plants, but still the rations were limited. Most people liked to think that food would be plentiful once the fall harvest happened. I knew better. That harvest was going to have to get us through the winter, and the rations were only going to get smaller.

"I can read your mind, too," Todd said.

"Can you?"

"I know exactly what you're thinking of . . . correction . . . *who* you're thinking of."

I wanted to argue, but there was no point. He was right. In the middle of all of this Lori was pretty well in the center of my thoughts. That bothered me. In the midst of terrible turmoil, tragedy, and death, I was spending my time thinking about her. I should have been spending more time thinking about other things—such as my father. What sort of person was I to feel any happiness when he was still out there, alone, by himself, hundreds of miles away?

Lori came out of the tent and walked right by us. "I don't even want to hear about it," she said as she passed.

"Hear about what?" I asked.

"It was my food and I chose not to eat it, so I can do anything I want with it," she said.

"I didn't say anything!" I protested.

"I know what you're thinking."

"Suddenly everybody thinks they know what I'm thinking!"

"I *do* know!" Todd said. "Do you want me to tell her?" he asked. He was bouncing up and down, his hand in the air, a goofy smile on his face.

"I want you to shut up!"

"I knew you were going to say that, too!" he yelled out.

"Look," I said to Lori. "I understand completely, and it is your food to give. It's just that you can't give them enough to feed everybody."

"I'm not trying to feed everybody, just Madison."

"And what about her mother?" I asked.

"It would be nice to feed her, too," she admitted.

"Tomorrow, after our flight, I want you to come with me and talk to Leonard and his family."

"Talk to them about what?"

"About how they're doing there in the forest, living off the land. I was hoping they could help Madison and her mother understand how to live off the land, too. They could learn from them."

"Really?" Lori asked. "That would be so nice."

"In fact, that's more than nice—that's downright *sweet*," Todd said. "One of us should give Adam a kiss—probably you."

"I think that could wait until later. Here, this is for you." I dug into my pocket and gave Lori two PowerBars.

"Thanks, but I'm not really hungry."

"Good, because it isn't really for you. Give them to Madison when you see her tomorrow. Each bar is good for one person for one day."

Lori took the bars and threw her arms around me, and for a moment the world seemed good.

19

The next day, the skies cleared and I was finally able to get back into the air. I felt like a weight was being lifted off my shoulders. Even better, Lori was at my side. Around her neck was a pair of binoculars and on her lap was a rifle, with a second strapped to the rack behind our heads. And, of course, I had my pistol on my side. Protection had a whole different meaning these days.

I banked to the left—still not as sharply as I would have if I'd been on my own but much sharper than I would have if anybody else had been with me. It was such an added bonus that Lori liked being up in the air and had no fear of flying, even in the open cockpit of my ultralight. I still felt like I had to protect her, but I had learned that having her along was also protection for me.

"I'm glad your father is okay with you going up with me," I said in the headset.

"So am I. He says you're very trustworthy."

"That's me, trustworthy."

I continued the bank and kept us low. Lori had asked if we could come in over top of the tent town so she could wave to Madison. Below us was Erin Mills Parkway. As far as the eye could see in both directions the road was clear and open. All of the cars for almost a mile in each direction had been removed. Gasoline was getting more and more scarce, so even cars that ran couldn't be driven. It was also an emergency landing strip for me and would be, if all went well, where I'd be taking off and landing with the Cessna. They were still working on it, since there was much more wrong with the engine than they'd thought, but they were hopeful of putting it up in the air. I was hopeful, too, but a small irrational part of me felt like I'd be cheating on my ultralight if I flew the Cessna and I didn't want to get it mad at me.

"I can see the tents!" Lori yelled into her headset.

"You don't need to yell," I said. "I can see them, too."

"Can you get any lower? I want them to see us. I promised."

"This is low enough. We need to keep an envelope of air to stay safe. They'll see us."

I reduced air speed and went slightly lower, doing what she'd asked without compromising our safety any further. As we came over top Lori began screaming and waving. I was sure they'd hear the roar of the engine and her yelling, too. I banked slightly to the right so she could look down on them.

There were now probably seventy-five tents in the woods close to the wall on the southwest corner. Many looked like they were going to take up more or less permanent residence, but others were just there for a night or two, camping and then leaving as they continued to move farther into the country or to whatever place they thought was safer.

"The little camp continues to grow. I'm so happy for them. More people means it's safe—right?" she asked.

"Safer." But certainly not safe.

"Brett told me he didn't like having the tents there," Lori said. "He said they were squatters and a security risk."

"What did you say to him when he told you that?"

"I told him he was an idiot and if he didn't like them being there he didn't have to go there."

"I'm sure he liked that. You don't have to be bothered about what Brett thinks because he has no influence on the committee," I said.

"That's good."

What I didn't tell her was Herb's opinion wasn't much different from Brett's, and Herb did have tremendous influence. He'd told the committee that that corner of our neighborhood—where the tent town and forest sat—was our weakest point of defense. He said that from those trees there was cover for people to fire RPGs and that the only protection would be to take down the trees—the shelter in which the tent town hid. To remove the trees was to remove the tent people. So far he hadn't suggested removing them, but I got the feeling that topic would come back up for discussion at some point. Herb wasn't cruel, but his focus was on what was best for us inside the walls, not those huddled beyond them.

I couldn't help but wonder what would happen if we did force them out. Where would they go, how would they live, and how would that affect us? We would be the villains. Then again, if Herb was right—and he almost always was—if we didn't force them out, we might not be villains but victims.

There was no point in trying to think through the possibilities. There was enough in the present to worry about. I put my mind back onto the controls and the ground below as we continued flying south along Erin Mills.

"There's our school," I said.

"It makes you wonder what happened to everybody, how all of our friends are doing," Lori said.

"Some are doing fine, I'm sure." And some were doing terribly. Some might not even be alive. Without thinking, I asked, "Do you ever wonder how your old boyfriend Chad is doing?"

What a stupid thing for me to say!

"I think about a lot of our old friends, including Chad. Actually, I think I can see his car." She was looking through the binoculars.

"It's down there. I was part of draining the gas out of it and every other car in the parking lot," I said. "I'm the guy who smashed the window so we could pop open his gas tank."

She laughed. "I bet you enjoyed that!"

"I did . . . and I've got a confession to make. I enjoyed it so much that I smashed two other windows just for fun."

She laughed even harder. "I guess I wonder about a lot of things, but Chad and his car are pretty low on the list. He's my *ex*-boyfriend. What I worry about a lot more is my present boyfriend being up in his plane flying around."

"There's nothing really to worry about," I said.

"How about the engine failing?"

"Mr. Nicholas and his mechanics keep this engine in tip-top shape. There's nothing to worry about there."

"Then how about somebody taking a shot at you?"

"That's not a big danger, or I wouldn't be bringing you out here."

"I guess I believe you, sort of. Is that the truth or a reas-suring lie?"

"I'd like to think of it as a reassuring truth."

She laughed again. I loved her laughter. It was more than just music to my ears. It was a little escape from reality.

"I've been thinking a lot about our farm," Lori said. "Have you flown over it lately?"

"I haven't been in that direction that far since you left. If danger is coming it's most likely to come from the city side, so I mainly patrol there."

"But something *could* come from the country, right?"

I knew where this was going. "It wouldn't hurt for me to do a pass over your farm sometime."

"Sometime, like today?"

"Of course today." I banked the plane to start us off to-ward the west.

She laughed in delight. Making her happy was important to me. There was so much I couldn't do for her, but this I could.

There was less chance of seeing anything in that direc-tion, but also less chance of any troubles and really lots of open space to put down in if I needed to. There was no harm in going over the country, and maybe some good might even come of it. I could then do an extended flight in the other direction toward the city. A longer patrol just meant sharing more time with Lori and more time in the air. That was a win-win situation for me.

I traveled in a straight line, using Burnham to guide me. There was movement along the road below: bicycles, people on foot, and the occasional car. All of them were moving among the abandoned vehicles that still littered the road.

The number of houses dwindled as we came up on the highway and then stopped completely—it marked the place where country began. The fields were uncultivated. Here was farmland that could be used to feed people, and it was being left unused. Everybody was desperate for food, but nobody out here was growing any, it seemed.

"I can see our property," Lori said. "Those pine trees are the eastern boundary. Can we go lower?"

I started to descend and at the same time tapered off the gas—the gravity on the drop would more than compensate, and our speed would be constant. The first few fields, those farthest from the house, were empty and open. I wondered what Mr. Peterson would think about his fields not being used.

"By this time of the year you'd usually be able to see the crops growing even higher than they are in the neighborhood," Lori said.

"Our crops are doing pretty well," I said.

Those closest to harvest were the crops being grown under glass in the makeshift greenhouses. They'd be followed quickly by the first harvest of potatoes. Mr. Peterson was going to turn those fields around and was hopeful of a second potato crop being brought in before winter came.

Strange, all this talk about harvests and crops. Before all of this I'd never really thought much about food being grown, or worried about the rain coming, or worried if there was going to be enough to go around. Before, food simply involved going to the grocery store, or opening the fridge or cupboards, or ordering in, or going to one of the dozens and dozens of restaurants scattered about. Food was never a problem because it was always there.

"There's our farmhouse!" Lori exclaimed. "And there are vehicles in the driveway that aren't ours."

There were four trucks and a few cars in the driveway. And the field right beside the house was brown soil—it was being worked. Then I noticed motion—it was a tractor in the nearest field tilling the land. Behind it the ground was fresh and brown, and there were small white dots—seagulls—landing or flitting around. There was something about the tractor. It just seemed so small. It *was* small. It was more like a big ride-'em lawn mower than a real tractor. There were also other figures out in the field and they were carrying tools—no, they were aiming them our way and they weren't tools!

I banked so sharply that Lori gasped. There was no time for me to be considerate. Out of the corner of my eye I caught sight of her gripping the seat. I leveled it out, but we were now headed away from the farmhouse.

"I saw weapons," I explained.

"I saw them, too, and they were aiming them up at us."

"Nothing to worry about. There's practically no chance of anybody hitting us," I said.

"How many people do you think are living there?"

"I have no idea, but that was a lot of vehicles."

"It's so wrong to have strangers living on our farm, in *our* house."

"We knew it wasn't going to stay vacant," I said. We also knew people would have killed Lori and her family to make it vacant so they could move in.

They would have kept defending it until more men with more weapons took it from them. I wondered how long before this group was overwhelmed by an even bigger force.

Then I had another thought. If they were able to grow food, they might be a group we could ultimately trade with. Maybe they had invaded and taken over the Petersons' farm, but we still might need to do business with them. Food was food, and we needed more. Possibly we had something they needed. I'd talk to Herb about it when we got back.

"I don't think it's smart for me to go back over the farmhouse," I said. "Sorry."

"That's okay. I'll see it again, someday, up close, once this is all over . . . right?"

"Guaranteed," I said. She reached out and gave my leg a little squeeze.

But what wasn't guaranteed was when this was going to be over. In some ways it was a big assumption that it was ever going to be over. Even when the power came back on, it would only throw light on a world that had changed so much that we might not be able to even recognize it. How did you get back from burned-out buildings, looted stores, starvation, and shooting strangers, to make it what it used to be?

Well clear of the western boundaries of the farm, I started the bank to the south. The lake was miles away, but with the sky almost cloud-free my visibility was all the way to the horizon. There were three smoke stacks—the chimneys of the power plant—thrust into the air like three fingers, the middle one the tallest. Normally they would have been spewing out smoke. Now the sky above them was unstained. They were going to be my mark—dead reckoning—about five miles away.

"Keep your eyes open," I said to Lori.

"What am I looking for?"

"Anything different, but anything that could be of value, you know, sections that have blocked themselves off the way ours has."

"Do you think there are a lot of them?"

"I've seen some, but Herb thinks there will be hundreds and hundreds of them scattered throughout the city and suburbs. Did you know in medieval England there were close to six thousand castles?"

"Um, no, but I don't understand what that has to do with this."

"They were built for the same reason, to defend the local peasants from barbarian raiding parties," I explained.

"Is that what we've become, peasants fearing for our lives from barbarians?"

"Hopefully, we're more than peasants and able to defend ourselves against the barbarians."

"I just don't understand why I can't see more people," Lori said.

"We're pretty high up."

"I can see *some* people, but I can't see *many* people."

"I guess they're in their houses."

"Or gone away," Lori said. "There used to be so many people everywhere. Where has everybody gone to?"

"I don't know." Some had left. Others were dead. Lots of others.

"What's that over there?" Lori asked.

"I don't see where you're looking."

She pointed and I tried to follow her outstretched arm. I banked ever so slightly to alter my view and aim in the direction she was pointing. I still didn't see anything.

"What are you looking at?" I asked.

"There, there!" she said. She was bouncing in her seat, pointing. "Far away and down by the lake."

I altered course again to try to align with her aim. This was taking us farther away from the smokestacks, and farther away from our neighborhood. Still, what did Lori see—or think she saw? I'd flown enough to know that from the air, to the untrained eye, lots of things that looked like something were really nothing. She was probably seeing a park, or mall or a school stadium or the burned-out hulk of an apartment building or something I couldn't even imagine.

Up ahead was a big subdivision. As we got closer, I saw what she was talking about. It was like there was a big hole in the middle of it. It wasn't a park or a school yard, but what was it?

"I can see it," I said. "I just don't know what I'm seeing."

There were some blackened parts—signs of fire. Were we simply seeing the results of another fire? Had the entire center of a subdivision been burned out? We were still too far and too high to tell much of anything. We were coming closer already, but I needed to shed some height. I tapped Lori on the leg and when she looked at me I pointed down. She nodded.

I could feel the drop in my ears. We were cutting across roads, houses, shopping malls, and schools—your basic suburban neighborhood—and from this height it didn't look like anything was wrong, except for that gash right in the middle of the neighborhood. There had been a fire, I could see by the blackened edges of the opening, but it was a strange shape. It looked like a golf divot, like something had taken out a swath of houses, as if a gigantic arrow had struck the neighborhood.

I kept dropping down lower until we were no more than a hundred feet in elevation. And then I saw it. Sticking out of one of the destroyed houses was the gigantic tailfin of a commercial airplane—the logo of my father's airline, shining red on silver. A commercial jet had crashed, undoubtedly killing everybody on the plane and everybody on the ground nearby. There it was, right before my eyes. I could hardly believe it.

What were those people thinking as the airplane plowed into them? Did they even see it coming? And what about the passengers—they probably only knew something was wrong just minutes before it crashed. The pilot and crew would have known, though. I could picture the cockpit and imagine what it would have been like for the pilot and the crew desperately trying to bring the plane back online, not knowing what had happened, why all the instruments had failed, struggling to keep it in the air, and then those last few seconds of complete terror.

Thank goodness my father was on the ground when that virus hit. At least that's what we told ourselves, right?

I pulled up on the yoke and banked sharply to the side. I didn't need to get any closer. I didn't need to see more. Or think more. I just needed to get home.

20

"Okay, you two, it's time for bed," my mother said.

"But it's Friday night! It's not like it's a school day tomorrow," Rachel protested.

"And even if it was, it isn't like it's real school," Danny added.

"It is as real as school can be these days," my mother said.

"Sure, whatever," Danny mumbled.

"Regardless, you still have weeding to do just like any other day," she said.

Each day the younger children were supposed to spend two hours working in the fields. On weekends they were expected to double that to almost four hours. We had all sorts of early-summer crops ripening, lettuce and other greens, herbs. Most important, the first crop of potatoes was almost ready to harvest. Lots of kids complained about the dirty work—including Danny—but we all had to make a contribution. Some days I went out with them, when Herb didn't have me busy with other things.

"We could still stay up later, sleep in, and do our chores in the afternoon," Danny protested.

"Afraid not. Especially not Rachel," my mother said. "She has to be up extra early."

"Why especially me?"

My mother smiled my way, and I said, "Because that's the best time for Lori and you to go horseback riding."

"Really? That's incredible!" Rachel started dancing around.

Lori had taken Rachel for short rides around the neighborhood before, and she was always this thrilled. What Rachel didn't know was that this ride was going to be longer and farther.

"Yeah, great," Danny said sarcastically. "Just please be quiet when you get up so you don't wake me."

"No dice, lazybones," my mother said. "You have to get up early to do your chores."

"I've got all day."

"Not if you want to go out on patrol with me," I added.

"I'm going up . . . in the ultralight?" He looked at my mother. She had never allowed him to fly with me despite him practically begging her. She gave a slight nod, and he jumped up into the air whooping and doing his own little dance.

"So you two need to get to bed," she said.

"I'll go to bed, but there's no way I'm going to sleep," Danny replied.

"Either way, go upstairs and get ready, and I'll be up in a few minutes to tuck you in."

They both said good night, jostling each other as they rushed up the stairs. Usually they complained about brushing their teeth, since the last of our toothpaste was long gone and we were making do the old-fashioned way, with baking soda, which tasted nasty.

"Lori won't go too far with Rachel on the ride, right?" my mother asked.

"She promised they won't go out of sight of the walls or the guards, and it's not like she's going out unarmed, so don't worry."

"I think worrying is the right thing to do."

"She'll be careful on the horse ride, and I'll be careful in the air. I'll just do some big, lazy circles around the neighborhood and then bring Danny back before I do the major patrol."

"Thanks, sweetheart. And did Herb agree to go back up with you on that patrol?"

"He agreed."

"It always feels safer to me if Herb is in the seat beside you."

I actually felt safer when he was there as well—although I had to add, "You know, it's not like he can flap his wings and keep us up if we have engine trouble."

"I don't even like to hear you talk about engine problems, but who would be better to have with you if you had to put down there miles away from our walls?" she asked.

"Some people would say Brett."

"And some people would be wrong. Nobody has more experience out there than Herb."

"I guess Brett's on patrol now," I said. Since the committee had given approval for night patrols he and his crew had been out every night.

"I'm sure he is. Don't get me wrong, he's doing an important job that nobody else would want to do," she said.

"The way he talks about it, I really think he likes being out there," I said.

"It's more than that," my mother said. "It's like he *needs* to go out there."

"Yeah, he's talked to me about how the adrenaline gives him this crazy high."

"And that's the problem, Adam, that's what worries me. He's an adrenaline junkie, and all any addict wants is more, more, more."

I looked at her. "You think it's that extreme?"

"To get the same high he has to keep doing things that are more dangerous, more risky. I just think it's only a matter of time until something happens, either to him or somebody who's out with him, and I don't want that person to be you."

"Me? There's no way I'd ever go out there at night with him."

"I'm glad to hear that." She looked genuinely relieved. "Some other guys have been chomping at the bit, though."

"I'm not one of them, but I know he's impressed some people. They talk like he's a real hero," I said.

"I've heard the same talk," she said. "Unfortunately, so has Brett. It's not just that he's impressed other people but that he's becoming too impressed with himself." She paused. "I've had a couple of confrontations with him to get him to understand whether he's inside or outside the walls he's still under my command."

"I get the feeling he doesn't like to take orders," I said.

"And that's why I don't trust him."

"Herb says he can control him," I said. "He understands what makes Brett tick."

"And that's the only reason I feel any comfort with Brett going out there, because of what Herb has said."

"And do you really trust Herb?" I asked.

"Don't you?" she asked.

I hesitated before answering.

"It's just that sometimes I wonder about what he tells us and doesn't tell us."

"You and I both know there are some things that he keeps to himself," she said. "I don't think we'll ever know everything, either about what's going on in his mind or about his background. Probably you know more about him than anybody else does."

I wondered if my mother was fishing to get more information out of me.

"I have complete confidence that Herb would do anything in the world to keep us safe. He really does think highly of you," she said. "I know he still feels bad about that stunt he pulled with the prisoner." She paused. "I know it was, how shall I say, troubling to me that he did that. I was wondering, are you still angry?"

"I'm not angry—well, at least not that angry—but yeah, that's the sort of thing I mean."

"I think he's just doing that, holding back information, because he doesn't want to worry people unnecessarily. It's sort of the way a parent does."

"Are you keeping information from me, too?"

She shook her head. "I tell you more than I probably should. It's just with your father not here . . ." She let the sentence trail off.

"And you've told me everything about Dad, right?"

"Everything I know, everything anybody *could* know. Which is only a guess. But he was on his usual schedule that day, and wouldn't have been up in the air for his return leg until hours after the grid went down and all the trouble started."

My mother knew I was still thinking about the downed plane Lori and I had seen and reported back to the committee. It had been five days, and I still hadn't been able to shake that scene out of my head. One more terrible image added to the slide show in my mind.

"I can't help thinking about the planes that were in the air at the time and how they'd have dropped out of the skies all over the world. Do you know how many planes were up in the air when it happened?" I asked.

"I don't know. I hadn't really thought about that," she replied.

"I've thought about it. A lot. There were over six thousand planes in the air. There were always six thousand planes in the air at any time."

"Really? Are you sure?" She sounded like she couldn't believe that number, but I knew it was true.

"I'm sure."

"I can't even imagine that . . . the carnage . . . the deaths."

"There would have been thousands and thousands of passengers in those planes. And they were all gone in an instant. Dad's plane, his passengers, him—they would all have been gone, too, if he'd been in the air."

"But he wasn't. He was on the ground," she said. "We know his plane was still on the ground."

I nodded, in both agreement and hope. I looked deep into her eyes for any sign of doubt or subterfuge. There was none. But that still left one more question unanswered. We had been tiptoeing across an area we'd left basically unspoken. I didn't want to upset her, but I needed an answer.

"Do you think he's still alive?" I asked, my voice practically a whisper.

"Your father is alive."

"You can't know that."

"We can't *know* he isn't," she said.

"But he's out there all alone, so far from home and—"

"And he's your father. If anybody could survive this it would be him." She paused. "I *need* to believe that he's fine, kiddo, that's he out there, somehow working his way back to us, that someday he's just going to appear at our front gate and come strolling down the street and walk in our front door."

We both looked at the door, waiting as if on cue for that to happen. The door stayed closed.

21

"Couldn't we just stay up in the air a little bit longer?" Danny asked.

"I can do one more pass over the gate on Burnham, and then we have to get down."

"Lori and Rachel are back inside the walls, so we could go farther now," he said.

The sky was crystal-clear with no breeze whatsoever. Perfect flying weather. I had been circling lazily over the neighborhood but always keeping an eye on them as they'd been out riding. I just didn't know it was so obvious that even Danny had noticed. That meant the girls would have noticed me from the ground as well. I hoped Lori would see my worrying about her as a positive.

"Could we go as far as the river?" Danny asked.

"We definitely could go that far, but why there?"

"I've heard all about Burnham Bridge, but I've never seen it before. I want to see it with my own eyes."

"There's not much to see, just a bridge that isn't there any-more . . . but I guess I can take you there."

"That would be great, thanks!" Danny exclaimed.

I banked away from the neighborhood and toward the river.

Funny that Danny wanted to see the place. I had watched the bridge's destruction and ever since had worked hard to avoid going anywhere near it if I didn't have to. If I was flying in that direction, I'd make a point of crossing the river valley well north or south of the site. I could even justify it in my mind. North and south were the two bridges that still crossed the river, so it made sense for me to avoid flying over a bridge that didn't exist and instead focus on where trouble could come from. Or so I tried to convince myself.

It had taken a long time to get the scene out of my mind— those trucks plunging down, the plumes of smoke and dust. I didn't want to replay the scene anymore.

"I can see the pillars!" Danny exclaimed after we covered the few miles in silence.

I could see them, too. The bridge's massive supports rose up two hundred feet from the valley, supporting nothing but air.

"It's hard to believe it was destroyed with just some fertilizer and chemicals and stuff," Danny said.

"I guess. But we used lots and lots of *stuff*."

"I was at the walls, and even from there I heard it blow. Everybody could see the smoke rising up. Was it amazing for you to see it directly with your own eyes?" he asked.

"I'll never forget it. Never."

"I wish I could have been there," he said. "It would have been so cool to see all those—"

"People die?" I asked, interrupting him. "Four hundred people. We can't forget that, Danny."

"But they were *bad guys*!"

"You bet. But they were still *people*. I know we had no choice . . . we had to do it, but they were still people."

I dropped down and banked so that we were coming in right over the river, right between the silent pillars. Below us the river was pooled into a lake, blocked by the fallen concrete and asphalt. We were low enough to see people gathering water and fishing. There were some hints of color in between the trees—tents in ones and twos, or clustered together in little tent towns. What would they do when winter came? People looked up as we passed, and some waved. I might have known some of them. Suddenly I had to get out of there. Now. I pulled back on the yoke to get us higher, to gain some distance. I wondered if I'd be visited in my sleep tonight by the vision of the bridge going down.

I'd put down just long enough to drop Danny off, refuel from one of the canisters in our garage, and then pop back up in the air with Herb at my side. With Danny I had to be big brother, protector, and pilot. With Herb, I was just the pilot. I hadn't realized how heavy a load it had been having Danny with me until I finally landed. Now I felt free and safe—or as safe as I could be anywhere.

Today we were flying well away from the neighborhood, toward the city.

"I'm sorry the Cessna isn't flying yet," Herb said over the intercom.

"I want them to get it right rather than soon. I know it's coming along."

"And then we'll need to train another pilot so we can have two aircraft up when needed."

"Training a pilot is not such an easy task."

"I'm counting on you to do it. If we have two aircraft, we need two pilots. Maybe three would be even better," Herb said.

"If my father was here, we'd have a second pilot who was better than the first," I said.

"Your father would have been a great contribution, but I'm not sure if any pilot could have been better than you," Herb said.

"Hah! That's nice to hear, even if it isn't necessarily accurate."

"It's accurate. You've shown real leadership, even to those of us who are supposedly in charge of this crazy situation. You've helped this neighborhood survive, and maybe just as important, survive with its morality intact."

"My father would have helped with that, too. I just wish he was here."

"So do I. Sometimes I've felt bad because there were a lot of situations I had to put you in that I wished I didn't have to."

"I did okay," I said.

"You did better than okay. I know what you've been up against better than anyone."

"Does any of it bother you at night?" I asked.

"I've had a lifetime of memories I'd rather forget. At night, in my bed, in the quiet, in the dark is one of the times those things come back most vividly," he said. "Some things you never get over thinking about."

That wasn't what I wanted to hear. "I flew over the destroyed bridge today. Danny wanted to see it."

"That is one of those things that stick in my mind," Herb said. "I've never seen that much destruction and that many people killed in one fell swoop. If it hadn't been so tragic, that explosion could have almost been beautiful. In a strange way it was like watching a thunderstorm or a waterfall."

This sounded a little bit crazy to me. Did Herb actually hear what he was saying? I didn't have a chance to argue, because suddenly we were back to the mission.

"Look, there's another one!"

I banked in the direction Herb was pointing. We were out looking for small neighborhoods like ours—places that had banded together, like Olde Burnham before it had been destroyed.

I couldn't see it at first, but then the outline became clear. It was a cluster of houses, maybe three or four dozen, whose residents had built a crude wall. Inside there were obvious clearings where crops were being grown.

"How many does that make?" I asked.

"Over twenty little pockets of civilization. We humans are such industrious little insects. No matter what, we struggle back."

"Maybe we're more like wild animals than insects. We do whatever we need to do to survive, even if it means others won't."

"True enough. I guess we always have to be prepared to show a little animal ourselves."

I instantly thought of Brett, and it was like Herb could read my mind.

"We need people like Brett, Adam, just like the government needed me, to keep us all safe."

I saw some smoke rising in the distance to my right and banked sharply to head us in that direction for a closer look.

"Do you see something?" Herb asked.

"Smoke."

"Good thing to check out," he said. "If there's smoke there's fire, and if there's fire there are people who will want to find a new home."

I brought us around until the smoke was dead ahead and visible to both of us. At least I thought he could see it now.

"Over there. Can you see the wisps of smoke rising up in the air?" I asked.

"I see it. Looks like somebody is burning garbage. With no collection they have to dispose of it somehow," Herb said. "Burning makes the most sense."

The engineers seemed to be able to turn almost anything into something we needed. Even so, we were burning some garbage ourselves, whatever we couldn't compost or recycle in some way.

As we closed in, the smell kept getting stronger and more putrid. There was no point in getting any closer, so I banked to the side to curve away from it.

"No," Herb said. "Get us closer . . . and lower. I need to see."

"Sure." I didn't see the point, but I wasn't going to argue. Still, why did he want to get closer to burning garbage? At least if I swung to the right we could come at it from upwind.

As we closed in, I recognized the place—it was a park off Dundas Street. The park was a sort of depression, like a bowl, with slopes rising up on three sides, topped by trees and bushes at the edge of the top rim. I'd played baseball there before—although nobody was going to play baseball there again for a long time. The whole infield was covered in smoldering garbage. It extended beyond the infield.

I banked, circling the park from the north, moving counterclockwise. As I continued to curve around it the smoke blew back into our faces. It smelled awful but familiar, like burned meat at a barbecue.

I looked down. It wasn't smoldering garbage—it was human bodies, a half dozen or so, burning in a fire being tended by a small crew.

"Oh my God," I mumbled. It was a makeshift crematorium and burial ground. "They've disposed of hundreds of bodies down there," Herb said.

There were bodies everywhere, tangled and twisted and blackened, with white bones sticking out, some burned to a crisp, some still wearing the remains of charred clothing. The sight, the smell, brought back memories of what Brett and his crew had done weeks ago after our attack on the bridge.

I banked sharply away and pulled back on the yoke. I needed to get up and away and into fresh, unstained sky.

22

I rested, my back against a rock, basking and baking in the sun. It was warm and wonderful, and I felt myself starting to drift off.

Then I jerked awake and got to my feet. A sleeping guard was no guard. I'd had another night with too little shut-eye and too many images. Pictures in my head of more dead, more bodies. I'd spent the evening with Lori and Todd, playing penny-ante poker, trying to get the images from my flight with Herb out of my mind, but even hanging out with those guys couldn't drive away those scenes. Why had it bothered me so much? It wasn't like I knew any of them, or knew what had happened to any of them; it wasn't like I hadn't seen death, over and over and over. Still, the smell seemed to linger in my nostrils.

I shifted the rifle from one shoulder to the other and started to walk alongside the riverbank. Behind me was a group of our people fishing, some using rods and others nets. The nets were made from a bunch of old volleyball nets we had found at the elementary school, with lengths of rope tied on the ends to make them wide enough to stretch across the river.

I was one of a dozen armed guards protecting our crew. We were far from the only people fishing along this stretch.

Leonard and his family were just upstream from us. Along with them were Madison and her mother and some others from the tent town that continued to grow on our southwest corner. Lori had told them we were going down to the river—and I'd had word sent out to Leonard's grandfather. While we weren't officially there to guard anybody except our own people, we were still going to take care of them as best we could. It didn't cost us anything, and if they could catch some fish it would make them more able to fend for themselves, which was in our best interest.

People were continuing to beg at our gates, and we could see that those passing by were becoming thinner and thinner. It was getting harder for people on the walls to keep saying we had nothing to give, nothing to share. It was one thing to defend against men with guns, another to turn away women and children who simply wanted something to eat.

It was even harder to think about those people living within sight of our walls—people like Leonard and Madison and their families. These weren't just anonymous strangers passing by, but people we knew, even cared for.

But hunger was becoming an issue inside our walls as well, with complaints growing. Rations had become smaller, and people were blaming Ernie—like somehow he could snap his fingers and there would suddenly be more food.

What they didn't know yet was that the committee had decided that daily rations were going to have to get even smaller in the coming weeks. Our stores of basics like flour and dried beans were getting low, and the only way to stop from running out of food completely until the big harvest in the fall was to stretch out what we had. I would have liked more food, too, but I was surprised at how little you could get by on—even if you were doing something really physical, like working the fields.

Ironically, now that some of the fields were starting to be harvested, it seemed to be even harder. People could see food and were wondering why they just couldn't have more of it. What they didn't think about was that some of the food we were growing was going to have to last for an entire year, until the fall harvest of *next* year. Winter would come eventually. I guess some people didn't want to look that far in the future. Grumbling stomachs clouded judgment.

I'd heard the discussions in the committee, heard the breakdown on supplies, and understood that even if we kept rationing the food there was not going to be enough to get us through the year. Nobody knew how long this was going to last, but so far there had been no sign, no indication that anything was going to happen to "save" us. If we were going to survive, that survival was based solely on what we were doing inside our walls—and of course the things we were trying to do today to bring in more food.

I'd noticed that the hungrier people got, the more irritable they became. Things that hadn't bothered anybody before now caused arguments and fights. Small disputes, fights in the school yard between kids, happened almost daily. My mother had to send more and more officers to respond to dust-ups between neighbors, husbands and wives, parents and kids. Rather than pulling together, people were starting to pull apart.

Yet in a strange way, things were going too well for the neighborhood, there was too much calm. Who would have thought that a lack of a problem was a problem? Not that we were wishing for it, but Herb had predicted that a big, visible outside enemy would have actually settled people down and brought them together.

We weren't relying solely on food being grown, of course—teams were going out daily to scavenge. Howie often led a team out during the day to search for things that we needed. They'd gone "old tech" and used the Yellow Pages phone book to locate stores that might still have some of what we wanted. It was interesting how looted and stripped stores still had some things of value hidden among the rumble that remained.

A whole group had learned about foraging in the fields and forests. They were looking for things like chicory, pine nuts, spruce needles, leaves that could be used for salads, roots that could be boiled like potatoes. Hunters had killed a few more deer, but more meat was coming from sources nobody wanted to talk about. I hadn't seen a squirrel within our walls or a dog outside of them for a long time. Traps and snares had been fashioned that caught rabbits, raccoons, and birds. Who would have thought that I would be eating starlings and raccoons—and enjoying them? Meat, any meat, was welcome. Somehow beans and potatoes and greens didn't fill the hole in your stomach that meat did. I would have killed for a big steak. Maybe I shouldn't have been thinking things like that, but I knew I wasn't the only one.

Today was more of the same. It felt good to actually be doing something about our situation. Fish certainly seemed more appetizing than some of the other meat we'd been eating. The salmon were running, and we hoped we could bring back enough to stretch our food supply.

There was also another part to our people being here—they

were outside the neighborhood, some of them for the first time in weeks. It was like watching prisoners who'd been released from their cells. But while they may have been feeling freer, the outside world was getting more dangerous by the day.

The away teams were continually coming across bodies. Everybody had heard stories of bodies not just tucked away in corners or in abandoned buildings but left out on the streets, clearly the victims of some kind of violence. It meant that at times like this we had to be even more careful—we couldn't afford even one guard to fall asleep in the sun.

I caught sight of Lori and we waved at each other. She was standing by to help load the catch into the truck. Todd was out again with an away team today, foraging. It was rare that those guys didn't bring us back something useful, even if it was just information. They only went out in daylight and in groups of at least twenty-five, often more. Very different from Brett and his boys.

Each evening, just before last light, the ten members of Brett's night patrol would set out. There was something eerie about them, all dressed in black, even their weapons rubbed down with dirt and their faces blackened. They often snuck over the walls instead of through the gates. Brett said he didn't want anybody out there to see him coming. I thought he was getting even more paranoid, but whatever they were doing seemed to be working. They often came back with supplies—sometimes weapons and ammunition they'd "liberated" from groups they'd encountered.

Brett and his squad—who were all in their early twenties—hung around together all the time. They used one guy's house as their headquarters. They reminded me of a football team, but with guns instead of helmets and pads. Actually, they wore their body armor all the time and kept their weapons strapped to their sides, ready to leave at a moment's notice.

I'd also noticed something else about them. None of them seemed to be losing any weight or complaining about being hungry. I couldn't help but wonder—were they bringing back everything they found? Then again, when you considered what they were doing, maybe they deserved a little more. They were still bringing back things that the community needed, and they were risking their lives to do it.

My mother told me that Brett's squad reminded her of the SWAT—special weapons and tactics—team she worked with at her precinct, who always had a little extra swagger in their step, even for police officers. She said Brett and his squad had to be a little cocky to do their job, but she was trying to make sure they stayed in line.

There was a whistle behind me. I turned back to see several of our people, in big rubber hip waders, start across the river, bringing one side of the net to meet the other. We'd soon see what the net had caught. Everybody close at hand had stopped in their tracks, watching, waiting, and hoping. The waders reached the near side, and others on the bank helped them pull in the net from both ends. As the net reached the shallows, I could see something bubbling at the surface of the water: fish, dozens and dozens and dozens!

Once the net was completely out of the water, people began laughing and yelling while holding fish above their heads. It was incredible to see everybody so happy. And then I got worried.

I looked up and down the river. We'd caught fish—and everybody's attention. That wasn't good. It was best that people who weren't from the neighborhood not see what had happened, but out here, in the open, that wasn't possible.

I pulled the rifle off my back. I wanted those people who were watching not just to see the fish but also to see the weapon, to notice all of us with weapons. I wasn't afraid of Leonard and his group or Madison and her family, but there had to be others in the woods along both sides of the river.

Suddenly, I noticed a half dozen figures standing atop a ridge that marked the highest point along the river. They weren't directly above us, but they were way too close for comfort. They were posed there like statues, silhouetted against the sky. I couldn't tell if they had any weapons, but there was something unnerving about the way they stood so still and seemed to be peering down on us.

With a hand signal, I caught Howie's attention, and then pointed to the watchers up above. He stared in their direction, and also seemed unsure of what to make of them. With my head rotating on a swivel I hustled over to him.

"What do you think?" he said.

"There's something about them I don't like."

"Me neither."

"Should we settle down our folks?" I said.

"They're just happy. Can you blame them?"

"I just don't want to get anybody who's desperate and hungry to try to get any of our fish . . . or us."

"You're right," Howie agreed. "I'll lead a group up there to chase them away."

"No, you need to stay here. I'll do it."

Howie hesitated for an instant and then nodded. "I'll get you ten guards. The rest stay with me."

I turned my attention to our observers, still peering down at us. I tried to will them away. If they left, I wouldn't have to go up after them.

Howie went over and gave some orders. A few of the sentries shouldered their weapons and started in my direction. Suddenly the thought of having only ten people with me didn't seem enough; having thirty guards in total out here didn't seem enough.

In my mind I was seeing not just the few figures poised at the top of the hill but hundreds of armed men, ambushing us from out of the forest. Those men—the people who had escaped from the compound—were never far from my thoughts, and I knew they were out there somewhere. If they came charging out of those woods right now, we couldn't possibly stop them. Still, I had to think about what we *could* stop.

Soon I was surrounded by the people I was going to lead, six men and four women. They were not necessarily the people I would have wanted at crunch time. I suddenly wished for Brett and his squad to be there. But once again it wasn't what was best but what was best given the circumstances, and that was me with them.

"We're going up there. Do you see them?" I asked.

There was a nodding of heads.

"What do you think they want?" one of the men asked.

"I don't know. We're going to go up and ask them. Let's go," I said.

We started off, quickly leaving the river behind and entering the cover of the trees. That meant we couldn't see the top any longer and they couldn't see us. I had to figure, though, that they'd seen us going into the trees and knew we were coming toward them. They'd either leave or get ready for us to be there. The first possibility was so much more appealing and so much less potentially deadly.

The path we were on climbed sharply and came to a fork. Both ways angled off but were headed in the same general direction of where they were standing. I divided the group into two, sending half to the right and leading the rest to the left. As we started climbing again I couldn't help but wonder if dividing us up was the right thing or the wrong thing. Herb would have known. Brett would have known.

I could feel the climb in my lungs, straining to get air, sweat coming down my side. I wondered how much of this was from the climb and how much was from a sense of fear that was growing inside me.

The trees thinned and I suddenly popped out, standing at the top of the slope. The second crew came out to my side. They saw me and waved, and I waved back. I could see them. I could see the river, but I couldn't see anybody else. Had we come up at the wrong spot or had the watchers taken off?

"Spread out, keep your eyes open, your guns ready," I ordered.

Where had they gone? Less than a hundred yards away was more forest. Had they reacted when they saw us coming and fled? I could only hope, although now they could be in the cover of those trees and we were here, exposed, open, vulnerable.

"Everybody back into the trees," I ordered. "I don't know where they've gone, but the important thing is that they have gone."

There was a sense of relief as my orders were instantly followed. Any hesitation to come up here was replaced by an urgency to get away, get back to the bottom, to our people.

The rest of the afternoon, I'd kept my attention focused on the ridge, to the place the watchers had been. It remained unoccupied. That didn't mean we weren't being watched, and it certainly didn't settle down my imagination, but that danger hadn't resurfaced.

The fish were almost all loaded into the bed of the pickup truck by now. I could see some of them flopping around, trying to jump out. I felt for them trying to get out, get back in the river, and I almost hoped one of them could get back to freedom, but really we needed all of those fish. Food was food. Now, with the fish loaded, the guards all went back to their position. That gave me an opportunity to do what I needed to do.

I walked over to Lori. "Can you help me with something?"

"Sure, if you don't mind being around somebody who smells like fish."

"On you anything smells good."

"Boy, you really are laying it on. It must be a big favor."

We walked away from other people. "I want you to talk to Elyse and suggest that we take her and Madison's fish back with us."

"You want to take their fish?" Lori sounded shocked.

"I don't want to take their fish. I just want them to come back with us—with their fish. Once they're safe in the neighborhood, they can take their fish over to their home," I explained. "Those people who were watching us from the ridge are gone, but that doesn't mean they're still not around and aren't a danger. I'm afraid that somebody is going to try to rob Elyse and Madison when they head back."

"Okay, I understand. I can talk to them."

"Did you really think I was trying to steal their fish?" I asked.

"Of course not. I'm just worried about them, that's all."

"So am I. Tell them they can count the fish and we'll give them the same number back. I'm going to talk to Leonard's family and tell them the same thing."

Lori reached over and gave me a hug and a kiss.

"You were right," I said. "You really do smell like fish."

She tried to pull away and I gave her a bigger hug. "I like fish. The smell of any food is very appealing."

"You're lucky you're kinda cute," she said.

She walked off in one direction and I headed off to talk to Leonard. He and his mother and grandfather were among a larger group of tent people who now lived all around them. They'd come together, the way we had, as a sort of loose group. While they didn't have walls, the trees, the creek, and the isolation had protected them from marauders. So far.

"How are you doing?" I asked as I walked up.

"We're doing well," his grandfather, Sheldon, said. "Although from what I can see not as well as your group."

"We got lucky, but you probably did better than us if you think about it. You don't have nearly as many mouths to feed as we do. How many of you are there now?"

"There are forty-five of us," Leonard said.

"I can see the camp growing as I fly over," I said.

"We see you up there all the time," Leonard said.

"It looks like a lawn mower with wings," his grandfather said.

"That seems to be the general consensus."

"I always wave at you. Do you ever see me?" Leonard asked.

I shrugged. "Not really," I said. "I'm pretty occupied keeping that lawn mower flying. What I *can* see is that there are more tents. It's good that there are more of you. More people means more safety."

"And more mouths to feed," Sheldon added.

"We wanted to thank you for inviting us to come along with you today," Leonard's mother said. "It does feel safer with all of you here."

"I actually wanted to talk to you about that, Amy. I think it might be better if, instead of heading off by yourselves, all of you, and your catch, come with us when we leave."

Sheldon looked all around, scanning the hills. "Did you see something else?"

I shook my head. "Sort of, but just because I don't see a danger right now doesn't mean it isn't there. We have vehicles; you can drive to our gate, and then after sunset go around the side, up the creek, to your tents."

He looked at his daughter. "Probably best not to leave a trail back for somebody to follow. Thanks for being concerned. We'll take you up on the offer. When are you going to leave?"

"Not for a while, as long as the fish are jumping. We do want to be safely home before dark, though."

"That's what we had hoped for, so that's perfect." He turned to Leonard and his mother. "Can you two spread the word to the others in our group, please?"

They headed off.

"Could I ask you another question, son?" he asked as they walked away.

"Sure, of course."

"I noticed that your people have pretty well cleared out the entire forest surrounding your walls. Your crew with all them chainsaws is hard to miss."

I hesitated for a second. I didn't know where he was going, but this was maybe an area I shouldn't be talking about. There were so many areas I shouldn't be talking about.

"They just wanted to make sure we had good sight lines from the walls," I said.

"Those are awfully long sight lines when they're taking out trees a hundred yards away, down on the opposite side of the creek."

"Um . . . I think there's some talk about planting in that field, maybe."

"I can't see your people planting crops that they can't protect," he said. "Besides, I've seen what they've been doing with the timber, cutting it up and bringing it back inside the walls."

"I hadn't noticed," I said, and shrugged.

"Son, you're not much of a liar."

"I'm not . . ." I was going to say "lying," but that would have been a lie, too. "I'm not allowed to talk about things."

"I can appreciate that," he said. "I'm going to tell you what I think, and you don't have to answer."

I nodded.

"The only reason to stockpile wood is because your people think you're going to need it for heat," he said. "And there's not going to be a need for heat until winter."

I listened, trying to keep my face as neutral and blank as Herb would have.

"Your people think that this is going to go through the winter, don't they?" he asked.

"Nobody knows that."

"But that's what they're thinking, isn't it?" he demanded.

I nodded ever so slightly. That was what we were preparing for, what Herb and the committee thought, but Herb kept drumming it into my head that our only real advantage was that we knew things before other people, and then acted before they acted.

"Son, you've been fair to us, decent, and I know there's not a lot of either of those things happening much these days. I need you to be fair with me now. My daughter and my grandson, all of us, we're living in tents. That's okay for now, for the short term, but we can't survive in tents throughout the winter. We need to know what's coming."

"Look, I really don't know . . . Nobody does. Would you be willing to talk to somebody who might know more?"

"I'd talk to anybody who could be honest with me."

"I'll arrange for you to talk to Herb."

"Thanks, Adam, thank you so much." He took my hand and shook it.

I could guarantee him a meeting. What I couldn't guarantee was that Herb would tell him the truth when they did meet.

23

I did a final pass over the river, low enough that I could see the smiles on the faces of our fishing team and wave back at them.

The first fishing day had been so successful that it had led to a second and now a third. Yesterday I had been back on the banks, but today I was guarding from a higher vantage point. I pulled back on the yoke and started to climb again. It was no wonder people were happy. Ernie and his crew had done masterful work, making fresh fish stew to feed everybody the last two nights. I don't think I'd ever tasted anything that good. There was more than enough for a few more meals, leaving most of the catch to be filleted and dried out for later. Which gave us more to be happy about.

I cleared the banks of the valley and kept climbing. I'd been flying for hours and needed to get fueled up. I banked toward the neighborhood, and as I did, I could see smoke rising into the sky, coming from within our walls.

Fires had been becoming more and more common. People who were used to gas stoves, electric lights, and propane barbecues were trying to get by with candles and wood fires. The fire chief and his three firefighters had repeatedly gone door to door and talked to people about fire safety, and so far we'd been lucky enough that any small fires had been quickly contained.

But this was different—bigger, thicker, darker. The smoke was rising almost straight into the air. I opened the throttle up all the way. Getting closer, I could feel my heart pounding harder. The smoke was rising from somewhere in the southern section. I was relieved it wasn't on the side of the neighborhood where my house was, but then immediately felt guilty.

Closing in, I could see that the smoke and fire were coming from a house up on Wheelwright Crescent. Any fire could easily spread to other houses. Thank God there wasn't any wind to carry the embers.

I could now see dozens and dozens of people organizing a bucket brigade from a nearby swimming pool, but the fire was already too out of control for them to fight it without proper equipment. Farther back there was a large crowd, people who had come to watch.

Slowly I circled. As I did I noticed that the guards on the nearest walls were looking in, toward the fire, instead of out. If I'd been down there I would have had Herb or Howie talk to them. Actually I could land on the upper part of Wheelwright, away from the fire, instead of on my street. There was a fuel depot in a shed behind one of the houses. I came down low, making sure the street was clear.

I eased off the throttle, pushed the stick down, and settled into my approach. This street had a little more curve to it than the section in front of my house, but it still wouldn't be any problem. One more scan up the road—no obstruction and no people. They all must have been down the street, staring at the fire.

My wheels touched down and I rumbled along the road, gently applying the brakes and rolling to a stop. I took off my helmet, undid the harness, jumped out, and ran toward the blaze.

The crowd watching the blaze was huge, with hundreds of people. I now knew basically all of them at least by face. I scanned the crowd for Lori or Todd, my mother or Danny and Rachel, or Howie or Herb. I couldn't see any of them, but the crowd was so big that they could have been somewhere within it.

The whole house was now engulfed in flames, oranges and reds and black smoke, pouring out of every window and through holes in the roof.

"Pretty amazing, isn't it?"

I turned around. It was Brett, the one person I didn't feel like talking to.

"I thought you'd be asleep," I said.

"Soon. I couldn't miss this."

"Do you know whose house it is?"

"No idea."

"Did everybody get out? Is everybody all right?"

"No idea about that either. It's daytime, so nobody would have been sleeping. Everybody probably cleared out," Brett said.

"We can hope."

Suddenly the roof collapsed and there was a collective gasp from the crowd as smoke and embers billowed into the sky in a gigantic plume! A wave of heat washed over us.

"Whoa," Brett said. There was something about his voice that made me turn and look at him. His mouth was slightly open, and his eyes had a dazzled look. I'd seen that expression before—when he had killed the deer.

"It was just a matter of time until a fire happened in here," he said.

"I've seen a lot of burned-out buildings from the air."

"The air?" Brett snorted. "Being up in the air isn't much different from hiding behind the walls. You don't really know what's happening until you see it up close and personal."

"I've been out."

"Not at night. That's when the men are separated from the *boys*."

I knew in his mind I was nothing more than one of the boys.

"Not that *you* should go out at night. Out there is like that fire. It's out of control, raw power, it's—"

"A rush for you."

He smiled. It wasn't a friendly smile. "At least you understand some part of it. It *is* a rush, being out there with my team, doing whatever needs to be done. *Whatever* needs to be done. Guaranteed."

I didn't know what he really meant and I was too smart to even ask.

"Well, you be good, kid." Brett slapped me on the back. "Much as I'd like to stay, I've got to get some shut-eye."

I watched him go, feeling more unsettled by him than by the fire at my back.

24

I climbed out of bed to close the window. Then I got back into bed and shut my eyes. It was pitch dark, hours before dawn. The smell of smoke was still lingering in the air. The wind must have shifted in my direction because the scent seemed to be stronger than when I'd first gone to bed. If I hadn't seen the fire finally being extinguished with my own eyes, I would have been concerned that it had spread.

Like everybody else, I'd spent hours watching until the fire was put out. Thank goodness the family hadn't been inside at the time it started. Later that evening at the communal dinner I'd heard that it was a mother and her two kids. I knew them like I seemed to now know everybody, but I didn't know them well. That made it better. I was happy that they had been taken in temporarily by some neighbors. Efforts were being made to gather things—clothing and household goods—and set them up in one of the two or three remaining vacant houses in the neighborhood.

After the meal Lori and I had gone for a walk together, but she told me that if I wasn't going to talk and was only going to stare into space I might as well go home and get some sleep. I took her advice. But even though I could always go to bed, getting to sleep was a different and difficult matter.

My eyes popped open. I heard sounds downstairs and quickly got to my feet. Without thinking, I grabbed my pistol and clicked the safety off. Then, a bit more clearheaded the next moment, I put the safety back on. It was probably just my brother or sister getting a drink of water or my mother getting ready to go out on patrol. With the pistol hanging at my side I opened the door and peered down the stairs to the front door.

My mother was standing there, balanced on one foot, putting on her shoes.

She looked up, seeming not at all shocked to see her teenage son checking up on things with a pistol in hand. "Sorry if I woke you, kiddo."

"I wasn't asleep. Where are you going?"

"There's some sort of disturbance."

"There is? I'll get my shoes and—"

"It's nothing," she said. "Just some movement outside the walls."

"On Burnham?"

"No, the west wall."

"I'll get my shoes," I said.

"There's nothing to worry about. You should go back to sleep."

"Do you really think that's going to happen?" I asked. "I'm coming with you."

She smiled. "I'd enjoy the company and I guess the twins will be okay for a bit."

I had fallen into bed in my clothes, including my holster, so I was ready to go. I slipped my gun into the sheath as I tiptoed down the steps. I grabbed my shoes and body armor and slipped outside behind my mom, pulling the door closed quietly.

"I'll drive!" I whispered after her. I pulled the keys from my pocket.

My beautiful beater of a car glowed in the moonlight. We both hopped in. I slipped on my shoes, then started the engine—it turned over on the first try and roared to life.

"I'm sure it's nothing," my mother said as I eased out. There was an edge to her voice.

"People on the wall are getting jumpy," I said.

"I just don't want it to become a boy-who-cried-wolf situation," she said. "We might not respond quickly enough to real danger if we keep getting false alarms."

I pulled up to the guard house and one of the guys waved at us, pointing toward the south. I quickly reversed and then headed back along Sawmill, circling the mall and heading to the southwest corner wall. Right outside the wall in that corner was the tent town.

I edged up as close as I could. Herb was there, as were Howie and a few other guards, but no Brett or any of his squad. They were already outside the walls on patrol and could have been anywhere.

"Update me," my mother said.

"We're hearing noises, people thrashing through the woods."

"But no discharge of weapons, right?" my mother asked.

"No, not that we've heard," Howie said.

"What if you turned on the lights?" I asked.

"They wouldn't penetrate the woods. We'd only make ourselves a more visible target to people in the darkness," Herb said. "I couldn't see anything with the night-vision goggles;

the trees are too close to the wall. It's time for us to cut down more of those trees, push back the forest away from these walls even farther."

"But the trees are sort of like the tent people's walls," I said.

"It's our walls I'm concerned about," Herb replied dismissively. "We have to—"

There was a loud, terrified scream—a woman's scream. A deadly silence followed. Then there was more screaming and yelling, and a shot rang out, and then a second, and there were more raised voices. Then came a fusillade of shots from what sounded like an automatic weapon, and still more cries and screams from the forest.

After a moment I could see flickering light—flames!

"We have to do something!" I yelled. "We have to go out there!"

"We can't," my mother said. "We can't risk lives, but we will do something." She turned to Howie. "Sound the alarm and start switching the lights on and off, repeatedly."

Howie rushed into action.

Herb and my mother conferred in urgent whispers.

Then my mom spoke to the assembled crowd. "Okay, people. Let's spread the word that we need all the guards on this side of the wall to get back into position but keep their heads down. At my signal they are to fire a shot into the ground just outside the wall."

"Why would they fire into the ground?" I asked Herb.

"We don't want them firing into the woods," he explained. "They're just as likely to hit an innocent. We want only the threat of their weapons."

My mom continued speaking to the group. "Then I need everybody—the guards, any rubberneckers from the neighborhood—I need us all to scream at the top of our lungs. I want it to sound like an army is here and rushing out into the woods. The idea is to get the attackers to flee."

A number of onlookers nodded grimly and then sped off to spread the word down along the watchposts. My mother followed, leaving just Herb and me.

"And then we go out?" I asked.

"And then we wait."

"Wait for what?"

"Until the first light. Then we go out—"

I tried to interrupt, but Herb held up a hand.

"I know you want to do more, Adam, but there's nothing else we can do without risking the lives of people we have a responsibility to protect. The lifeboat isn't big enough to hold everybody."

"Then maybe we need a bigger boat!" I snapped.

The siren started to blare, and I jumped. Three long blasts—which meant the west wall—followed by two short blasts—which meant the south wall. Together it let people know that the problem was at the corner of those two walls, right where we stood. The noise was deafening and frightening and reassuring all at once.

Howie apparently pulled the switch, and the area in front of the walls was bathed in colors from the strings of Christmas tree lights hanging off the wall. They were powered by car batteries that were recharged after each use by bicycles hooked up to a series of generators. But like Herb had said, the glow of the lights didn't extend into the forest. It was so surreal, the blaring siren and the reds and greens and blues, plus the flickering of flames amid the trees. It was like Christmas in hell. The lights went off again and the darkness was overwhelming. Strangely, the siren now seemed louder. And it probably was louder, since both the lights and the siren ran off the same batteries.

People from the neighborhood were now rushing out to the walls from nearby streets. Above the murmurs and scrabble of feet I heard Howie's voice over the bullhorn.

"Weapons ready!" he called out.

I went to take my pistol from the holster, and Herb put a hand on my hand to stop me. I looked up and he shook his head.

"On my order!" Howie called out.

Again the lights came back on and the siren faded slightly.

"Ready . . . aim low . . . no accidents . . . and fire!"

There was a chorus of gunfire, sharp and loud, as guns along the wall discharged. Almost before I could even hear the shots being fired, the ground in front of us jumped up in dozens of places where bullets had slammed into the rocks and dirt.

"Now!" Howie called over the bullhorn.

In response, hundreds of voices screamed out and a chill went up my spine. It was louder, more prolonged, and more frightening than the sound of the gunfire. The screaming and yelling went on and on. I couldn't help but imagine what people in the forest were thinking, what people in our neighborhood still tucked in their homes were thinking. It was terrifying.

The lights went off again, and almost on cue everybody

went silent. The silence was more overwhelming than the screaming. It was as if it hurt my ears. There was nothing. Nothing from the walls, nothing from the neighborhood, and then there was something—a small voice crying. It wasn't loud but it was piercing. It continued and everybody stood, frozen in place, listening.

"No, we can't," Herb said to me before I even opened my mouth. "Not yet."

The crying stopped. Either somebody had reached the child and offered him or her comfort or— Well, we had to hope the child was okay.

It was going to be a long wait until morning.

25

I looked at my watch. It was just before five-thirty; the sun would be up by six. I had been standing at the wall for a few hours, along with crowds of people waiting to see what had happened. Probably everybody in the neighborhood had been woken by the uproar, and many had made their way to the southwest corner. My mother and Howie had repositioned their people, putting extra guards on every wall. There was always the danger that getting us looking one way was nothing more than a distraction in order to attack from another.

It was still too dark to do anything, but I could see the outline of the trees more clearly at the edge of the forest and there was a hint of light in the other direction, toward the east.

The flames in the forest had died out almost as quickly as the voices—the cries. There had been just silence and darkness for hours. That wasn't much different from what was coming from inside the walls as well. My neighbors and I spoke softly so as to not disturb the night—or the dead. It wasn't just a fear, it was reality. Gunshots, fire, anguished cries. Something bad had happened. People had died. That was certain. The only questions that remained were who and how many and how bad was it, and those questions couldn't be answered until we went out there. What made it so much worse was that I knew these people. They weren't just anonymous strangers passing by our walls. I didn't even want to think how Lori would react if something had happened to Madison or Elyse. I looked at my watch again—another minute had passed.

Lori had arrived with her parents, who had worked to comfort her before they headed back to take care of the milking. She had fallen asleep, her back against the wall, and I'd wake her when it was time. Almost intuitively it seemed as if she knew I was looking at her, and her eyes opened. She got up and came toward me.

"Well?"

"Not long."

"You've been saying that for the last two hours," she said.

"Now I mean it. Ten or fifteen minutes."

"And then somebody goes out?"

"People have already gone out. Herb made a decision to send out two teams, one from each gate, along Burnham and Erin Mills Parkway."

"That's good, right?"

"That's *very* good. It secures the area."

Howie was in charge of one team. Brett, who had returned in the middle of the night with his squad, was leading the other. He said they weren't even close to the neighborhood but had heard the gunfire and then our response, and came racing back.

"If the area is secure, why can't we go out now?" Lori asked me.

"Maybe we should ask somebody who's in charge."

Herb and my mother were up closer to the gate, talking with some of the regular guards. We were going to go out with overwhelming force, as Herb called it. Every guard who wasn't going to be on the wall was going out—more than 150 people with weapons were flooding the area.

Lori and I stood slightly off to the side and waited for them to complete their conversation, the planning. Before we could even open our mouths, Herb turned and said, "Soon, we're going soon."

Herb rummaged around in a bag at his feet and pulled out some body armor. "You better put this on," he said, trying to hand it to Lori.

"I already have a vest."

"You do?"

She pulled open her jacket to show him. "Yes, Adam gave it to me."

"What a nice present for a boy to give a girl these days," my mother said. She threw me a hard look. "And just what were *you* planning on wearing?"

"This is *your* body armor?" Lori questioned.

"I wanted to make sure you'd be safe."

"And that you wouldn't be? How do you think I'd feel if you went out without anything and got hit?" Lori demanded.

"How do you think *I'd* feel knowing that I kept the armor and sent you out without—"

We were back to the same argument we kept having these days. Was it an argument? Or was it a conversation? I couldn't tell.

"This is all very sweet," Herb said. "Let's just not let 'sweet' get in the way of 'smart.' Adam, you know that nobody should leave the neighborhood without body armor."

"I know. Sorry."

"Sorry is good as long as you don't let it happen again." He handed me the extra armor and I slipped it on. "You're too valuable to this entire neighborhood to risk your life."

"And too valuable to *me*," my mother said.

Herb turned to her. "What's the situation on the walls?"

"We're all set," she said. "I'll be monitoring the patrols on the walls. Howie and Brett and their patrols are definitely in place by now. I just wish I could go out there, too, but the captain has to stay with her ship." She looked at Lori and me. "You two take care of each other."

I nodded. Herb hadn't wanted Lori to come out in the first wave, but I'd convinced him. She had the best relationship with the tent people, and having her there would be good for them if not necessarily for her.

"It's time to go," Herb said.

We walked along the inside of the wall to join a group of guards already assembled at the gate. Herb insisted that Lori be at the rear, which meant I had to be there, too. As we arrived at the gate Herb gave the word. Slowly one of the two heavy wooden doors swung inside. He stepped out first and was followed by the long column of guards. Lori and I followed behind the last two men through the gate. The line from my neighborhood stretched before us, and while the main group was filing down the path, others started to fan out along the edge of the woods.

"Your attention, please!" It was Herb's metallic voice blasting from the bullhorn. "We are coming out to offer assistance.

We are coming to help. Please do not fire, please do not fire on us!"

I could feel my adrenaline starting to surge with each step we took. Now I was glad not to be at the head of the line and equally glad that I had on body armor again. Giving it up had really been more stupid than sweet. I could have gotten Lori another suit instead of giving her mine.

We hit the edge of the forest. We were now more protected from view and more vulnerable to attack. Again, I was grateful to have so many people in front of me. The sounds of feet on gravel and bodies moving through the brush should have been reassuring but were ominous because there was no other noise. The air was tinged with the smell of smoke, the residue of last night's fires. We came up to Herb's side.

"You two stay right together, understand?" Herb said.

"Like glue," Lori said, and gave a weak little smile.

She looked scared and I was working hard not to be scared.

Herb gestured—a slight movement of his head—to the left. Among the trees lay two people, obviously dead, and three of our men standing over them.

Lori gasped and skidded to a stop.

"C'mon," I said as I followed Herb.

Now there was noise up ahead, the sound of many voices.

We quickly came upon the center of their little compound—the people who had been burned out of their condo had encountered tragedy again. There was utter chaos, tents shredded to pieces or burned to nothing, a few people standing around, or huddled on the ground, crying, yelling, and our guards everywhere.

I scanned the scene, desperately looking for Madison and Elyse—and there they were. They came running toward us. Both of them wrapped their arms around Lori. Madison was weeping and Elyse was talking, but her words hardly made sense. Repeatedly she tried to talk and each time just dissolved into tears, Lori comforting them as if they were both her children.

I felt uncomfortable, but I also needed to know what had happened. I edged away to where Herb was standing around the center fire pit, surrounded by other people from the tent town.

It was like everybody was talking, but nobody was saying anything. There was so much desperation in their voices, in their expressions.

"Everybody, stop!" Herb yelled.

I jumped. It was so rare to hear him raise his voice.

Everyone fell silent. Herb pointed at one man. "Friend, I need you and only you to tell us what happened. Understand?"

It was Mr. Armstrong. I knew him, but I didn't know if Herb even knew his name. His eyes were wide, his expression glazed, his face dirty, hair sticking up, and what might have been blood on his jacket.

Another man started to talk, and Herb held up a hand to silence him. Herb then looked from person to person to emphasize his point. They all looked too beaten, too scared to argue.

"Now, please, talk to us," he said to Mr. Armstrong.

"They came—there were a lot of them," he said. "We couldn't tell for sure how many. It was just so confusing. They were like shadows and they swept in before we knew what was happening. They began firing at people, shooting into tents, setting them on fire. It was all so fast we couldn't even defend ourselves.

"They shot people who weren't even fighting back, who didn't even have weapons. They just shot people who were standing there with their hands raised and—"

"Do you know how many were killed?" Herb asked.

Mr. Armstrong shook his head. "The woods . . . plus we haven't looked in all the tents and—" Mr. Armstrong stopped midsentence, overcome.

In front of me I noticed two men from our neighborhood tending a woman and a small child, huddled together on the ground. As our men unwrapped the victims' blanket I could see red, raw, burned skin on the mother's arm. I shuddered. One of the men was Dr. Morgan. I hadn't even realized that any of our medical people had come out with us.

"And then we saw the lights go on and the shots being fired from the walls, and then that horrible, wonderful yelling, and suddenly they were gone," Mr. Armstrong said.

"Thank you for what you did," one woman said, and others echoed her.

"I'm sorry we couldn't have done more," Herb said.

We all knew there was more we could have done, but didn't.

"We're going to have to take the injured inside the walls to be treated at the clinic," Dr. Morgan said.

I looked at Herb for his reaction. There was none.

"Thank you, thank you so much," a woman sputtered through her tears.

"But what about the rest of us?" a man asked.

"We'll have our men search the woods and make sure your attackers are gone," Herb said. "We have guards stationed up on the streets. You're safe."

"Will they be here tonight to protect us?"

"We can leave guards out tonight," Herb said.

"And after tonight?" the woman demanded.

"We'll talk to the committee. But we can offer you no guarantees."

"But what's to stop them from coming back?" the man asked.

"Nothing," Herb said. "Nothing. And they will be back. If not in two nights, then four. If not them, then somebody else just like them."

"But what are you saying?"

"You'd be wise not to stay here any longer," Herb said. "It isn't safe."

"But where can we go?" the man demanded.

"I don't have any answers," Herb said.

"You could let us into your neighborhood!"

I could see that every person was now listening, waiting, hoping.

"I'm sorry, but you can't come in," Herb said.

His words hit hard. The brief second of hope had been slashed.

"You don't have to feed us; we just need the protection of the walls," the man pleaded.

"We can't let you in and *not* feed you," Herb said, "so we can't let you in."

"But if we can't stay here, and you won't let us in, then what's to become of us?" the man asked.

Others joined in, trying to talk, asking questions.

Herb held up his hands and with that one gesture silenced everybody.

"We are not responsible for your lives!" Herb said. "For now, you're safe. For now, we'll take care of the wounded. Does anybody object to the wounded being cared for?"

"Of course not," the man said.

"Then we'll do what we can," Herb said. "You'll have to be grateful for what we can do instead of angry about what we can't."

26

Late that morning, the committee members sat around our living room after calling an emergency meeting to discuss the attack.

"To begin, what precautions have been put in place to protect the survivors in the tent town?" Judge Robertson asked.

"As Herb promised, I've made arrangements to establish a sentry line this evening," Howie explained.

"I'm worried about our people being outside the walls at night," my mother said.

"We should be worried," Herb agreed. "They're in danger and potentially could only stop a small force."

"Should I put out more guards?" Howie asked.

"That just puts more people at risk. We have to remember that if a sentry line could provide security, we wouldn't have had to build walls around our neighborhood. Our guards being out there guarantees nothing but that the guards themselves are at risk," Herb said.

"A risk we've agreed to take tonight," my mother said.

"Yes, of course," Herb added. "It's the least we can do . . . and probably the most as well."

"This is all so unfortunate, but in some ways it was predictable," the judge said. "We have been given reports by the away team of increasingly violent gangs operating at night, stealing and looting and preying on the unarmed and vulnerable."

Brett had been telling everybody that the area was a combat zone. I had been starting to wonder if he was just saying things like that to make him and his men seem more like action heroes. But after tonight, well, who could argue?

"It's unfortunate that our away team wasn't there to intercept this group," Councilor Stevens said.

"Or fortunate," Herb countered. "They could have been easily surprised, outnumbered, and overwhelmed. The death count could have been higher and would have included members of our neighborhood."

"Is there a final number?" the judge asked.

"Fifteen people were killed in the initial attack," my mother said.

"And two of the people who were severely burned did not survive," Dr. Morgan reported. "Given the severity of their burns and the limits in our facilities, there was nothing we could do for them."

"We all know you did your best," the judge said.

"We treated and discharged those with minor injuries. Three others still remain in our facility. I think two of them will be fine, but the third will require long-term care, assuming he survives."

"Please update us again tomorrow. So at present there are seventeen souls lost. What do we know about the actual attack?" my mother asked.

"From interviews with the survivors," Herb said, "an unknown number of heavily armed and masked men—"

Councilor Stevens sat up. "Masked? That's somehow even more horrible. Are you sure they were masked?"

"That's what we were told. They were wearing dark masks and dark-colored clothing."

I looked at Herb for his reaction, but he might as well have been wearing a mask himself—there was nothing.

"They swept into the camp and began firing their weapons. They simply discharged weapons into tents—more than half the people killed were found still inside, under covers—and they then proceeded to shoot down anybody they came across."

"Did they take anything?" Howie asked.

"There are no reports, but it's likely that they could have looted tents without any witnesses," Herb answered.

"Or perhaps the lights and display of force from the walls chased them away before they had a chance to steal anything," Judge Roberts suggested.

"Yes, perhaps that was it," Herb agreed.

I could tell Herb was just agreeing even though he didn't mean it. I was positive there was something more about this that he was thinking and not talking about. I'd gotten to the point that even if I didn't know what he was secretly thinking, I knew when he was doing it.

"As well as discharging weapons they proceeded to set fire to tents," Howie said. "Perhaps that was done as a way of creating a diversion."

Again I looked at Herb to see if he agreed with this. Again his mask was in place.

"Herb?" I called. He turned around. "You don't think what happened out there makes sense, do you?"

He stayed silent for a moment and then slowly shook his head. "I have some questions."

"What sort of questions?" my mother asked.

I didn't know if me calling him out would cause him to talk or to clam up, so I was relieved when he started telling us his theory.

"The whole thing doesn't add up. Why would somebody attack, wasting valuable assets—ammunition—and risk their lives for no gain?" he asked.

"Like the judge said, I was just assuming that we chased them away with our lights and gunfire before they could get what they were after," Howie said.

"What benefit was there in setting tents on fire? That would only destroy the things that any raiding party would be searching for. It was like they swept in with the intent of simply killing those people and destroying their shelters."

"We've certainly seen many acts of random violence," the judge said.

Herb shook his head. "This was not random. Did you find any bodies that belonged to this raiding party?"

"None," Howie said. "Maybe they took their dead with them."

"Perhaps, but I think that's unlikely. They swept in, destroyed their target, and left without a single casualty. These people were not just ruthless but organized and professional."

Ruthless, organized, and professional—those words seemed to hang in the air.

"I'm almost afraid to ask this next question," the judge said. He paused, and it was like it wasn't even necessary for him to speak because I was sure we all had the same thought. "Do you think this could have been the work of remnants of the force we destroyed at the bridge?"

Herb shook his head. "We have no way of knowing one way or another."

"So it could be them?" Howie asked.

"If it is, it's a new tactic. Their previous actions were always aimed toward strengthening, gaining, robbing, finding more resources—always getting something."

"So you think it wasn't them," the judge concluded.

"Herb didn't say that, either," my mother interjected. "Maybe this attack on the tent town was a way to test our defenses."

"But why would they do that?" Howie asked. "They can't possibly think that they could successfully attack us now. We destroyed their forces . . . most of them anyway."

"What Howie's saying makes sense," the judge said.

"We can't assume that they haven't recruited more members, but it's possibly the work of another group altogether," Herb said. "The group from the compound is not the only evil out there. All I know is that they chose to attack in the one spot where we are most vulnerable to an attack."

We were back to a subject that kept coming up but had never been resolved.

"Can we strengthen the walls there?" Councilor Stevens asked.

"The issue isn't the strength of the walls but the closeness of the forest. No matter what we do, our walls would be pierced by an RPG round. We need to take down the trees and cover for at least a hundred meters on all sides."

I knew that the whole tent town was within that distance from our walls.

The judge let out a big sigh. "I know we have discussed this issue at great length. It might be wise for us to revisit this situation."

"It's clear that the tent town can no longer exist," Herb said.

I felt a rush of anxiety.

"Are you suggesting allowing the tent people to come into our neighborhood?" the judge asked.

"No, sir, we cannot afford that. They have to go elsewhere."

Herb turned and looked to me. I felt afraid of what he was going to say next.

"I have a plan," he said. "But we're going to need Adam and, Mr. Peterson, your daughter to help us make it work."

"Lori isn't going to do anything that will hurt those people," I said. "And neither will I."

"You don't even know what I'm proposing, son. You might want to listen before you pass judgment."

27

We walked out of the little greenhouse.
Herb, Lori, and I were the tour guides for people from the
two tent towns. There were ten of them altogether, including
Leonard's grandfather from one group and Madison's mother
from the other.

"I can't get over all the things you've been able to do here,"
Leonard's grandfather said.

"It's amazing how people working together can get things
done," Herb said. "But people of our vintage know about
hard work, don't we?"

They both laughed. For Herb, connecting with the other
old-timer was mainly just strategy but also some degree of
admiration. They were about the same age and each a leader
of his respective community, so they not only had things in
common but also a mutual respect.

Along with the greenhouse we'd shown them the clinic,
the school, the fields, and the guard system along the walls.

"This has all been very impressive. But are you going to
tell us what this little tour is about?" Sheldon asked.

"Couldn't it just be one neighbor inviting some other
neighbors in for a visit?" Herb replied.

"We've been neighbors for three months, yet you've always

seemed to make a point out of keeping us outside, so I figure something is up," he said. "No offense."

"None taken. Why do you think you're here?" Herb asked.

"Well, the only thing that's changed is the attack on the other tent people two nights ago," he offered.

"And we do want to thank you for everything you've done for us," Mr. Armstrong said. He had become the unofficial leader of the other tent town.

"It was a terrible thing that happened to you," Leonard's grandfather said. "It could have been us. It's the thing we live in fear of."

"That fear is well placed, Sheldon," Herb said. "You're no less open to an attack than the other tent group was."

"I guess we're a little more protected because we're farther from the roads, and we do have a lot of armed guards," Sheldon said.

"There were a lot of men who attacked us," Mr. Armstrong said.

"We'd put up a fight," Sheldon said.

"I know you would, but that fight would have casualties and fatalities." Herb paused. "You all know that your present situations put you in extreme danger."

"It felt so much better knowing your men were patrolling the last two nights," Madison's mother, Elyse, said.

"We won't be able to extend that patrol for more than a few more nights. We can't expose our men to the risk. That's why we invited you in today, because we're asking both your groups to move."

"Are you inviting us to move into your neighborhood?" Elyse asked.

Herb shook his head. "We can't do that. We simply don't have the capacity to take on more people."

"So do you just expect us to pick up our tents and leave?" Sheldon demanded.

"Yes, I do," Herb said.

"You have no right to make us leave," Sheldon said defiantly.

"The threat isn't from us, but from outside forces," Herb said.

"We have guns and we'll post more guards," Mr. Armstrong said.

"You can't guard against winter. You'll need shelter, heat, warmer clothing, food, and better security as well," Herb said.

"We all know what we need," Leonard's grandfather said. "Knowing what we need and getting it are two different things."

"We want to help you get those things," I explained.

"The only place that has all of those things is your neighborhood," he said.

"Not here. There's no room in our boat," Herb said. He turned to me. "But, as a very wise person once said to me, we can help build a bigger boat."

———————

Forty-five minutes later, we were across the street from our compound, standing in front of a vacant house. I opened the door and we walked in, followed by Leonard's entire family.

"This is going to be ours?" Leonard asked.

"Your family is going to split it with one other family from your tent town," I said.

"Even cut in half it's bigger than our old house," he said.

"And a lot bigger than the tent," his mother added.

Penny ran up the stairs.

"It's a house, but that doesn't make it safe," Leonard's aunt—Auntie Mary—said. She had been reluctant to leave the tents behind and had threatened not to come.

"There's a concrete wall on the south, a high fence to west," I said. "We already have a crew working on the east side, and the north wall is across the street from us on Burnham. We'll guard that wall for you."

"It will be good to have walls," Amy said.

"And sleep in a bed," Sheldon added. "How many houses are in this section?"

"Just under a hundred and forty of them are vacant. Those are the houses your group and the other tent town will take over," I explained again.

"And the people who live here are okay with this?" he asked.

"I've been in conversation with them about many things," Herb explained. "They agreed to this."

"He helped them see there are benefits for everybody, including them," I added. "Our committee agreed to give them three rototillers, and Lori's father is going to come over with his tractor to help cultivate the seed we're donating. It's mostly potatoes, cabbage, and carrots, but you can start growing."

"I just wish it wasn't so late in the season," Sheldon said.

"The growing season will be extended with the greenhouses

our engineers are going to show you how to build, and of course we'll try to figure out the best place to dig a well for drinking water," I said. "And, oh, did I mention that the committee has agreed to allow our doctors to come over to take care of all the people who form this new neighborhood?"

"That's . . . that's all so amazing," Amy said.

"We're grateful, so grateful," Sheldon added.

"I still have a question," Auntie Mary said.

I turned to face her. She was standing at the open door, holding her rifle. She didn't have her finger on the trigger and it certainly wasn't pointed at me, but I still felt a rush of fear.

"Why are you doing all this?" she asked.

"Do we need a reason to help other people?" I asked.

"Yeah, you do. What's in it for you, for your neighborhood?"

I thought about saying "nothing," but there *was* something in it for us.

"We needed to clear space away from our southeast walls, and the one tent town was in the way."

"You could have just forced them to leave," she said. "You have enough men and weapons."

"That's not who we are," I said. "Honestly."

"Honestly?" she scoffed. "You still haven't answered why you're making that offer to us as well. We're nowhere near your walls."

"We couldn't stand by and watch what's going to happen, watch you all die when winter comes."

"Lots of people are dying out there," she said.

"We can't help everybody, but we can help a few people. This isn't just about surviving. We need to do more than just survive. We have to keep being human. That's all we're offering, a chance to help us all keep being human," I said.

Slowly she nodded. "I think I might believe you."

28

"Adam."

Once again I reached for my pistol in the pitch black of my room.

"Adam, wake up."

It was Rachel. I relaxed and then tensed all over again. What if I'd found my gun?

"I'm awake. What's wrong?"

"I don't know. Mom's arguing with somebody downstairs."

I sat up and looked over at my half-open door. I heard them, too. Something was going on.

"I'll find out. You go back to sleep."

"I won't be able to sleep," she said.

"Then at least go back to bed. I'll take care of it."

When Rachel opened my bedroom door to leave, I could hear the voices more clearly. It was my mother and Brett. What could they be arguing about in the middle of the night? I felt uneasy.

As usual, I was sleeping in my clothes. I grabbed my pistol as I climbed out of bed, stuffing the weapon into my back pocket, under my shirttail.

I went down the stairs and eased into the kitchen. The voices had gone silent, but the atmosphere was tense. My mother was standing, and Brett and Herb were seated at the kitchen table. Thank goodness Herb was there. Brett was sitting on a chair, chewing an apple. He looked up and glared at me, and suddenly I didn't think it was unwise to have my gun with me.

"We encountered resistance," Brett said. "Simple as that."

"Simple as that?" my mother exclaimed. "Two people were killed!"

"A lot more than two," Brett said. "Over twenty of them were killed."

"Two of our people, two of the men under your command were—"

"How about if we all just calm down?" Herb said. His voice was quiet, his words spoken slowly. They both nodded. "Good. Now, Brett, could you please start at the beginning."

Brett took another bite of the apple, chewed a couple of times, and swallowed. "We were out on the hunt, doing our jobs, and we ran into a bunch of guys who had weapons."

"Where were they?" Herb asked.

"They were in a truck. As we approached they stopped and a few of them got out and ran for cover."

"Is that when you noticed the weapons?" Herb asked.

"I didn't need to see them to know that they had weapons. Everybody out there has weapons."

"But you did see them," Herb persisted.

"We saw rifles."

"If you saw they had weapons, why did you approach them?" my mother asked.

"If we ran from everybody out there who had a weapon,

we'd be doing nothing but running. Like I said, *everybody* out there has a weapon."

"And what happened next?" Herb asked. His voice remained calm.

"When I saw that they were going to flank us, that we were in danger, I took action," Brett said. "I opened fire."

"Did you give them warning?" my mother asked.

"Warning?" Brett asked.

"Standard police procedure."

"There's nothing out there that's standard, and what we're doing has nothing to do with policing," Brett snapped. "Do you have any idea what's going on out there?"

"Watch your tone, mister!" she snapped. "You're still under my command, and you're still a police officer."

"Am I a police officer?" he questioned. "I'm out there in a war zone trying to steal things we need to—"

"You're not stealing, you're scavenging," she said.

Brett laughed. I hadn't expected that. "Call it anything you want. Write it down in some little book. It doesn't change anything. We're out there taking things, and other people are out there to either stop us from taking what they already have or are trying to get the same things we're after. We came back to the neighborhood with a truck, ammunition, and a number of weapons tonight. I think we did pretty well."

"Two of our people were killed!"

"And, like I explained, more than twenty of their men were killed. I think that's a pretty high kill ratio in our favor."

"What does that even mean?" my mother demanded. "This is not a war."

Brett laughed again. "Yes it is, and you'd know that if you were out there instead of staying here inside the walls."

"Maybe if I had been out there leading, nobody would have died—"

"If it wasn't for *me* being there, it would have been more," Brett yelled. "If they hadn't frozen, none of them would have died."

My mother looked shocked. "You're actually blaming the people who died for their own deaths?"

"Well, it's better than blaming me. I'm not responsible."

"You were leading, so of course you're responsible," she yelled.

"By that logic I guess *you're* responsible since you're the *leader* of all of us, our *commanding* officer," he said, sarcasm dripping from his words. "Look, you have no idea what a war zone it is out there."

"We know how bad it is out there," my mother said.

"Do you?" he demanded. "When was the last time that you were out there at night?"

"That's not my job," my mother said. "And perhaps it shouldn't be yours either, if you can't provide us with a plausible report of what went on tonight."

"Nobody ever seems to complain when I bring back the items this community needs to survive. Nobody complains when I wipe out the bad guys so they can't come in and kill other people. It's easy for you 'leaders' to sit here sipping coffee while you decide what should have been done," Brett snarled. "I was *there*. I did what needed to be done! I always do what needs to be done!"

"I think we all have an appreciation for the dangers, the

potential for casualties, and the necessity of having a squad out there," Herb said.

"Thank you!" Brett said.

"But you have to remember that while you're leading that squad you're also still under the direct command of the committee and your captain," Herb continued.

The smug look on Brett's face vanished.

"As the leader of the away team you *are* responsible for their lives," Herb continued, "as well as responsible for following the directives of your commanders."

"I don't ask the men with me to do anything I wouldn't do," Brett said. "And believe me, I'm always the one in front, doing whatever is most dangerous."

"That isn't the issue," my mother said. "As you yourself said, I am responsible for all of those lives and ultimately the lives of the members of this entire community. We're going to have to review what happens out there. When you go out, where you go, and what you do when you do get out."

"It sounds like you're trying to put me on a leash."

"And that leash is going to be a lot shorter if you don't follow orders!" my mother snapped.

"If you think that somebody else should be leading the away team, then you have my permission to replace me."

"Nobody *needs* your permission to replace you," my mother said. "There is a chain of command. You will follow it or you will be eliminated from that chain. Do you understand?"

His answer was too quiet for me to hear.

"Brett, we know you're just trying to do your best," Herb said. "All of us are. For now the first thing we have to do is inform the families of the deaths as well as check on the wounded man."

"Doc Morgan said it was a serious wound but he thought he'd be able to stitch him back together," Brett said. "If I'm dismissed, I'd like to go up to the clinic and be there when he comes out of surgery."

"That shows leadership," my mother said.

"I think all of my men are happy with *my* leadership," Brett said. That was a shot aimed right at my mother. "Am I dismissed?"

"Yes."

He pushed his chair back and stomped to the doorway, smirking at me as he passed, and then headed out the front door, closing it noisily behind him. He didn't slam it, but he made sure we all knew that he wasn't completely happy about what had just transpired.

It was time to go back to bed.

29

As on most mornings, I got up before anyone else and headed straight over to the Petersons' house. I knew they'd be up for sure, taking care of the livestock. Lori was my morning meditation. Being around her meant I could try to start the day with my head in a good space.

After a quick breakfast with her mother, Lori and I went out to the fields.

We walked hand in hand alongside rows of potato plants. The crops were getting closer to harvest by the day. It was so hard to believe that a few short months ago this was nothing more than a strip of scrub grass and weeds that acted as a buffer between the houses and the highway. Now the highway was silent and this strip offered survival.

Walking along with Lori, it was sometimes hard for me to think beyond the fields, beyond the walls, beyond the world we were living in. She made me happy, and happy was in even shorter supply than food.

"There's my father," Lori said.

"What?"

For a split second I thought she said "your father" and my heart soared and then crashed back to reality when I realized my mistake.

Mr. Peterson was standing between the rows talking to some of the people working the field. We started toward him.

"Hello, Adam," a man called out. He wore a floppy hat that half covered his face and was holding a hoe in his hands.

"Hi." I recognized his voice and he certainly looked familiar but I couldn't completely place him.

"Do you have a minute to talk?" he asked.

"Sure."

"Privately."

That surprised me a little, but I nodded. I let go of Lori's hand. "Why don't you go on and talk to your dad. I'll be with you in a minute," I told her.

She started off toward the hill and the man shuffled out of the field. His movement was very awkward. I wondered if he'd been injured or something, but when he came out from behind the row of plants I saw that his feet were shackled together and instantly I knew who it was.

"I wasn't sure if you recognized me," Quinn said.

"I didn't, at least not at first," I stammered. Seeing him out of context had thrown me. "But I guess the shackles sort of gave it away. Sorry about you having to wear them."

"Don't be. It's strange to have to be shackled like this, but I understand people not trusting me. I guess they figure between the shackles and the armed guard I'm not going anywhere."

It was then that I noticed an elderly woman standing just up the slope of the field, a shotgun in hand. She gave me a little wave. I waved back.

"I'm not even sure she could hit me if she tried," he said, "but really there's nothing to worry about. I'm just grateful for the fact that my life was saved, that I'm treated okay, and even being out working is better than being locked up all the time."

"Where do they keep you?"

"Still up at the hospital. There's a place in the back—I think it was a storage room for the pharmacy—and they lock me in there every night."

"I'm sorry about that, too."

"Don't be. What I did, what I was part of, makes me understand why they shouldn't trust me."

"Trust takes time. It's important," I said.

"Trust is important, and so is gratitude. I never really had a chance to thank you for what you did," he said. "That woman would have killed me."

Herb, my mother, and I were the only people to know the truth about that episode weeks ago—that it was staged by Herb to get Quinn to talk. Quinn had been in no danger, and instead of being grateful he should have been angry. We were talking trust, and I didn't deserve his. I'd wanted to go back at some point to tell him, but Herb had talked me out of it. Besides, he said, I had thought the threat was real, and I did try to save his life, so it wasn't all fake.

"That's okay. I'm sure you would have done the same thing for me," I said.

He shook his head. "I'm not sure I know anybody else who would have done what you did. You're a good kid."

"Our neighborhood is full of good people," I said.

"Yeah, there are lots of good people here. Almost all of them."

"Almost?" I asked.

"Look, I'm not complaining . . . I'm just grateful . . . and maybe he's your brother, so I'm gonna shut up now."

"I only have one brother. He's ten and everybody likes him, except maybe his twin sister sometimes."

He smiled. "Then maybe he's a friend of yours. Just forget I said anything."

Even without Quinn saying anything more, I was pretty sure I knew who he was talking about. Brett had been spending time at the clinic hospital every day visiting with the wounded member of his squad. I wanted to hear more.

"Look, I have lots of friends, but there are some people here I don't consider friends. How's the wounded man doing up there?" I decided I'd do a little fishing around.

"All right I guess. He certainly has a lot of visitors."

"And is it some of those visitors you're wondering about?" I asked.

He suddenly looked sheepish.

"There's one of them I don't like or trust either," I said.

"Yeah, one of them is, well, he's a real head case."

"Brett," I said involuntarily.

"None of them introduced themselves, but he's always swaggering about."

"That's Brett. The wounded man is one of his squad. He leads a small team that goes out at night to patrol the area," I explained.

"Patrol?" He laughed, in a way that was unnerving. "That's what we used to call it, too. He came over that first day and talked to me. He acted friendly—at least at first. He had lots of questions about how we did things, about how our leadership worked, and where he thought they fled to. I told them I didn't even know if the colonel was still alive."

"Was the colonel really a military man?" I asked.

"I don't think he was still in the military when this all

happened—I figured he'd had some sort of dishonorable discharge and I doubt he had that high a rank, but he still insisted that we all address him as the colonel."

"And he called you the division."

"Yes, he liked to think of us as an army," Quinn explained. "His army."

"Brett would probably like to have a chance to finish off what we started," I said.

"Funny, I almost got the feeling he admired what we had done."

Somehow that didn't surprise me.

"Strangest thing, the two of them even remind me of each other," Quinn said.

"I figured the colonel would have been a lot older."

"I'm talking about the look in their eyes. It's like there's no life, like there's nothing there."

"Nothing?"

"Deadness. No feelings, no emotions."

I'd seen that look in Brett and, if I was being honest, in Herb, too. Herb had learned to hide it, but Brett hadn't.

"When I didn't have the answers he wanted, he came over to the bars and told me that if it was up to him he would just slit my throat and he'd enjoy it. And, you know what, I knew he was telling the truth. Not just that he'd do it, but that he would have *enjoyed* it . . . getting up close."

He looked scared.

"Just like with the colonel. Thank goodness he was on one side of the bars and I was on the other."

"You have nothing to worry about. Brett doesn't make the decisions."

"You've got to make sure it stays that way. He can never be in charge," he said.

"Nobody is going to let him harm you."

"It's not just for me, but for everybody. I've seen what happens when somebody like that is the leader. Somebody like him can force people into doing things they don't believe in doing. Not that I'm looking for an excuse—I chose to follow the colonel. All I can do is try to make up for it."

That sounded so much like what Herb had said—he was trying to make up for things he'd done, too.

"And maybe if I do enough right, someday I can even earn the trust of people here," Quinn said.

"I trust you," I said. "I believe you."

"That means a lot. Especially because I'm going to tell you something else." He stopped and looked around. Only his grandmotherly guard was close, but not close enough to eavesdrop. "Ever since that first time Brett threatened to kill me, I've tried to pretend to be asleep when they come in. It's amazing what you can find out when people don't think you're listening."

"And what did you learn?" I asked.

"Something they did out there—well, it was something bad."

"What exactly?"

He shook his head. "That I don't know, but I know it's bad enough that they threatened to kill the wounded man if he talked."

"Are you sure you didn't hear wrong?"

"I could have, but I don't think so. That guy, his name is Jack. He's scared of that Brett guy, too . . . and I don't blame him.

"I just wanted you to know, well, because I trust you, and I owe you, and because there's one more thing you should know."

I looked at him, waiting for him to continue.

"Adam, *you* have to be careful."

"I think we all have to be careful."

"I mean around this Brett guy. I heard him talking. He doesn't like you, or your mother, and he doesn't have any respect for any of the people who run this place. If he could kill you and get away with it, he'd do it in a second. Make sure you watch your back."

A chill went up my spine because he was just putting into words what I already felt.

"I better get back to work. I don't even know what you can do with what I've just told you."

"I just appreciate you telling me," I said.

Now I'd have to figure out what to do.

30

"Are you all right with this?" Herb asked Dr. Morgan.

"I'm trained to help patients, not trick them."

"You're trained to save lives, and that's what we're trying to do here."

I hadn't known what to do with the information Quinn had told me, but I figured Herb might, and I was right. Now we were here at the clinic—Herb, Todd, and me—putting that plan into action.

"So you'll help?" Todd asked.

"It's strange, but I'll help," Dr. Morgan said.

"Then let's do it," Herb said.

Dr. Morgan nodded and then walked away, leaving us behind in the examination room off to the side of the waiting area.

"So can we talk about this one more time?" Todd said. "You know, just to be sure."

"It's good to be clear on things," Herb said. "I'd like you to explain it to us. That way, I'll know you understand everything."

Todd nodded. "Okay, we're here because Adam and I are going to talk to Jack or, I guess, to get him to talk to us.

We're not sure what he's going to say, but we think it has to do with something that the away team did."

"That's what we believe, but he may not say anything," I said.

"And the doc is going to help motivate him by giving him a shot of truth serum, which I thought was something that only existed in the movies," Todd said.

"The truth serum we're giving him is just a medication that's going to make him feel so awful, so bad, that he'll think he's going to die," Herb explained matter-of-factly.

"But he's not really going to die, right?"

"No, he'll just feel like it," Herb said. "We only want him to *think* he's about to die,"

"Man, I don't want to ever get you mad at me," Todd joked.

"We thought Jack would be more willing to talk to you than to Adam because you know him better."

"I guess I do."

He did. Jack, the guy from Brett's squad, was a few years older than us, but he and Todd had played on the football team together two years ago when Todd was a junior, and Todd had also dated his younger sister, Vanessa. No surprise there—Todd had dated everybody's sister. Jack's mother and Vanessa had been away when this all began, on a short trip to New York; they had never returned. His father had been away on business, too, so Jack had been left alone.

Dr. Morgan came out of the room, an empty syringe in hand, and nodded to us. "I added this to his IV drip while he was sleeping, and then I made enough noise to wake him up. He should be taking a turn for the worse almost immediately."

The doctor went to the other side of the outer room. Herb placed a hand on Todd's shoulder. "I know you can do this. There's nobody I'd rather have in there."

"Even Adam?"

"You're the best man for this job. Now go. I'll be out here making sure nobody else comes in and there are no surprises."

Todd and I exchanged a look and a nod. Then he pushed through the door and I followed behind.

"Hey, Jack, how are you doing?" Todd called out.

Jack was slumped in the bed. He gave Todd a smile and then, seeing me, let the smile fade slightly. Maybe it wasn't such a good idea for me to be in there even to begin with.

"Hey, man," I said. "How are you doing?"

"He's doing great!" Todd said before Jack could answer. "This guy is as strong as an ox. It would take more than a bullet or two to kill him!"

"So you're doing well?" I asked.

"I'm getting there. Some days are better than others."

"And today?"

"Not good . . . especially not right now," he said.

That was to be expected considering what the doctor had just dosed him with.

"Maybe we should leave you alone," Todd said.

"No, stay . . . company is good," Jack said.

Todd settled himself on the bottom of the bed, while I sat in a nearby chair. "I guess you're looking forward to getting better and going back out with the patrol," Todd said.

"Yeah, I guess." He didn't sound like he was looking forward to anything.

"In the meantime, I was wondering what you'd think about either me or Todd filling in for you and taking your spot on the away team?" I said.

"You?" he exclaimed, his eyes widening. He shook his head vigorously. "There's no way they'd let you go out there . . . not the committee and not Brett."

"I guess I understand," I said. "What about Todd?"

He turned directly to Todd. "You don't want to go out there. Even if they ask you, you just say no. It just wouldn't be right for you to—"

He sat bolt upright, gagged, and threw up all over the bed. The vomit sloshed onto the floor between Todd and me.

"I'll get the doc!" I shouted. I jumped to my feet and rushed through the door.

Dr. Morgan and Herb were waiting on the other side. Before I could even say anything Dr. Morgan started to move.

Herb grabbed him by the shoulder. "Just a minute. Think this through and remember what you have to say. If you get it wrong, we did all of this for nothing."

Dr. Morgan nodded. He didn't look confident. He closed his eyes and took a deep breath. Then he rushed through the door and I followed him. He went right over to Jack and started asking questions, probing him with his fingers, and running the stethoscope all over him.

Todd and I stood back and watched. The doctor's performance couldn't have looked more convincing.

"Jack, I'm so sorry," Dr. Morgan said. "I think your injury has just ruptured. There's nothing I can do."

"What do you mean?"

"From what I can tell it's a case of massive internal bleeding. There's nothing I can do."

Jack's whole body shuddered. "Can't you . . . can't you . . ."

"There's nothing, son, I'm so sorry. I just don't have the proper facilities. The pain is going to only get worse. I'm going to go and get you something to take it away, to put you out."

Dr. Morgan got to his feet and I started to follow after him, to leave Todd alone. That was the plan.

"Adam, wait!" Jack called out. "Wait."

I stopped.

"I want you to stay . . . It's better to have more people here . . . at the end."

Those words made me flinch. What we were doing to him was cruel—and it was at least partly my idea. But it was for the sake of the neighborhood. I had to put away my feelings so that this wasn't all for nothing.

"I'm sorry, Jack," I said, sitting back down in the chair. "We'll make sure people know about what you did. How you died a hero."

"Hero? You have no idea what we . . ." His words trailed off and then he convulsed again in pain.

We watched in silence. When he recovered he picked up where he left off.

"If you knew what I did, you'd know I wasn't a hero. None of us are heroes. We did things . . . I didn't want to do them, but Brett . . . He just made us . . . made us believe it was right."

"What sort of things?" Todd asked.

"Todd, don't go out there with him," Jack whispered. "It will kill you even if you don't die. Please don't go out there."

"I won't," Todd said.

"Neither of you," he said, looking at me. "You, he'd just kill if he could. He hates you, Adam . . . *hates* you."

Those were Quinn's words coming at me again. But we needed more than just vague reports about Brett's emotions.

"This is the time," I said. "You have to tell us what you did, what Brett made you do. You can't take this with you."

Jack gagged again and threw up the rest of his breakfast.

He started sobbing. "I'm so sorry. Those poor people— We just slaughtered them."

"What people?" Todd asked. "What people?"

"So many of them. There were just so many of them. We just shot into the tents . . . set them on fire and—"

"It was the away team that attacked the tent town?" Now I was about to lose my breakfast.

"Brett told us to. That's the only reason. We did what he said. We just followed orders and—" Jack began sobbing uncontrollably.

Todd sat at the foot of the bed, his head hanging down, staring at the floor.

I got to my feet, practically toppling over, and stumbled through the door.

Herb was there with the doctor. The shocked expression on Herb's face told me he'd heard it all. Herb was never shocked, or at least he never showed it.

"It was them. He confessed. They were the ones," I said to him.

Herb didn't say anything. The shock on his face suddenly disappeared, replaced by a look in his eyes so intense, so dark, that I stepped back.

"What now, what happens now?" I asked.

"Now I'm going to talk to Jack."

"And what do I do? What about Todd?"

"I'll send him out. I want you and Dr. Morgan to step outside as well." He pointed at the outer door of the clinic, which led to the parking lot. "You three stand guard at that door. Nobody comes in. Nobody. Not even any of you."

31

I squirmed uneasily in my seat, Todd so close I could hear him breathing, but in the darkness I couldn't see him even though he was no more than five feet away. It was early the following morning, and we were both behind the glass—the one-way glass in a little panic room in Herb's basement. The door was concealed so well—it just looked like another piece of paneling—that even though I'd been in Herb's basement a hundred times I didn't even know the room was here. It was small and held nothing more than two chairs and a little cot.

From the outside, the little window looked like a mirror hanging on the wall. On the other side of the glass Herb sat at his desk, his back to us, scribbling notes on sheet after sheet of paper. I had no idea what he was working on, but he was quietly going through things, reading, marking, and shuffling pages. He reminded me of a teacher grading papers between classes. Well, except most teachers didn't have a 9-millimeter handgun sitting on the corner of their desk like a deadly paperweight. He looked so calm.

I wished I could be calm. Instead my whole body was tingling, sweat dripping down my sides. I wanted to believe that part of it was because of the heat in the little room. I was still shocked that I hadn't known that Herb even had this room in his basement, but on the other hand I shouldn't have been surprised by him. Nothing he did, said, or possessed should ever surprise me. I wiped one hand on my shirt and then the other. I didn't want perspiration to get in the way of my grip. I was holding a rifle, as was Todd, each aimed through a small opening. Those openings were behind pictures and couldn't be seen from the outside. Now there was nothing to do but wait until Brett arrived.

At that same time my mother, Howie, and sixteen trusted people would start to fan out across the neighborhood. In some ways more people would have been better, but the larger the group the greater the chance of word leaking out, and that had potentially fatal consequences. As it was, there were such mixed emotions—anger, disbelief, acceptance.

They were divided into groups of three, and each group was going to find one of the other six remaining members of Brett's squad and follow the agreed-upon plan: confront, disarm, and capture. One at a time, maybe they could be taken without a shot being fired. They'd just come in from night patrol and after eating breakfast they'd all go their individual ways. Some, maybe most of them, would be captured in bed.

With Brett it was going to be different. Herb wanted to interview him, get as much information as he could before he let him know what was happening. I thought there was also one other way this was going to be different. This was personal for Herb: he wanted to be the one who took Brett down. He'd sent word for him to come into the basement to meet up after he had breakfast. That was something they often did, so it shouldn't have sounded any warning bells in Brett's mind.

After another ten minutes or so I heard the sound of heavy boots stomping down the steps.

"Was it a good patrol?" Herb asked without lifting his head from his papers.

Brett slumped into the chair beside the desk. He looked tired but relaxed. He was, as always, dressed completely in black clothing and he still had on his body armor and wore a holstered gun at his side. I wondered if he had a black mask in his pocket.

"Brought back everybody I took out. No casualties."

"No casualties or just none for your men?"

"None—period. So not the perfect night. It's always best when we can take down some bad guys," Brett said.

"Yes, there is some satisfaction in taking down bad guys," Herb said.

I thought I saw a slight flicker in Brett's face. Had he read something into that statement? His face went back to his usual smug expression quickly enough.

I also started thinking about where I should aim to avoid the body armor—did I go for a head shot or the legs? His vest was undone at the top. A chest shot was probably the best.

I did a mental double-take. Here I was hiding in a room in the dark, peering through one-way glass, trying to figure out where I should shoot somebody. Maybe the bigger question was, *Could* I shoot him if he resisted? Did I have what it took to shoot a man?

"I'm going to crash soon. You never bring me down here for small talk, so what's happening?" Brett asked.

"I wanted to offer my congratulations," Herb said.

"Congratulations?"

"Yes." Herb paused. "I know what you did."

Brett didn't answer. At least not at first. "I've done lots of things, so just what are you congratulating me on?"

Herb laughed. "Didn't you think I'd find out eventually? I knew it was all more than coincidence."

Brett remained silent. That smug expression of his stayed in place. If Herb was trying to rattle him it wasn't working.

"First the apartment building. Setting the fire was a brilliant and daring move."

The apartment building—Brett had set the fire? Wait, did Herb know that or was he just making a guess?

"Do your team members even know about that?" Herb asked.

Brett smiled. "Only two of them."

"That might even be two too many, because this has to be kept quiet. You knew that nobody, especially the committee members, would understand."

"Don't worry, my men are loyal . . . and afraid of me. Nobody would ever dare say a word," Brett said with a smile. "I have to admit that I was starting to wonder about you."

"Me?"

"You're on the committee, and it was starting to sound like you agreed with everything they wanted to do or not do."

"It was important for them to believe it, and I must have been believable if I managed to even fool you," Herb said.

"I figured you were probably just playing a game with them, but I wasn't certain."

"You and me, we're two of a kind," Herb said.

Brett sat up straighter in his seat. He looked like he was bursting with pride.

"We both know you have to do what needs to be done. That's all you were doing out there, what needs to be done," Herb said.

"I picked up the hints," Brett said. "I listened to what you said about that apartment building holding high ground on us."

"And then the need to remove those tent people," Herb added.

"It had to be done, so I did it. But that time my whole team was part of it."

"Of course it had to be done, for the safety of the community," Herb said.

"Doesn't it bother you to have to pretend to take orders from idiots like that captain and the judge?"

"They don't understand," Herb said.

"They don't understand anything that's going on out there, but even if they did they wouldn't have the guts to do what's needed."

"You have to understand that they're all working with a handicap," Herb said.

"Lots of handicaps!" Brett exclaimed.

"You're right," Herb said. "They have morals, a conscience, a belief in the sanctity of human life. They are laboring under the restraints of basic human values, while you, on the other hand, are both a plastic action hero and a *true* sociopath."

"Yeah, I am an action hero and . . ." The sentence trailed off as he realized what he'd been called. Even Brett knew that being called a sociopath was not a compliment.

"I guess it takes a sociopath to know a sociopath. You're no different from me," Brett said.

"I *was* no different from you when I was your age, except maybe I was worse, did more damage, took more lives," Herb said.

"Don't count on that. You have no idea just how many lives I've taken."

"Spoken like a true sociopath, proud of your death count." Herb paused. "It's over. The committee knows."

"How do they know?" Brett demanded. His smiley-guy routine had slipped away completely.

"I told them what I found out from Jack."

"He talked?"

"He made a deathbed confession."

"But I thought he was getting better."

"He is, but he was easily fooled into believing he was dying," Herb explained.

"He's an idiot. I should have taken care of him out there instead of bringing him back. I let my emotions get in the way."

"Most sociopaths don't have emotions. Is poor Brett trying to become a real boy, like Pinocchio?" Herb asked.

Brett looked confused by the comment. "So what happens now?"

"You're going to be disarmed, arrested, tried, and punished," Herb said.

"Tried by those idiots on the committee?"

"The only reason you're alive this minute is because of the members of the committee, because they believe in decency, justice, and fair play. If I were actually running the show I would have simply put a bullet in your head the minute you walked in."

"That's what I would have done," Brett said. "We're really two of a kind, and you know it."

"No we're not. I did terrible things because I was given an order to follow, and even then I felt remorse and regret. You have done terrible things for pleasure. You have enjoyed it."

Inexplicably, Brett smiled again. "I still might enjoy it. Do you really think my team is going to let this happen?"

"As of right now your team has already been arrested. There's nobody to help you."

If Brett was shocked by this, he didn't show it.

"And it looks like there's nobody to help you, Herb. It's just me and you," Brett said.

"It certainly looks like that."

Why hadn't Herb mentioned that we had two rifles trained on Brett? I looked down the sight of the barrel, right into Brett's chest. I heard Todd's breathing quicken.

"Disarming me might be harder than you think. Other than you reaching for that gun and shooting me, what's to stop me from shooting you between the eyes?" Brett asked. "Do you really think you can beat me to the draw? I'm fast and you're old."

"I would imagine there's only one way to find out if you're faster than I am. Please, go ahead and try."

"You really don't expect me to just give up, do you?" Brett asked.

"Not really. I thought I'd give you a chance to go out in a blaze of glory, a chance to get away. And even if you didn't, wouldn't it be better to die that way than live like a caged rat?"

Why was he saying any of this? Was he goading Brett into doing something?

"So it's going to come down to me and you, right here, right now. Either I kill you or you kill me, and . . ." His expression changed again. He had doubt and fear on his face. "You'd like me to go for my gun, wouldn't you?"

Herb didn't answer.

"You set this game up. Your house, your time, your plan. You always have a backup plan. You taught me that. This isn't just me and you, is it?"

"I never said it was," Herb said.

"You want me to draw my weapon, don't you?" Brett asked. "That's why you wanted to meet me down here, away from outside eyes, so nobody would see me get cut down."

Herb remained silent.

"That way you can say to the committee that you had no choice but to shoot me."

Was that the reason? Was that what he was doing?

Brett looked all around. "Is it going to come from behind? How many weapons are trained on me right now? It can't be many, because you would want no witnesses . . . or only witnesses you can trust." He laughed. "So it must be your friend Adam."

A shiver went up my spine.

"Come on out, Adam, and face me like a man. No, wait, you aren't a man, you're just a boy." He turned directly to Herb. "Do you really think he has what it takes to shoot somebody down? Do you think he'll fire at me if I go for my gun? Are you really willing to bet your life on him?"

"I have bet my life on Adam before, and I would do it again. I know he'll do the right thing," Herb said.

"And is the right thing murdering me?" Brett asked. "Because that's what it would be. Or is that part of your plan, too? You used me to do the things that needed to be done, you aimed me like a weapon, and now that I'm a liability you'll terminate me. Now you'll give Adam a taste for blood, you'll make him into a murderer, your next killer who'll do the dirty work so you can keep your hands clean."

Brett was trying to get into my head, hoping that my trigger finger wouldn't function. I didn't know if I could *kill* him, but I knew I could *shoot* him.

"Can you hear all of this, Adam? Now you know what he's doing. Can you still do it? Can you murder a man in cold blood, cut him down like a dog?"

"Adam wouldn't be the one to shoot you," Herb said. "That would be me."

"Not likely. Either Adam kills me or I kill you. You have no chance of getting to that gun before I can draw."

"Not that gun," Herb said. "But certainly this one." Slowly raising his right hand from beneath the desk, Herb produced another pistol—a big one. It was aimed directly at Brett. Herb would have shot him dead before Brett could have possibly pulled out his weapon—before I could have reacted.

"There's special ammunition in this one," Herb said. "It will go through my desk and your body armor as if it were cutting through butter. Five bullets in the blink of an eye. You'd be dead before you even knew what hit you. The way those people in the tents were dead before they knew what had hit them. The difference is that they didn't deserve to die. *You* do."

I could see sweat dripping off Brett's nose.

"So I'll ask you again. Wouldn't it be better to go down in a blaze of bullets than live as a prisoner?"

He was still taunting Brett, daring him to go for his gun even though he had no chance.

Slowly Brett started to raise his hands. "Adam!" he yelled out. "You can see I'm surrendering. If he shoots me you have to tell your mother, tell the judge that he murdered me. Then he's got to be punished as a murderer or you're all just a bunch of hypocrites."

Brett got up slowly, his hands well above his head. "I'm giving up. You didn't expect that, did you?" he said to Herb.

"Actually I did. Cowards and bullies seldom fight when they think they might lose. Now, with the little finger and thumb of your left hand, I want you to remove your pistol and place it on my desk," Herb said.

Brett did as he was told.

"Adam and Todd, I would like you, one at a time, to come out here while the other has his weapon aimed squarely at Brett's chest."

"I'll go first," I said to Todd. I withdrew the rifle and got up. My legs were numb and shaking, and I was bathed in sweat. I pushed open the door and my eyes reacted to the light.

"So it wasn't just one of them. Even you didn't trust Adam. How does it feel not to be trusted, kid?" Brett asked.

"A lot better than standing there with my hands in the air and three guns pointed at me."

"So do you really think you could pull the trigger?" he asked me.

"Shut up or you'll find out right now."

"Big talk from the little man. If it was me and I had the chance, I'd blow you away. You and your mother, your brother and sister, and that little girlfriend of yours . . . Of course I'd have a little fun with her before I—"

"Another word and I shoot you," Herb said, "and you know *I'd* do it."

Brett shut up.

"Adam, you know I trust you, but I also like to have as many backup plans and guns as I might need. And speaking of backup guns"—he gestured to Brett with his pistol—"I'm going to need all of yours. I want you to unbuckle your pants and let them drop to the floor."

"What?" Brett asked.

"I know you're carrying at least one backup piece, probably a second, and I know you like to have that knife with you. Strip down."

Brett didn't move.

"Do it now or I'll pop one in your knee and you'll be in so much pain that you'll beg me to finish you off." Herb aimed the gun right at Brett's right leg.

Brett undid the buckle and the pants fell down. There was a knife strapped to one leg and a pistol to the other.

"Now the shirt. And please feel free to do something that gives me an excuse to fire," Herb said.

Slowly Brett took off the body armor and then removed his jacket. I could see bulges under the shirt. He had at least one more gun. He unbuttoned the shirt, and as it opened it revealed a third pistol in a holster and a hand grenade taped in place.

"Adam, I want you to remove both of those. Todd, keep

the gun aimed at his chest and don't hesitate to shoot if he does anything."

"Don't worry about me. I'm not as good a person as Adam. Me, I could kill him and not lose sleep tonight," Todd replied.

"More big words," Brett said.

"Just go for the gun," Todd said. "*Please* go for the gun."

In response Brett raised his hands even higher. Carefully I pulled the gun out of the holster and then removed the grenade, making sure that the tape didn't catch the pin.

"Now your boxers—drop them to the ground and step out of them," Herb ordered.

"What sort of weapon do you think I'm carrying in there?" Brett asked.

"Take them off or I shoot them off," Herb said.

Brett started to take them down.

"Left hand only," Herb said. "Keep the right hand on the top of your head."

Awkwardly Brett complied.

"He's got a gun taped to his butt!" Todd exclaimed.

I reached over and removed that gun as well. Herb tossed me a pair of handcuffs. "Hands behind your back."

"Can't I get dressed first?"

"You're not getting dressed. You leave like this so anybody who's out there can see what you are once we strip away the weapons and the body armor. You're just a scared little kid, a bully, and now, well, you're nothing."

"There's only one way I could be a nothing," Brett said. "And that's if you kill me and we all know that's not going to happen."

"Don't count on that," Herb said. "Some governments take the lives of convicted murderers—especially mass murderers. You'll have a fair trial and then we'll see what the committee wants to do with you. You always said I could convince them to do anything I wanted. You'd better hope you were wrong."

32

After news of the arrest of Brett and his squad spread through the neighborhood, living through the next few days felt like riding a roller coaster. There was a wave of bad feelings flowing through the streets. The committee was working hard to keep that wave from becoming a tidal wave.

It wasn't just that people were disturbed by the allegations against Brett and his squad but that they now felt less safe. Even though almost all my neighbors didn't agree with what he'd done, they had liked having him out there taking on the bad guys. It was as if they didn't understand that Brett and his men *were* the bad guys.

Each member of Brett's squad had been interviewed, and more information had come out. Not only had the condominium tower been set on fire and the tent people slaughtered, but the away team had gone into other little neighborhoods and taken whatever they wanted, killing whoever tried to stop them. Sometimes Brett killed people who weren't trying to stop him. He just killed them.

Some of the squad had been followers and now that the truth had come out, there was almost a sense of relief that it was finally over for them. They had done what they had done, but they felt awful. Guilty. Others, like Brett, seemed to have not just committed the crimes but enjoyed them. Brett had shown no remorse, had offered no apology, and only seemed to regret that he had been found out and stopped. It was like that part of his brain that controlled remorse, that made us all human, was missing for him.

Lori, Todd, and I had spent some time going over it, trying to make sense of it. This was really too big to keep to myself—or to ask Todd to—so we just talked it all out.

But in the midst of the shock and anger, good news arrived: the Cessna was finally working!

"Well, what do you think?" Herb asked. It was a bright, sunny day and we were checking out our new flying machine, which had been towed out behind my car to our makeshift runway.

"All the controls feel right, and the engine sounds good," I said.

"So we're ready to take it up?"

"As ready as we can be. Everything that could be done has been done. The only real way to see if a plane is airworthy is to fly it."

"Then let's do."

Hundreds of people lined the wall, and almost as many stood outside the neighborhood on the far side of Erin Mills Parkway. It was a straight clear section, three lanes wide and long enough to take off and land the Cessna. It didn't need a long runway compared to a jet, but I was used to my ultralight, which could practically land on a dime. Who would have ever thought that I'd feel safer in an ultralight than in a Cessna?

It probably would have been better not to have Herb or anybody else up with me, but if I had to have one person I just wished it could have been my father. The plans always were for him to be there when I soloed. It would have made him proud and happy.

I eased off the brakes and fed more gas into the engine. It roared in response and we started inching forward. I opened up the throttle more, and the speed and sound increased. The plan was to taxi it the length of the runway, testing it out, and then come back the other way, taking off into the wind. We picked up speed, but I kept full flaps down so that there was no risk of us taking off into the air. Gently, ever so carefully, I played with the rudder to nudge us a little left and then right of the center line of the street. So far, everything was reacting the way it was supposed to. I slowed us down, hit the right rudder and left brake hard, and spun us around, aiming back up the runway and into the wind.

"This is it. Last chance to get out and watch from the ground," I said.

Herb chuckled. "There's a much better view from up there."

I pushed the yoke back and forth, turned the wheel and worked the pedals one more time, and then watched as the rudder and ailerons performed. There was nothing more that could be done on the ground. This was the moment of truth!

I opened the throttle and the plane instantly responded. More gas, faster and faster. We were quickly approaching takeoff speed. I had enough road ahead to safely abort the flight if I needed to—but I wasn't going to do that. I pulled back on the stick, and the rumbling in the wheels eased and then went silent as they lifted away from the surface and we soared upward. Out of the corner of my eye I could see the reaction of the people lining the way, raising their hands, jumping up and down, and screaming out cheers that I couldn't possibly hear over the engine.

"It's nice to see their excitement," Herb said. "They needed something positive to happen."

We all did.

I banked slightly to the right and we quickly came up on my high school and the police station. I was almost shocked by how fast we were traveling. I had become so used to the ultralight that I'd forgotten the speed of a Cessna.

"Let's not go too far," Herb said.

"Of course. It's best to keep our landing strip close at hand."

I tightened up the bank so we'd come around faster.

"Ultimately you'll be able to travel much farther, but right now I think it's important for the people in the neighborhood to see you up here. They need some good news, but more important they need to feel protected," Herb said. "For now I want you up in the air at least twice a day," he continued. "I want people down below to see you up there protecting them, and you should have more sets of eyes with you."

"I can bring Todd and Lori with me." Unlike the ultralight, the Cessna had four seats, two in the front and two in the back.

"Good. We are less safe now than we were," Herb said. "We have one less patrol out there and another twenty people occupied guarding our prisoners."

The neighborhood came underneath us again.

"So what's the time line on what's going to happen to Brett and his squad?"

"The first step is that Judge Roberts is arranging the trial, seeking people to sit on a jury."

"That could be a problem. I've heard that some people feel the away team shouldn't have been arrested, that what they were doing was all for the good of the neighborhood," I said. "Those people on a jury would find them innocent of doing anything wrong."

"I've heard those rumblings, too, but once people hear all the details that attitude will change. A few sentences about the children they killed in cold blood in the tent town should be enough to convince even Brett's most ardent supporters."

"And if the verdict is guilty?"

"That's the hard part. A couple of them can possibly be turned around, kept on a short leash, and counseled. They might become useful again," Herb said.

"But not all of them. Not Brett."

"Not Brett. His kind can't be changed."

"But didn't you say *you* were his kind?" I surprised myself by even saying that.

Herb didn't answer and I wondered if I'd offended him. I should have kept my mouth shut.

"I'm sorry for saying that," I said.

"You shouldn't be sorry. Since all of this happened I've been thinking a lot about that same thing. I wondered what sort of person I would have become if I had been that young and put in the same situation as Brett. I might have been even worse. He and I are both animals, but I believe that we are basically two different *types* of animals."

"You're not an animal."

"At the core we're all animals, just trying to survive and take care of our babies. I know that the agency aimed me at different targets, but my actions were no less final or fatal or brutal than those perpetrated by Brett. I want to believe that our actions were motived by different things. I like to believe, perhaps falsely, that I was motivated by a sense of duty."

"Doesn't Brett say the same thing?" I asked. "That he was doing that for us, to protect the neighborhood?"

"He says it, but I don't think even he believes it. He delighted in the kill. I have spoken to him at some length and found out things. The setting of fires, the cruelty, the rush he gets in killing animals."

"I saw that when we shot those deer. There was a look in his eyes."

"Blood lust. He enjoys the kill. He is a true sociopath. I'd like to believe that I was forced to do sociopathic things— the taking of lives—but was never a true sociopath."

"Of course you're not!"

"Don't be so certain. The best sociopaths are those who can convince others that they're not. They usually end up making wonderful politicians."

"I knew something wasn't right about him from the beginning," I said.

"I knew, too. I just thought I could control him, aim him in the right direction. In the end all of this is my fault. I didn't pull the trigger, but I loaded the gun and handed it to him."

"You wanted to kill him in your basement, didn't you?"

"It would have been cleaner and simpler. I *should* have simply killed all of them, the entire squad."

"But, but . . . how?"

"I would have gone out on patrol with them. It wouldn't have been difficult to put a bullet in Brett's head. Cut the head off a snake, and the rest is harmless."

"You would have just killed them all."

"If I'd done that we could have kept what they did away from everybody and they would have died as heroes instead of being tried as murderers. It would have united the neighborhood instead of dividing it."

"But you didn't kill them," I said. "Isn't that what makes you different from Brett, better than him?"

"That's the irony. He *was* needed. Before he got out of control that sort of ruthlessness—disregard for even his own life—was something we required. I still don't know if we as a neighborhood are capable of doing what we may need to do at some point."

"I'm not worried. We'll do the right thing."

"The right thing isn't necessarily the correct thing. Ruthlessness has its place."

"What's the right thing to do with them?"

"As I said, one or two can be reclaimed. One or two we can simply expel from the neighborhood and they'll cause us no harm."

"And Brett?"

"He can't be retrained, treated, or released. He is a threat to all people who are trying to simply survive. Expelling him from the neighborhood would only result in the deaths of countless innocents. Even worse, he would mostly be a threat to us. His hatred of life, which is general, would be aimed directly at our neighborhood, and very specifically at you and me and the committee members. He blames us for his downfall. He would be out there plotting and planning, gathering strength, gathering followers. Do you want him out there waiting for us?"

That thought sent a shiver up my spine. "So what do we do with him?"

"Either he has to be kept in custody forever or he has to be executed."

"Killed?"

"Execution is state-sanctioned killing."

"And which do you think should happen?" I asked.

"Being in custody takes resources and is risky. The permanent solution would be better. He needs to be killed."

I should have said something, objected, talked about the importance of human life. All the things I used to believe in. Now, I didn't disagree, it was just a question of how—and who.

"It would be me," Herb said. I hadn't asked, but he had answered. "I would be the one who kills him. I could never ask anybody else to do that job. Back there in the basement of my house Brett was right and wrong. I did want him to go for his gun, but I was the one who was going to take the shot. I had my finger on the trigger the whole time. I wasn't counting on you to be his executioner."

"I knew you weren't, but I was ready. My finger was on the trigger, too . . . And for a few seconds I even wished he had gone for it. I was ready to kill him."

"For your sake I'm glad you didn't have to. Taking a life does something to you. Something I hope you never need to have happen."

"I've been part of taking lives," I said.

"Part is different, very different. Okay, I think it's time to take us down. Is it true that landings are the most dangerous part?"

"Right now, everything seems to be the most dangerous part. I'll bring us down."

33

After that first flight, we set up a patrol schedule, and I started taking Todd and Lori up with me. I didn't see anything new to worry about outside the walls, and sometimes I could even forget about Brett and the upcoming trial. In the Cessna I could go farther from our neighborhood than I had before, but I still missed the ultralight and started to take it up as well. It felt like an old friend. One morning, after I had just come back from a mini patrol in the ultralight, my mother came out to find me tying it down for the day.

"After being in that Cessna for a few days I didn't think you'd still be going up in the ultralight," she said.

"It's easier to just walk out to our driveway and take off from the street," I explained.

The Cessna was kept up in the parking lot in the strip mall and needed to use Erin Mills Parkway as a runway, so it meant taxiing out through the gate and getting the guards to block off the road for takeoffs and landings so that I didn't hit somebody walking by our neighborhood.

"For short patrols this just makes more sense," I said.

What I didn't say was that while everything seemed mechanically fine with the Cessna, I just trusted my ultralight more. Or maybe I just trusted me in it more. I'd spent so much time behind the stick, I felt like I could read it better.

"It must be nice to be away from the neighborhood," she said.

I nodded. "A lot of people are tense because of the trial."

"They're our own people, but some of the comments have been disturbing to me," she said. "It's like people are prepared to overlook what Brett and his crew did."

"How does somebody overlook murdering innocent people?" I said.

She let out a big sigh. "Ultimately what they did is on my shoulders. Brett was under my command."

"He was under nobody's command. Although it's funny—Herb feels like it's his responsibility, too."

"There's probably enough blame to go around for both of us. For now, though, I think I need to go up to the gate and—"

"You need to get to sleep," I said. "How long have you been up?"

"A while. It's just that we're a little short-shifted on the walls now that we need to guard our prisoners."

I knew that was not only necessary and a drain, but uncomfortable for those who had to do it. Guarding against outside forces was one thing, but keeping our own as prisoners was different and difficult.

"Right now, just as people need to see you in the air, they need to see me around to feel more confident. They need to be reassured."

"How reassured do you think they'd be if they saw you fall flat on your face? Why don't you go inside and sleep for at least a few hours?" I asked.

"I've got a committee meeting at eleven, and I have to get some breakfast first and—"

"And you can grab something and go to sleep. Rachel and Danny are with friends. The house is empty and quiet. I'll go and see Lori or spend some time with Todd. Go in and go to sleep, okay?"

"I'll lie down for a while," she agreed. She gave me a hug and a kiss. "You need to take it easy yourself."

"I sleep every night." Although it was never that solid or that long a sleep, I still got a lot more than she did.

My mother went into the house, leaving me alone to finish my job. Just as I finished the last tie, a go-cart came roaring along the street and bounced up onto our driveway. I whirled around, afraid the loud engine would disturb my mother.

"Is the captain here?" the driver asked as he got off the little machine.

"She's unavailable right now. Is there something I can help with?"

"There's somebody up at the gate wanting to come in," he said.

"There's always somebody at the gate wanting to come in, so why does she have to be involved?"

He shrugged. "I don't really know. They just sent me to get the captain. They said she'd want to deal with this one."

"She's not able to deal with it. Tell whoever it is to go away. If that doesn't work, maybe I can find Herb." Then I realized that Herb probably needed to be left alone as much as my mother did. "Wait, on second thought, I'll come up."

"That might work. I better get back to the gate."

"Can you do me a favor, please? Could you just push the go-cart until you get to the corner?"

He looked confused, but when I quickly explained he nodded.

"Thanks. I'll be up soon."

He pushed the cart out of the driveway and all the way to the corner before he jumped in and cranked the engine. Even from a distance it was pretty loud.

I continued to secure the last of the ties, then stood up and started to walk to the gate in a foul mood. Everyone understood that nobody was to be let in, so why did they need my mother or Herb or even me? Why hadn't I just insisted that the guards turn the stranger away? Brett would have liked that. Get somebody else to do the dirty work at the walls while I flew high above everyone and everything.

As I walked along the streets I could see all the front lawns were filled with crops either still growing or getting ready to harvest. Food was going to be plentiful and whole teams had been assembled to pick, process, and preserve. Some of that had already happened. Tomatoes were being turned into sauce, cucumbers pickled, potatoes stored in cold cellars, and some vegetables canned to last us through the winter and into the next harvest.

Mr. Peterson was hopeful that the greenhouses could be used well into the fall and again in the early spring to produce second and third crops to supplement our food supplies. Even with that we still needed more. Sixteen hundred people required a lot of food.

The wall was up ahead. It was high and solid and reassuring. It was good to be on the inside. There were so many terrible, bad, tragic, and dangerous things going on out there. I walked up to the guards at the gate. I knew them all. They were good people, just trying to do the best they could, and I knew that turning away people was the hardest part of the job.

"Good morning," I said. "Sorry my mother couldn't be here. I was told there's somebody who wants in."

"He said he lives here."

That was different. We had an obligation to let in people who lived here—the committee had agreed to that.

"We've had so many people falsely claiming to be from here that we couldn't just let him in," the guard said. "We need somebody to talk to him to verify it and give approval."

"I don't know if I can give approval, but I can talk to him. What did he tell you?"

The guard shook his head. "It was the last shift that talked to him, but they told us he didn't make a lot of sense, that he's in pretty bad shape. I was told he mentioned your mother."

"My mother? What did he say?"

"Like I said, I didn't speak to him."

"I'll go out and speak to him right now."

"I'll have a couple of guards go with you," he said.

"Does he seem dangerous?" I asked.

"He hasn't moved since we got here, and from what they told me the only danger was that he was going to fall over. The guy can't weigh much more than a buck twenty-five."

"Does Howie know about this?"

"We sent word for him when we sent word down to your mother. He's occupied at the south gate and sent back a message he'd be here in an hour at the most. Do you want to wait?"

"I'll be okay. I have my gun," I said, gesturing to the pistol in the holster on my shoulder. "But could you have the people on the wall keep an eye on me? Just open up the gate."

"Yes, sir."

I didn't get called "sir" often and it unnerved me, especially since the man saying it was older than me. The gate opened.

"He's just out there, sitting on the far curb," the guard said. "He hasn't moved in the last thirty minutes. He might have fallen asleep."

Or died, I thought, if he was in as bad a shape as they said. I hesitated at the opening. I bent down and pretended to check my shoelaces, but what I was really doing was putting my hand against my second gun—the one I now had almost permanently tucked into a holster on top of my sock on my right foot. Maybe I was just getting paranoid, but if Herb thought it was necessary to carry a second weapon, who was I to argue? It was almost an unspoken motto—better to have it and not need it than to need it and not have it.

I inched out of the gate and they closed it behind me—standard policy. That was unnerving. It was always dangerous or potentially dangerous. I looked around. There were a few people on the road, no vehicles, and nothing that could be seen as a threat. At first I didn't even see the man. He was sitting on the curb, curled up, arms folded over his head. His clothes were worn and ratty, and he only had one shoe, the second foot clad in a sock with rags wrapped around it.

I started to have my doubts. How wise was it for me to be out here, especially alone? He looked to be in desperate shape. I probably would have to tell him he couldn't come in, and couldn't predict how he was going to react. Desperate people with nothing to lose were the most dangerous. For a second I figured it wasn't too late—I could still turn around and ask for help. But really I couldn't. I knew that those people on the wall were watching me. And even though Brett was safely locked away I felt like he was watching me, judging me. Worse, in one way Brett was right. I didn't really know what it was like out here.

I stopped in front of the man. He didn't move, didn't seem to be aware that I was even there.

"Hello?" I tentatively called out. He coughed—a big guttural sound that came out of his chest. At least I knew he was alive.

"Hey, are you okay?"

He looked up and a smile seemed to crease his thick beard, and I saw my father's eyes looking back at me.

34

Days later, my father ran his hand along the side of the Cessna. "It's beautiful, really beautiful," he said.

Beautiful was having him here.

"I don't think it's nearly as nice as *our* ultralight."

He smiled—his big crooked smile clear now that the beard was gone. "It is *our* ultralight, isn't it?"

"I'm just sorry you couldn't be here when I took it up the first time."

"I'm sorry, too . . ." He got that faraway look in his eyes, and I waited for him to continue. "I'm just so glad to be here."

"We're all glad you're back," my mother said. She wrapped an arm around him. She was beaming.

It had been five days from meeting that haggard bearded man to being here. The first two nights he'd spent up in the clinic, an IV in his arm and my mother at his side. He was sick, anemic, and had broken ribs that had only partially healed and a big scar on his side where he'd been slashed by a knife.

Dr. Morgan had assured us he was going to be fine with rest, food, and medicine, but my father still looked like death warmed over. There were times I hardly recognized him. He looked familiar, like an old uncle or a grandfather we'd never known, but not like our father. He had aged tremendously. It was as if the pounds had poured off and the years piled on.

Rachel and Danny had been ecstatic. They didn't even like to let him out of their sight and they clung to him as if they were afraid he'd disappear. I guess I understood that. They were both late for field duties today because they couldn't say goodbye. Finally he'd walked them to the field and then joined us up here.

"So can we take her up?" he asked.

I looked at my mother for approval. She nodded ever so slightly.

"We can go up. You and me," I said.

The houses grew smaller beneath us.

"Perfect takeoff," my father said.

That was a high compliment coming from him. If his being back was a dream come true, then being up in the air with him was beyond a dream. How many daydreams had I had about this? Besides the rare occasions on which I'd ridden up front on holidays when he was at the controls of his jet and the flights we'd shared in a Cessna, how many times had we shared the cockpit? This time of course there was one big, big difference—I was the one at the controls and he was beside me. I banked so that we could do a long, slow circle around the neighborhood. I didn't want to go far from our landing strip.

"She flies as nice as she looks," my father said.

"Do you want to take the controls?"

"It's your flight, your plane."

"Technically, it belongs to the whole neighborhood."

"You're the captain, so when it's in the air it belongs to you. Besides, I want to just sit back and enjoy the view. I never thought I'd see the world again from the air."

"There are lots of things we thought we'd never see again," I said.

"Like me?" he asked. "Did you figure I was gone?"

"I knew you'd be back. I just didn't know how."

"I wasn't that sure myself, and I didn't think it would be on foot."

"It's just so amazing that you walked twelve hundred miles," I said.

"It was so much farther than that. I couldn't travel in a straight line and had to avoid bigger centers. Cities are just, well . . . not a good place to be."

"I had fantasies about coming to get you in the ultralight," I said.

"There was no way for you to do that, no way for you to find me. Besides, they needed you here. I'm so proud of you, so amazed at how you've all pulled together and what you've been able to do," he said.

"We've all worked together to make it happen."

"But you've been a big part of it. You and your mother."

"And Herb. I don't know where we'd be without him."

"He's a good man fighting some demons. I guess now I know more of what that's like. You have no idea what it's like out . . . out there. "

He had only given us little glimpses of what he'd been through. I wasn't sure if it was because he couldn't bear to talk about it or didn't want to burden us with all of it. I know there were things I wasn't comfortable telling him—not now and maybe not forever.

"It's like the Garden of Eden in the neighborhood," he said.

"Or the Garden of Eden Mills."

"In some ways it's even more remarkable when you consider all that's going on all around us . . . all around everywhere."

"If you ever want to talk about it—need to talk about it— I'm here."

"I know you are. You've always been here. I'm just so sorry that I wasn't . . . so sorry that I let you down." He started to cry.

I was surprised, but not. Tears had come often to him since he returned.

"You walked halfway across the country to get here. You did more than anybody would have expected. You coming back has given the whole neighborhood hope. Almost everybody has somebody who went missing or never came back. They'd just about given up hope of ever seeing them, and then you walk in our front gate and everybody believes that anything is possible."

"I'm sitting in a plane that my son is flying. I didn't think I'd ever be in a plane again. I'm with my family. I never thought I'd see any of you again." He gestured out the window. "Look what's been done down here. You have to think that anything is possible. Anything."

I took one hand off the wheel and placed it on his hand.

He looked over at me and brushed away his tears. "I have to keep convincing myself this is all real."

"Sometimes I think the same thing. I wake up and can't believe any of this is real, and then it all comes rushing back."

"I know it's real. I know it happened. I just can't believe that through it all—all that I've seen, all that I've had happen—I'm back here with my family. That we're together."

He was right. That was even more amazing.

35

My father, Rachel, and Danny were laughing and arguing over a game of Balderdash. It had become an evening ritual for us to play a board game, all of us together, starting before the sun set and then using candles to continue playing. We now had teams making homemade candles out of beeswax and there was no longer a danger of running out of them. Tonight my mom had some business to attend to, and I had been out spending some time with Lori. I almost felt guilty. Here my father was, back with us, the thing I'd dreamed and prayed for, and it seemed like I was already taking him for granted. It was nice for Danny and Rachel to have that special time just with Dad, though.

I heard the front door open and instinctively kept my eyes focused on the hall until my mother appeared. She came over and gave the kids and my father a hug.

"How's it going out there?" I asked.

"Didn't we used to have a rule that work stayed at work?" my father asked.

"We did until work surrounded the house," I said sharply, and then felt bad for saying it. "Sorry."

"No need," my father said. "You're right. How *is* it out there?"

"Very quiet. The walls are secure and all the guards are in place."

This now included the people guarding our prisoners. It was a drain on resources to have three shifts of six men, around the clock, seven days a week guarding them. The jury had finally been chosen and the trial was coming up in less than a week, but that probably wouldn't be the end of the problem or the need for guards—well, unless Brett and his squad were found innocent, or asked to leave the neighborhood.

Judge Roberts not only was the head of the committee but was going to be the presiding judge in the trial. Brett and his squad had been given one lawyer to represent them all, and another lawyer was going to be the prosecutor. They had wanted to be tried by their peers, with a jury reaching a verdict. There were still some people who felt they'd only done what they needed to do for the rest of us. That sort of sympathy was scary. If even one member of the jury voted for innocence, then the jury would be hung and the whole thing would have to begin again.

"I think we should all get a good night's sleep," my mother said. "Tomorrow is going to be a big harvest day."

"Anything is better than going to school," Danny said.

"It'll be nice for me to make a contribution to the neighborhood," my father added. "I'm looking forward to it."

"Will you be working in the fields, too?" Danny asked me.

"I'll be working *above* the fields," I said. "They want me to fly perimeter patrol for a good chunk of the day."

"So while we're working you're going to be playing."

"If you think flying a tight circle for four or five hours

while I keep my eyes glued to the ground is play, then I'm just going to have a riot up there."

"Maybe I could be your copilot," Danny said.

"I'm afraid that seat is taken, kiddo. Herb is going to go up with me."

"How is he feeling?" my mother asked.

"He's fine, just a little tired, I think," I replied.

"I'm worried about him," my mother said.

My mother and I had both mentioned he'd lost the spring in his step and his hand had developed a slight tremor. He even looked older than he had a few months ago. But then, so did a lot of us.

"I can understand being worried," my father added. "He really has aged since the last time I saw him . . . not that I'm anybody to talk about that."

Our father was recovering, but he was still gaunt, and there were lines etched deeply on his face that had never been there before—or at least I'd never noticed them. Now I found myself staring at him a lot, maybe just to confirm that he was really, really there.

"Herb is important to all of us. I just think he needs to take things easier at his age," my mother said.

"He went to sleep early tonight," I said. "He's going to get a good night's sleep and then tomorrow he only has to sit beside me in the ultralight."

I was happy to have that chance to be with him. Now that my father was back, I felt like I hadn't seen Herb much. It would also give us a chance to talk. It seemed like when he was free of the neighborhood he was freer to tell me what he was thinking.

"And we have a winner!" Danny yelled out.

"That just means you're better at lying," Rachel said.

"Or telling when somebody is lying. That is what Balder-dash is all about, you know!"

"Enough!" my mother said. "It's time for bed. Both of you go up and get ready for bed."

The twins got up, continuing to argue with each other as they left the room.

"I'll go and help settle them in," my father said.

"I haven't been home all week to do that, so let me. You just sit," my mother said.

She went upstairs and I could hear her shushing the bickering.

"Why don't we do the dishes?" my father suggested to me. "You wash and I'll dry."

I started to gather up the dishes, and my father went to run water in the sink before he caught himself. He chuckled. "I spent so much time out there, knowing that there was no water or electricity, but then I come back here and expect everything to be the same."

"I understand. Do you know how many times I've reached for my cell phone or grabbed the remote and tried to watch TV? Pretty stupid."

"Not stupid, it's habit. Reassuring, comforting habit."

"We do have water; it's just not in the pipes." I lifted up the big container and poured a few inches into the bottom of the sink. He added a tiny bit of soap and swirled it around to get it sort of sudsy. We were down to our last bottle.

"I guess we should be grateful for what we have," he said. "Nobody here is going without water for drinking or washing or irrigation."

"A lot of thought and planning and work went into that. I just hope there will be enough food for everybody."

"It certainly looks like a lot of food, but there are a lot of mouths to feed."

As my father talked I studied him without trying to look too obvious about it. He had managed to put on a few pounds, but he was still not much more than skin and bones. There was a noticeable shaking in his hands, and he didn't seem to be able to stand for long. How had he been able to walk halfway across the country when sometimes it looked like he could hardly walk halfway across the house?

The glass I was drying slipped from my hands and, before I could recover it, crashed to the ceramic tiles, shattering into a million pieces. My father jumped and spun around, a look of terror on his face.

"It was just a glass . . . I'm sorry."

He took a deep breath and seemed to relax. "It's okay . . . I guess I'm still a little jittery."

I swept up the mess and then we finished washing and drying in silence. Now and then came laughter from upstairs—the twins having fun with Mom.

"I used to hate doing dishes," he said. "But now I have to say it's kind of wonderful."

"I still hate it," I said, and he laughed.

"Listen, about tomorrow I just wish there was more that I could do to contribute to the family and to the neighborhood."

"You still need your rest, Dad. As I said, I'm going up on patrol in the ultralight tomorrow. But we'd be a lot safer if you'd take the Cessna up as well at some point."

A slight grin came to his face and grew into a smile. "I'd

like that, but how about the first couple of times I go up, you be the copilot?"

"You don't need me to do that."

"Just the first couple of times. I've been up in the air a lot less than you in the last few months."

"It's like riding a bike," I said.

"No it isn't. Fall off a bike and you skin your knee. Fall out of the sky and you lose your life. You've had a lot more training than me on the Cessna. I'd just like you to walk me through it, that's all."

"I can do that. How about the day after tomorrow?"

"You have yourself a deal. Now let's just finish up the dishes and get to bed."

36

Late that night, I felt my bedroom door open and squinted one eye to see a slightly lighter dark rectangle against the background of the hallway before the door swung closed again.

I heard someone come over to the bed. In my still-asleep state I didn't even start to reach for the pistol on my night table—I'd been trying to train myself to stop doing that. The last thing I wanted to do was shoot somebody in my family.

"Mom, is that—"

A hand suddenly pressed down on my throat and a piece of cold, sharp metal touched the side of my face.

"It isn't your mommy," a voice whispered hoarsely. It was Brett.

My whole body froze.

"If you make a sound, if you struggle, I'll gut you," he whispered.

This was not a nightmare, not the sleeping kind.

Brett pressed the metal—a knife—harder, and I could feel the blade prick the skin of my cheek.

"Where is your gun?" he whispered.

"It's . . ." I tried to talk, but his hand against my windpipe wouldn't let any air escape. He slightly released the pressure. "The night table . . . it's on the night table . . . beside the bed."

He kept the one hand against my throat and removed the knife ever so slightly. He reached out and grabbed my pistol.

"Get up," he said. He now removed his grip and stood up beside the bed. My eyes had had enough time to come awake and adjust to the light. He loomed right over top of me and in the faint light from the window I could see the gun—my gun—aimed right at me.

"Now!" he breathed.

He backed away and I slowly got up. I was wearing pants and socks, my spare pistol still in the holster on my ankle, pressed against my leg.

"We're going to leave, and you better move quietly. If anybody hears, if anybody comes out to try to stop us, I will kill them. Believe me."

"I believe you," I said quietly. "Why are you taking me?"

I could only think of one reason—that he wanted to kill me and didn't want anybody to hear—so his answer came as a shock.

"I need you to fly the plane."

"The Cessna?"

"It's too valuable to leave behind. Move. The longer we talk, the more likely somebody will hear and come to investigate."

There was no choice. "Let's go," I said.

He grabbed me by the arm and swung me in front of him. I almost fell over, but his iron grip on my arm kept me up. I opened the door and hesitated. It was dark, the doors to all the other bedrooms closed. I stepped out into the hall, Brett right behind me. I was aware of the gun in my sock but more aware of the gun aimed at my back. As quietly as possible, I went down the stairs. I knew by heart which of them was going to creak under my weight, and I avoided them. Brett followed suit. We reached the main floor and the house remained silent. Thank goodness nobody had heard us.

Then I had a terrible thought. What if he'd already killed my family? What if they were upstairs in their beds, dead?

I stopped and turned around as we reached the front door. "How do I know my family is all right, that you haven't hurt them?"

"You don't." Even in the dim light I could see a sick smile come to his face.

"Adam?" It was a small, high sound—Rachel.

I froze in my tracks and Brett pressed against the wall, trying to disappear into the gloom.

She was at the top of the stairs. Just a shadow in the darkness. "Is that you?" Her voice was quiet, like she was trying not to wake anybody.

"Of course it's me," I said, working hard to control my own voice. "I'm just going out to my plane for a bit. Go back to sleep. Okay?"

"Sure . . . okay."

"Rachel, I love you."

"I love you, too. Goodnight."

I heard the door to her room softly close.

"How touching," Brett mocked. "You saved her life. Not that she'll ever see you again to say thank you. You should have said goodbye instead of goodnight."

I bent down and grabbed my shoes. I'd need them, but

they would also give me an excuse to bend down later on—to pull out my pistol.

We went outside. There was slightly more light but not a lot more. Clouds were blocking the stars and the moon. It wasn't raining but it was supposed to start sometime tonight. What time was it?

A dark figure came out of the shadows from Herb's front lawn. But it wasn't Herb.

"Well?" Brett asked.

"Nobody has come out yet," the man said. I recognized him. He was one of Brett's squad—another one of the prisoners. He was carrying a rifle.

"He's got one more minute to get Herb, and then we leave," Brett said.

"You're taking Herb, too?" I gasped.

"We're killing Herb," Brett said.

"Why would you kill him?"

"He's the only one here who's a danger to us when we leave. Besides, after all he taught me, he'd be disappointed in me if I didn't try to take him out."

As awful, as terrible as that sounded, I knew he believed that. Sadly, so did I. I also knew that wanting to kill Herb and doing it were two very different things.

"Do you think your man can do it?" I asked.

"I sent in two men, and there are two more at the front door and two more at the back. Either my men come out or Herb comes out and walks into a bullet. Either way, he's dead."

I had to get inside Brett's head. "I knew you were afraid of Herb, but I didn't know just how afraid you were."

The second man looked to Brett for his reaction. There was no change in his expression. Herb would have been proud of *that*.

"We've already killed tonight, although maybe I should add one more to my count." He turned and faced me directly and trained the gun at my head. "One more word and I shoot you. We can get out even without the Cessna."

I tried to hide my emotions, control the fear.

"If you were going to kill me, you would have done it already," I said.

"You still might die. Getting you and the Cessna out isn't going to be easy." He paused. "Besides, I'd *enjoy* killing you."

I tried to remain blank, but my whole body shuddered. He saw it and chuckled. He *was* enjoying this.

There was a sound like muffled drumbeats—shots being fired. Four of them, close together. Almost immediately, two men came out of Herb's front door and hurried toward us.

"So much for Herb saving you," Brett said.

He pushed me forward and I staggered, almost dropping the shoes I was still carrying.

"Well?" Brett asked.

"In his bed, sound asleep. We put four shots into him. He never knew what hit him."

My head went numb. They were lying, they were wrong. Herb couldn't be dead. That wasn't possible.

"I almost wish it hadn't happened that way," Brett said. "He deserved to go down fighting, but this was easier. Let's get going."

There were now seven of them as the others joined from the back of the house. I had that gun tucked in my sock, but

I'd lost my chance. There was no way I could do anything except wait for the moment and hope it came.

I found myself in the middle of the pack. Each man had a rifle and a pistol. I knew them all of course. Some I knew from before and had actually liked. I felt sorry for them being dragged into this. Others were no different from Brett. They were cold-blooded killers, and my life meant no more to them than it did to Brett. It didn't matter, though—I had no chance to do anything with this many of them watching me.

"You know the plane won't hold eight people," I said.

"We're not stupid. Three are going with you in the plane."

"And the rest?"

"They're going over the wall with me," he said.

"You're not coming in the plane?"

"I want the plane, but I don't ever want to fly in anything that you're piloting."

"So you're going to leave three others to do the dangerous part. Do you think the guards are just going to let us push the plane out through the gate?"

"Maybe you're right," Brett said. "It's too dangerous. We should all just go over the wall." He gave me a push forward. "Your only value is with the plane. No plane, no value. I might as well kill you now." He aimed the gun right at my head.

I should have been afraid—terrified—but I wasn't. If I was going to die, at least it was going to be fast and clean. At least my parents would know what had happened to me. I wasn't going to give Brett what he wanted—my fear.

"Now or later, does it really matter?" I asked.

"We're all going to die, so the only thing we can do is try

to live a little bit longer. Do you want to live a little bit longer?" he asked.

I nodded ever so slightly.

"So do you think you can convince the guards to let you and my men out?"

"I can convince them."

"And how are you going to do that?" Brett asked.

"I'll be in the plane with your men, and I'll taxi it forward toward the gate and motion for the guards to open it up for us to pass. Nobody will question anything."

"Nobody ever questions anything the little prince does, do they?" he said.

"Why do you hate me so much?" I asked.

"Does it bother the little prince that he isn't loved by all his subjects?" Brett said with a sneer.

"It's better if some people don't like you, even hate you. It just means you're doing the right thing."

"Brave words. I guess we'll see how brave you really are when you don't have your mommy to hide behind." Brett then pointed at three of the men. "You three are with him in the plane."

I needed to do something to change the numbers. "It would be better if there were only two with me," I said.

"Better for who?" Brett asked.

"For everybody. Two people can hide away in the backseat and not be seen. A third would have to be up front. If the guards see one of your faces, do you think they're going to let me out?"

"Sounds more like you want to reduce the odds in your favor a little," Brett said.

"Do you have such little faith in your men that you figure it takes three guns pointed at me instead of two?"

"Then two it is." He pointed at two—Owen and Tim. Interestingly, they were the two the committee had talked about being the least involved, the ones who had been more witnesses to the crimes than participants.

Why was Brett giving me to them? Was this his way of seeing if they were trustworthy? Regardless of his reasons, it could work in my favor. They were the ones I knew the best, the ones who were closest to my age.

"I know you two *men* can do the job," Brett said.

When Brett emphasized that word—*men*—I heard Herb speaking. Brett had indeed learned much from him.

Herb. My heart nearly stopped and for a minute I couldn't breathe. *Was he really gone?* What would happen to the neighborhood without him? I could only hope that I'd live long enough to find out.

"We want him alive, but if there's trouble make sure you put a bullet in his head," Brett said. "Understand?"

They both nodded obediently.

Suddenly Brett spun around and slapped me, the smack exploding into my head and knocking me off my feet. I sprawled across the ground, shocked. "What the—"

"Just because I'm not going to kill you doesn't mean that I'm going to treat you well. Get to your feet now or I'll put the boots to you as well."

I gathered up my shoes and stood. There was a look of cruel, cold joy on Brett's face. He had enjoyed slapping me and was looking forward to doing it again—or worse—once he had me where I couldn't be saved. I wasn't going to let that happen. Either I was going to escape or die here trying.

We started moving again, walking through the fields, protected by the crops and the darkness from prying eyes. Everybody would be asleep in the houses, and those on the walls would be looking outward, not into the neighborhood itself. There was nobody who was going to help me get away. Even if a patrol saw us, what chance would they have? They'd be outnumbered, outgunned, and would be reluctant to fire on people they couldn't identify in the dark. Brett wouldn't be restrained by anything.

We came to the top of the field. The shadows of the stores at the mall were right in front of us just across the road. The plane was sitting on the other side of them in the parking lot. I knew there were no guards watching it.

All that was left was to get there, get it started, taxi to the gate, wave to the guards, and then go out on the parkway and take off. Once I started it the noise would attract attention, but there was probably nobody who would be able to get there in time to notice them in the plane or to question me as I taxied out. I wasn't a "little prince," but people didn't question me or what I was doing. They'd let me taxi out of the neighborhood.

"We're leaving you here," Brett said to his two men. "We're going to go over the wall. Hopefully we can get away without attracting attention. Give us ten minutes to make our escape. But if you hear gunfire, go right away. That will be the diversion. Use it as your excuse to get into the air—just say you have to catch the bad guys. Understand?"

"Yes, sir," one of them said, and the other nodded.

"Good. I have faith in you. We'll meet at the agreed place, although you'll be there hours before us. See you then."

Brett led four men away. They quickly disappeared into the darkness.

"Nice, leaving the two of you to do the real dangerous job," I said.

"He trusts us," Owen said.

"I'm sure he trusts you, but we all know that you two aren't like him."

"What do you mean?"

"Everybody knows, starting with the committee, that you two were only doing what you were told. You were going to be released by the judge, sort of put on probation. I heard them talking."

"Really?" the second—Tim—asked.

"Really. I wouldn't lie to you," I said. Of course that was a lie. I'd heard them talking, but the decision would be made by the judge, the jury, and the committee—and there'd been no guarantees.

"You don't have to do this," I said. "Neither of you. You have a choice."

"We have no choice," Owen said.

"Of course you do. He's taken off to save his own skin. You can just give me your guns, turn yourselves in, and we'll work this out. You'll be let free, welcomed back into the neighborhood."

"It's too late," Owen said.

"It's not too late. We can do it right now." I held out my hand. "Just give me the guns."

"We escaped."

"And you can turn yourselves in, right now. You can explain how Brett made you do it. I'll testify in your favor, tell people, my mother, the judge, everybody, that you did the right thing."

"You don't understand," Tim said. "Five of the guards who were watching us, they're . . . they're dead."

"Brett killed them?"

"Not him," Owen said, his voice barely a whisper. "Each of us killed one of them."

"But we didn't have a choice," Tim exclaimed. His voice was very loud. "Brett gave us the guns and told us we had to do it, that we had to shoot them."

"You just murdered them?" I said.

"We didn't want to," Owen added. There was a catch in his voice like he was on the verge of crying. "It was different from out there. We got to know the guards—we even knew a couple of them from before."

"And still you shot them."

"Brett ordered us to," Tim said.

"He might have shot us instead," Owen said. "Brett doesn't tolerate people not listening to him."

"We had to do it," Tim pleaded. "It was them or us. He made us kill the five guards."

I could hardly believe what they were saying. They'd killed the five guards—but wait. "You said five, but weren't there six guards on duty?"

"One of them is still there," Tim said. "He's tied up. Brett let us pick one to live. He said it was too risky to tie them all up."

"Why would it be risky to tie up one and not all six?" I asked.

"Brett said it. I don't know."

They were too brainwashed or too afraid to even question him. I was scared but not too scared to think. I thought I knew why he had left one alive. "Did the guard who was tied up see the others being killed?"

"Yes," Owen said. "He was there, watching the whole thing, waiting for his turn, but it didn't come."

"Brett even put a gun to his head and pulled the trigger, but there was no bullet in the chamber," Tim said. "The man wet himself."

"And Brett probably laughed," I said.

"He told us he let him live so that everybody would know that we had done the killing," Owen said.

"So there was no way back," Tim said.

"And he's right," Owen said. "We can't come back here. Ever."

"He set you up, just like he's setting you up right now to do the most dangerous part. He's manipulating you, and you're letting him get away with it," I said.

"I know," Tim said. "And that's why there's no choice any-more."

"There's always a choice."

"We can't stay."

"Yes you can, I'll explain it all. People will understand."

"No they won't. How can they let us get away with killing those men? How can we face their families?" Tim asked.

"Then you could just take off. Don't meet Brett at the rendezvous," I said. "Go out over the fence."

"How would we live out there?" Owen said. "The two of us wouldn't be able to survive. We need his help, the help of the whole squad."

"Besides," Tim said, "if we didn't show up, he'd come look-ing for us. You have no idea what he's capable of doing."

"I've heard the reports."

"No, you only know a little bit of it. If you knew the whole truth you'd be— Well, we know the whole truth. We've seen it with our own eyes. It's better to be dead than have Brett come after you."

"We have no choice." Tim pushed the gun against my chest. "We have to go . . . Now!"

37

Quietly we padded across the open roadway. It was empty, dark, and deserted. If anybody did see us, they didn't act or react, but why should they? Nobody was looking for danger from within. We filed down the narrow passage between two of the stores.

The parking lot was filled with cars, many with their tires and windows removed. The windows were being used in the makeshift greenhouses. Most of the cars still had a tankful of gas, stored until it was needed. In a clearing right by the Baskin-Robbins sat the Cessna. Beyond that was the wall, manned by unseen guards. Even if they did look back this way they wouldn't have been able to make us out as we darted between the cars, staying low.

Both Owen and Tim had their rifles slung over their backs and their pistols in their hands, roughly aimed in my direction as I led them to the plane. We all stopped behind a truck to catch our breath. They seemed to be panting hard—even harder than me. It wasn't just the run. They were afraid, even more than I was.

"I guess they're over the wall now," I said. "No shots and no trouble. They're going to the meeting spot, but I'm not sure how we're going to meet anybody. It's not like I can put this plane down in a parking lot. It takes a lot of space to land."

"Brett's taken care of it."

"I'm not sure he even knows enough to realize just how much space it takes to land a Cessna. If we get up there with no place to land, we're all dead."

"You can definitely land a Cessna there," Owen said.

"And now you're an expert, too?" I asked.

"Not an expert, but it's been done before. We know that. The Division used to land a Cessna there all the time."

"The Division?" That could mean only one thing. "We're going to land at the compound, aren't we?"

"We shouldn't be telling you that," Tim said.

"You already did. He's meeting you at the compound. That's just crazy. How do you even know that those men, the Division, haven't come back? We could be flying into a trap and be captured."

"We won't be captured," Owen said. "It isn't a trap."

Now I had one more terrible revelation. "It's not a trap because you know that the remnants of those men are back there. You're going to join the people who were trying to kill us all. You've already partnered up with them, haven't you?"

Neither Owen nor Tim answered, which was the clearest answer imaginable.

"Look, there's no telling what they might do. We land and they might just kill all three of us and take the plane," I said.

"They won't do that," Tim said. "They won't harm us."

"Brett arranged an alliance with them," Owen said.

"When did he do that?" I demanded.

"A couple of weeks ago, before it all exploded, before we

were taken prisoner," Tim said. "Brett, he's always got a backup plan, and that was it."

"He said he didn't know if the neighborhood would survive, but he knew that those men would," Owen said.

"He wanted to be part of them? What about the people in this neighborhood?" I demanded.

"Shut up," Tim hissed. "I've had enough of your lecture. We're going. Either you get us out of here or I just put a bullet in your head right now."

I'd pushed him too far. Maybe I'd push him a little further.

"You shoot me, and the guards will be here soon enough. You'll be shooting yourself. You'll both be dead."

"Maybe, maybe not, but you'd be too dead to find out what happens to us," Owen said. "So which will it be?" he asked as he aimed at my head.

"We're going."

We were going to the plane, but there was no way we were going to that compound. I'd try to stop them before we got up into the air, but if we did get airborne none of us was going to land in one piece. I'd crash the plane before I'd let that happen.

"Follow me," I said.

I moved past the last three rows of cars and came up to the Cessna. They were right behind me, so close that I could hear them breathing. I went to the wheels and kicked out the blocks holding the plane in place. We'd positioned the plane when I came back so it could taxi out of the lot, along the road, and through the gate without having to be turned around.

I opened the cockpit door. "Climb in," I said.

Owen put a foot on the strut, but Tim stopped him. "You first," Tim ordered me.

I tossed my shoes onto the seat and pulled myself up and in. Owen tried to climb in through my door, going over the top of me to get to the copilot's seat, and I stopped him.

"Get into the back," I said, "unless you're going to fly it."

He scrambled over the seat and then Tim climbed in after him, also going to the back.

"Once I start the engine everybody is going to be looking this way. You have to stay low and not let them see you," I said. "Lay the rifles down and then get out of sight."

Both ducked down, but the tops of their heads were still visible.

"You have to get lower."

They both disappeared from view. I turned the ignition switch and the engine roared to life. There was no question that the guards on the wall heard it. I flicked on the running lights and now we were visible as well. I opened the throttle and gave it the gas, and we started rumbling forward.

I looked over my shoulder. Tim and Owen were neither visible out the windows nor able to see what I was going to do. I reached down with one hand and removed the pistol from my sock. Slowly, helped only by the slight illumination from the control panel lights, I brought it up and clicked off the safety, the sound covered by the noise of the engine. I could just lean over the seat and shoot them both, one and then the other. They'd never know what hit them. It would be simple.

But I couldn't do it. I couldn't execute the two of them. I

had to give them a chance even if they weren't giving me any chances.

I turned off the engine and they both looked up at me looking down at them.

"What's wrong? Why have you turned the engine—" Owen began.

He saw the gun in my hand.

"Don't move. Put down your pistols or I'll shoot."

Owen looked like he was going to comply, but Tim didn't budge. "There are two of us, Adam. Do you really think you can shoot us? Brett always says you don't have what it takes to pull the trigger."

"Are you going to stake your lives on what a maniac like Brett thinks?" I asked.

"We have no choice."

Tim swung his gun up. I saw Owen's arm start to go up as well, and then I pulled the trigger and fired and fired and fired and fired until the firing pin just clicked and clicked and clicked on the empty clip. Fumes of sulfur and smoke filled the cockpit, and my ears felt like they had been shattered, the explosions echoing in my head.

I pushed open the door and tumbled out of the plane, smashing heavily onto the pavement. My stomach retching, vomit flowing out and onto my legs and to the asphalt, I tried to get up. But my legs collapsed under me. I pushed over and away from the vomit and propped myself up against the wheel of the Cessna.

I heard the dull thumping of feet and saw lights bouncing toward me—guards were rushing at me from all directions.

"Put up your hands! Put them into the air!"

"He's got a gun!" somebody else screamed.

I'd forgotten I was still holding the pistol. I let it drop to the ground and raised my hands.

"It's me!" I screamed. "It's me—Adam!" My stomach churned again and I vomited once more.

"It's Adam, it's Adam! Put down your weapons!"

I looked up. It was Howie.

He bent down beside me. "Adam, are you all right? What happened?"

I tried to answer but couldn't find any words. I was too stunned to talk. I gestured to the plane.

Howie stood up and flashed a light inside the plane. "Oh, my God . . . What happened?"

"I . . . I killed them."

"It's the prisoners," Howie gasped. "Two of them . . . But how? Why are they here?"

"They escaped. All of them. Brett is gone . . . over the wall. They killed all the guards but one."

Howie barked out some orders, sending some men to the house that was being used as the jail.

"I'll send for Herb," Howie said. "He'll know what to do."

"No," I said, shaking my head. "He won't. Herb is dead. They killed him."

I staggered to my feet, my legs wobbling, threatening to buckle again. Howie offered me his hand for support.

"I've got to get to my house. I have to make sure my family is all right."

"Why wouldn't they be all right?" Howie questioned.

"Brett was in my house. He took me from there. He said he wasn't going to hurt them if I went with him. I have to check."

"Somebody, bring me a car!" Howie yelled.

People started to scramble, but before they could even react car headlights swept over the parking lot and an engine roared. I knew the sound of that motor—it was my Omega. It squealed to a stop and my father jumped out of the driver's seat, my mother came out of the other door, and then Rachel and Danny climbed out after them from the backseat.

I ran across the parking lot and practically jumped into my father's arms. My mother and then the kids all came together, wrapping me into the middle of their embrace. They started to ask me questions, but I had no words.

I just started to cry, and that started my mother and father and the twins crying. They were here, and we were together and safe.

No.

Safe might never happen again.

Ever.

THE RULE OF THREE: FIGHT FOR POWER

bonus materials . . .

HOME EMERGENCY SUPPLIES

by Jim Cobb

As the Rule of Three books show, a little preparation can mean the difference between life and death in an emergency—particularly the global blackout that changes everything for Adam and his suburban neighbors. In almost all potential scenarios, home is the preferred location to be in the aftermath of a major disaster. While some sort of nomadic existence might appeal to the adventurous romantic hiding inside many of us, the truth of the matter is that having a stable base of operations provides for a much safer existence. In the event of a crisis, the primary plan should be to hunker down at home, unless home has become unsafe for some reason.

Sheltering in place at home will, of course, require a certain degree of planning to ensure you and your family will be able to meet your basic needs for the duration of the crisis. The good news is that many homes already have a fair amount of supplies on hand, so it might just be a matter of expanding a bit more upon what's already there.

Food and water top the list of must-haves for emergencies. Power is one of the first things often affected by disasters. This means your microwave oven, and perhaps your stove if it is electric rather than gas, will not be working. Forget all about nuking bags of popcorn or pizza rolls. While it is certainly possible to use outdoor grills, patio fire pits, or even campfires for cooking, these sorts of solutions are also affected by weather conditions. If it is pouring rain with high winds, you're not going to be doing much open-fire cooking.

Since you can't reliably predict whether you'll have the ability to cook or even warm up some canned soup, concentrate on stocking up on food items that are ready to eat right out of the package. These include things like granola bars, protein bars, nuts, dried fruit, crackers, and peanut butter. Think about it like this: If you are able to cook, whether on the stove or over a campfire, that opens up additional options, but don't count on it, just in case. That said, having a few extra cans of soup, stew, pasta, and such will certainly be welcome if cooking is feasible.

Depending on the nature of the disaster and whether you rely on city sewer and water or you have a well and a septic system, you may or may not have access to clean water.

Rather than just crossing your fingers and hoping the faucets will still deliver clear and safe H_2O, plan ahead and stock up on bottled water. Common thinking among disaster readiness experts is that you should plan for at least one gallon of water per person, per day of the crisis. A case of water typically contains twenty-four half-liter bottles. One gallon is equal to about four liters. So, a case of water is equivalent to about three gallons.

Having the ability to filter and purify water is also beneficial. Rain is pure until it hits the ground. Water from lakes, rivers, and streams must absolutely be filtered and purified before drinking. To do otherwise is to risk getting extremely ill. Bringing water to a rolling boil is sufficient to kill any nasty invisible organisms that might be floating in it. Companies such as Sawyer and Lifestraw make very good filtration gear that doesn't cost an arm and a leg.

Of course, the question is, how much food and water is enough? The best approach is to take it one step at a time. Your first goal should be to have enough on hand to last your family for a solid week. Once you've hit that goal, go for two weeks, then a month. Keep working at it until you've reached the point where you and your family are comfortable with how much food and water you have stored.

Once you have food and water taken care of, next on the list is first aid and hygiene. Every home should have a first-aid kit, even if all the supplies aren't truly kept in a single container. The most common injuries during and after a disaster include cuts, scrapes, burns, and bruises. The first-aid supplies kept in the home should be able to address these sorts of injuries, so be sure to have adhesive bandages, burn cream, antiseptic ointment, gauze pads, elastic wrap, and the like. If the opportunity to take a first-aid class comes up at school or with a community group, I would encourage you to enroll. Whether you or a family member has had formal training or not, your first-aid supplies should include a good manual, too.

On top of those first-aid supplies, you might want to have some basic medicines on hand in order to deal with common illness symptoms, such as an upset stomach, head and chest colds, and fever.

As for hygiene, remember what we said earlier about water? If you're only limited to a gallon of water each day, you aren't going to be able to take nice, long, hot showers or baths. Now, if your plumbing has been unaffected by the crisis, great! If not, though, you'll be glad you planned ahead. Hand sanitizer, rather than soap and water, should be used to wash hands after going to the bathroom. A wash cloth, soap, and just a little water can go a long way, believe it or not. You might not be sparkling clean, but at least you won't feel like you crawled out of a sewage pit.

Toilets may still flush, even if there isn't any water pressure coming into the home. You can refill the toilet tank with rain or pool water. If for some reason the toilets won't flush at all, you'll need to come up with an alternate plan. Gross, I know, but it needs to be addressed. You can line the toilet with a heavy duty trash bag. After a few uses, close the bag, tie it up, and put it outside for later disposal. Be careful you don't overload the bag.

With the absence of electrical power comes the lack of light after sundown. Flashlights and headlamps will be necessary to see what you're doing and to keep you from falling down stairs and such. Dynamo flashlights, the type that run off of crank power rather than batteries, are great to have, but often aren't the brightest lights available. Granted, you don't need something that would allow you to display shadow puppets on the lunar surface, but you'll want a few flashlights that are bright enough to illuminate your backyard when you're checking for critters of either the four- or two-legged variety.

Candles, lanterns, and oil lamps will also be useful, but you need to be very cautious about them. Any sort of open flame is an invitation to a house fire if you're not careful.

If disaster hits during the winter months and you live in a cold climate, being able to keep warm would be a real concern. One of the best solutions is to have the family gather together in a small room, such as a bedroom, and huddle up with one another. Cover windows and doors with blankets to help insulate the room. The body heat from just a few people will help keep the room warm. It won't get hot by any stretch of the imagination, but it will keep you from turning into a Popsicle.

The last essential component of your home emergency supplies is a crank-powered radio. Cell phones, tablets, laptops—all those great tools for communication and entertainment require electricity to operate. At some point, if the disaster goes on long enough, those batteries will die. A crank-powered radio will allow you to gather information about the ongoing situation as well as help to pass the time. That information may turn out to be absolutely critical. Knowing what is going on in the world around you will allow you and your family to react quicker to dangerous situations that may arise.

While none of us look forward to dealing with a crisis, certainly not at all on the scale of what Adam and his family and friends are going through, planning ahead and setting aside some emergency supplies at home could turn a disaster into nothing more than an inconvenience.

JIM COBB is the owner of Disaster Prep Consultants (DisasterPrepConsultants.com) and has authored several books on the subject of disaster readiness, the most recent of which is *Countdown to Preparedness*.

GO FISH

ERIC WALTERS

What did you want to be when you grew up?
I had a fifth-grade teacher who said I could be a writer when I grew up. I thought that was stupid since I was go-ing to be in the NBA. Apparently, one of us was stupid.

When did you realize you wanted to be a writer?
I started writing for my fifth-grade class. They were a won-derful group who were good at three things: gym, recess, and lunch. They didn't like to read or write but were pretty good at making up stories (usually when they were trying to avoid being suspended again). I started writing for them and was amazed by the process. If you can find something you love doing, it pays well, and it isn't illegal, you should basi-cally keep doing it.

What's your most embarrassing childhood memory?
That didn't happen until my teen years, and then there were countless embarrassing moments.

What's your favorite childhood memory?
Spending summers at the cottage, swimming, catching frogs, and reading.

As a young person, who did you look up to most?
Bugs Bunny. He was not only a rascally rabbit, but always seemed to get out of whatever trouble he got into.

What was your favorite thing about school?
I liked almost everything about school, but loved gym and reading—although not at the same time.

What were your hobbies as a kid? What are your hobbies now?
Playing sports and hanging with my friends. I particularly liked basketball, soccer, and track. Now, playing sports and hanging with my friends.

What was your first job, and what was your "worst" job?
Delivering groceries in a basket on the front of my bike all across the city was my first real job. Painting steel girders was the worst—I am afraid of heights, but the money was amazing.

What book is on your nightstand now?
The Fault in Our Stars by John Green.

How did you celebrate publishing your first book?
I brought my kids all to Toys"R"Us and told them to buy whatever they wanted.

Where do you write your books?
I've written while on the slopes of Kilimanjaro, lost in the Sahara Desert, and at food courts in the mall.

What sparked your imagination for The Rule of Three series?
I love the whole "what if?" question and this was the ultimate what if book. Placing it in my actual neighborhood made it even more real and alive—sometimes too real. I started stocking food in our basement and considered whether or not getting a gun would be a good thing. I settled for extra food.

What kind of research did you do for The Rule of Three series?
I read so many survival guides—the real things that would need to be done in the event of an emergency or societal meltdown. I had a consultant who was a pilot and a second who was an environmental engineer.

What was the most interesting thing you learned while researching?
This stuff could happen. I had a reviewer talk about how "unrealistic it was" that society would break down in a couple of weeks. The unrealistic part is that it wouldn't take that long. I was overly generous. Big blackouts usually have looting within hours.

Why did you decide to set the book in your neighborhood?
I love being able to visualize things. I'm a very visual writer. Adam lived in my house, landed his ultra-light on my street, and went to the high school my kids attended.

How would you survive if a *Rule of Three*–style disaster struck?
I'm a writer, so I'd be able to problem solve things. I'm also big, rather determined, and grew up poor and tough. I'd take care of business if I needed to.

Do you have a favorite dystopian book?
Monument 14 by Emmy Laybourne.

What challenges do you face in the writing process, and how do you overcome them?
Organizing a trilogy that's this long and complicated involved a great deal of plotting, planning, and strategy. It was like juggling a combination of gravel, rocks, and boulders all at once.

Which of your characters is most like you?
Herb. My kids always kidded me that I acted like I was in the Secret Service and I'm always trying to figure things out.

What makes you laugh out loud?
Great comedy, Celebrity Jeopardy on *SNL* and real *Jeopardy* (sometimes hard to tell them apart), *Tosh 2.0*, and *Louie*.

What do you do on a rainy day?
Get wet unless I'm indoors. Then I watch TV, read, and most of all, write.

What's your idea of fun?
Being with my family, spending time with my wife and grown kids, spending time at the cottage or travelling, being in Kenya at my orphanage.

If you could live in any fictional world, what would it be?
You mean I'm not?

What's your favorite song?
Today, at this moment, it's by Grover Washington: "The Best Is yet to Come."

Who is your favorite fictional character?
Yossarian from *Catch-22*.

What was your favorite book when you were a kid? Do you have a favorite book now?
Owls in the Family by Farley Mowat. Probably now, it's either *Hatchet* by Gary Paulsen, or *Catch-22*, or almost anything by Kurt Vonnegut Jr. or Steinbeck.

If you were stranded on a desert island, who would you want for company?
Somebody who knew how to build a boat from available material.

If you could travel anywhere in the world, where would you go and what would you do?
I'd be in Kikima, Kenya, at my orphanage, just chilling with the kids.

If you could travel in time, where would you go and what would you do?
It would be the future—distant future—a time when the Toronto Maple Leafs have a winning hockey team.

What's the best advice you have ever received about writing?
Write, write, and write some more.

What advice do you wish someone had given you when you were younger?
Buy Apple stock.

What do you want readers to remember about your books?
I hope they were entertained, but also went away thinking.

What would you do if you ever stopped writing?
Probably lay very still in my coffin. My plan is to compose until I decompose.

If you were a superhero, what would your super-power be?
Flight would be pretty cool, although my fear of flying might make that interesting. I'd fly very low to the ground.

What do you consider to be your greatest accomplishment?
Convincing my very wonderful wife to marry me . . . and stay with me.

What do you wish you could do better?
I'm too old to dunk any more. I wish I could still dunk.

THEIR WORST ENEMY
MAY BE THEMSELVES

Read on for a sneak peek of the stunning conclusion to the
RULE OF 3 series.

1

"I . . . I killed them," I stammered. "They were going to take me and . . . I shot them."

I was standing in a parking lot, in the dark, in the middle of the night. Beside me, inside the plane, were the two people I'd shot. *The two people I'd killed.* That rattled around in my head.

I'd killed them. Shot them dead before they could shoot me.

"Adam . . . what happened?" my mother demanded.

She, my father, and the twins were there with me. We stood in a huddle, with my family trying to calm and comfort me.

Howie, my mom's lieutenant, stood nearby.

My whole body had started shaking, as if I were standing out in the freezing cold. But it was actually just a cool late-summer night.

In the lights cast by the several patrol cars that had gathered, the whole scene was now as bright as day. Here I stood in the parking lot of the strip mall—the mall where I used to go to get an ice cream or to run an errand and pick things up for my parents at the grocery store or the drugstore, or the bakery. The place I'd come to get a slice of pizza.

Although the stores were mostly abandoned, the mall looked pretty much the same as it always did. The differences were the nearby high fence that marked one edge of our community, the armed guards at the gate, and of course the airplane with the two bodies inside it.

Those things were more different than anything I could have even imagined a few months ago, before the blackout hit.

I tried to gather myself.

The twins—my younger brother and sister—were holding on to me, crying.

"I didn't have any choice," I said. "I shot them. I had to."

"You shot who?" my father questioned.

"Two of the prisoners, Owen and Tim. They were trying to force me to fly them away."

"Oh my lord!" he exclaimed.

"They killed the guards and they all escaped and—"

"Brett has escaped?" my mother asked.

I could tell by her expression how shocked she was. More than that, there was fear.

"Yes, all of the prisoners. He and the others are probably already over the walls and gone."

My mother launched into police-captain mode, barking out orders to Howie, who rushed off to notify the guards on the walls.

She turned her attention back to me. "But why were you even out here to begin with in the middle of the night?"

"It was Brett," I said. "He was in our house."

My sister gasped.

"In my room. He had a knife." Even as I said the words it didn't seem real, more like a bizarre nightmare. "He told me if I didn't come along quietly he'd kill me and everybody else in the house. I had to go with him. There was no choice."

"But why? Why did he want you to go with him?" my father asked.

"He didn't want me. He wanted the plane. Once we were outside the house, we met up with six others, and he ordered two of them to come along with me. They tried to make me fly it out for them and—"

Then I remembered.

"We have to get to Herb!"

"What?" my mother asked.

"They shot Herb . . . We have to get help . . . We have to bring the doctor! He could still be alive!"

I broke free of my family and started running.

I heard them shouting out after me, but I couldn't stop.

I raced through the parking lot, dodging the abandoned cars, and ran out into the street. I pounded down the hill back toward Herb's house, where I pictured him lying in a pool of blood, having been shot in his bed by two of Brett's militiamen.

My feet and legs, which moments before had been so shaky that I could hardly stand, were now pulsing with power, carrying me over the pavement like I was really flying.